Two horsemen pounded out of the night, bent low in their saddles, seeming to race shoulder to shoulder to see which would lance Conan first. Snarling, the Cimmerian leaped to the side, away from the long-bladed lances. The two riders tried to wheel on him together, but he closed with them, thrusting at the closer of them. His blade struck a metal plate in quilted brigantine, then slid off and between the plates. The movements of his attack were continuous. Even as his steel pierced ribs and heart, he was scrambling onto the dying man's horse, throwing both the corpse and himself against the second enemy.

**THE
VICTORIOUS**

The Adventures of Conan,
published by Tor Books

Conan the Bold by John Maddox Roberts
Conan the Champion by John Maddox Roberts
Conan the Defender by Robert Jordan
Conan the Defiant by Steve Perry
Conan the Destroyer by Robert Jordan
Conan the Fearless by Steve Perry
Conan the Formidable by Steve Perry
Conan the Free Lance by Steve Perry
Conan the Great by Leonard Carpenter
Conan the Guardian by Roland J. Green
Conan the Hero by Leonard Carpenter
Conan the Indomitable by Steve Perry
Conan the Invincible by Robert Jordan
Conan the Magnificent by Robert Jordan
Conan the Marauder by John Maddox Roberts
Conan the Raider by Leonard Carpenter
Conan the Renegade by Leonard Carpenter
Conan the Triumphant by Robert Jordan
Conan the Unconquered by Robert Jordan
Conan the Valiant by Roland Green
Conan the Valorous by John Maddox Roberts
Conan the Victorious by Robert Jordan
Conan the Warlord by Leonard Carpenter

CONAN
THE VICTORIOUS

BY
ROBERT
JORDAN

TOR ®

A TOM DOHERTY ASSOCIATES BOOK
NEW YORK

This is a work of fiction. All the characters and events portrayed in this book are fictitious, and any resemblance to real people or events is purely coincidental.

CONAN THE VICTORIOUS

A Tor Book
Published by Tom Doherty Associates, Inc.
49 West 24th Street
New York, N.Y. 10010

Cover art by Boris Vallejo

ISBN: 0-812-51399-1

Printed in the United States of America

0 9 8 7 6 5

Conan
the Victorious

PROLOGUE

The Vendhyan night was preternaturally still, the air weighty and oppressive. No slightest breeze stirred, leaving the capital city of Ayodhya to swelter. The moon hung heavily in the sky like a monstrous yellow pustule, and most of the few who ventured out to see it shuddered and wished for even a single cloud to hide its sickly malevolence. There were whispers in the city that such a night, such a moon, were omens of plague, or of war, but certainly of death.

The man who called himself Naipal gave no heed to the whispers. Watching from the highest balcony of a vast palace of alabaster spires and golden domes, his by royal gift, he knew the moon was no omen of any sort. It was the stars that gave the night its promise, the passing of configurations that had blocked his way for months. He laid long, supple fingers on the long, narrow golden coffer held beneath his arm. Tonight, he thought, there would be one moment of transcendent danger, a moment when all his plans could crumble to dust. Yet there was no gain

1

without risk, and the greater the gain, the greater the danger.

Naipal was not his true name, for in a land noted for its intrigues, those who followed his path were secretive beyond the ordinary. He was tall for a Vendhyan, and they were accounted a tall people among the nations of the East. That height gave him a presence that he deliberately diminished by wearing robes of somber hue, such as the dark gray he now wore, rather than the rainbow silks and satins affected by men of fashion. Also the shade of charcoal was his modestly small turban, with neither gem nor plume to set it off. His face was darkly handsome, seeming calm beyond the ability of any disaster to shatter, with heavy-lidded black eyes that spoke of wisdom to men and of passion to women.

Seldom did he allow himself to be seen, however, for in mystery there was power, though many knew that one called Naipal was court wizard to King Bhandarkar of Vendhya. This Naipal, it was said in Ayodhya, was a wise man, not only for his good and faithful service to the King since the strange disappearance of the former court wizard, but also for his modest lack of ambition. In a place where every man and woman brimmed with ambition and plotting, the lack was considered praiseworthy, if peculiar. But then, his sort did peculiar things. It was known, for instance, that he gave great sums to the poor, to the children of the streets. This was a source of some amusement to the nobles of the court, for they thought he did it to assume a guise of kindness. In truth he had thought long before giving the first coin. He had come from those streets and remembered well wretched nights crouched in an alley, too hungry to sleep. The truth would have showed a weakness; therefore he fostered the cynical rumors of his motives, for he allowed himself no weakness.

With a last look at the sky, Naipal left the balcony, firmly clutching the narrow coffer. Golden lamps, cunningly wrought in the shapes of birds and flowers, lit the high-ceilinged corridors of his palace. Exquisite porcelains and fragile crystal vases stood on tables of polished ebony and carven ivory. The carpets layered thickly beneath his feet in a welter of color were beyond price, and any one of the delicately-woven tapestries on the alabaster walls could have been exchanged for the daughter of a king. In public, Naipal made every effort to efface himself; in private, he reveled in all the pleasures of the senses. This night, however, after waiting so long, his eye did not touch any of the ornaments of his palace nor did he call for wine, nor musicians, nor women.

Down he went, into the depths of his palace and beyond, to chambers with walls that glowed with a faint pearlescence as though glazed by the hand of a master, chambers hewn from the bowels of the earth by his powers. Few of his servants were allowed to enter those deep-buried rooms and passages, and those few could not speak of what they did or saw for the simple lack of a tongue. The world at large did not know of those chambers, for those servants who did not descend into them, and so were allowed to keep their tongues, fearfully and wisely averted their eyes and would not so much as whisper of them on their sleeping pallets.

A downward-sloping corridor opened into a great square chamber, thirty paces on a side, with softly-gleaming canescent walls that were all of one piece, without join. Above, a pointed dome rose twenty times the height of a tall man. Centered beneath that dome was an arcane pattern in silver, buried in the near translucence of the floor and encompassing the greater part of the room. That silver graving gave off its own unholy radiance of frosty paleness.

At nine precisely chosen spots on the perimeter of that figure were tripods of delicately worked gold, no higher than Naipal's knee and placed so that each leg seemed to continue a portion of the pattern. The air seemed sharp with dire forces, and the memories of foulness done.

Incongruously, the sixth part of the length of one wall was taken by a large grille of iron bars, with a locked door, also of iron, set in it. Near the strange latticework a table of polished rosewood held the implements and ingredients he would need this night, all arranged on black velvet as a gem merchant might display his wares. A large flat box of ornately carved ivory stood atop faceted crystal legs at one end of the velvet. The place of honor on that table, though, was held by a small, finely crafted ebony chest.

Setting the golden coffer beside a silken cushion before which stood another golden tripod, Naipal went to the table. His hand stretched toward the small black chest, but on sudden impulse he raised the ivory lid instead. Carefully he brushed aside layers of blue silk, as soft as the finest down, revealing a silvered mirror, its polished surface showing no image at all, not even a reflection of the chamber.

The mage nodded. He had expected no different, but knew he must not allow his certainties to stop him from proper precautions. This mirror was not so very unlike a scrying glass, but instead of being used to communicate or spy, it had very special properties. That silver surface would show no images save those that threatened his designs.

Once, soon after he became wizard in the court of King Bhandarkar, Mount Yimsha, abode of the dreaded Black Seers, had appeared in the mirror. It had been only curiosity at his ascension, he knew. They saw no threat in him, more fools they. In a day the image was gone, and never since had anything been reflected there. Not so much as a flicker. Such was the efficacy of his planning.

With a feeling of satisfaction, Naipal covered the mirror once more and opened the ebony chest. Within was that which made his satisfaction grow. In carven hollows in the sable wood lay ten stones, smooth ovals of so inky a hue that the ebony seemed less black beside them. Nine were the size of the last joint of a man's thumb, the last twice so large. These were the *khorassani*. For centuries men had died seeking them in vain, until their very existence became first part of legends, then the stuff of stories for children. Ten years it had taken Naipal to acquire them, a search filled with adventures and trials to make it fit for epics had it been known.

Reverently he placed the nine smaller *khorassani*, one atop each of the golden tripods that bordered the arcane figure within the floor. The tenth, the largest, he set on the tripod before the cushion. All was in readiness.

Naipal settled cross-legged onto the cushion and began to speak the words of power, commanding forces unseen. "*E'las eloyhim! Maraath savinday! Khora mar! Khora mar!*"

Again the words repeated, again and again unending, and the stone before him began to glow as though with fires imprisoned in its core. No illumination did it give, yet it seemed to burn with all light. Abruptly, with a hiss as of white-hot metal thrust into water, narrow streaks of fire leaped from the glowing stone, one to each of the nine *khorassani* surrounding the silver pattern. As suddenly as they were born, the blazing bars died, yet now all ten stones blazed with the same fury. Once more the slashing hiss sounded, and the encircling stones were linked by burning lines, while from each tripod another bar of terrible incandescence stretched both upward and downward. Within the confines of that fiery cage neither floor nor dome could any longer be seen, but only darkness stretching to infinity.

Naipal fell silent, studying his handiwork, then shouted, "Masrok, I summon you!"

A rushing came, as though all the winds of the world poured through vast caverns.

A thunderclap smote the chamber, and within the flame-barred cage there floated a huge eight-armed shape, twice as tall as any man and more, with skin like polished obsidian. Its only garb was a silver necklace from which depended three human skulls, and its body was smooth and sexless. Two of its hands held silver swords that shone with an unearthly light. Two more held spears with human skulls hanging below the points for decoration, and another grasped a needle-pointed dagger. Each weapon shared the glaucous, other-worldly glow. Large leathery ears twitched on the hairless head, and sharply slanted ruby eyes swiveled to Naipal.

Carefully the creature stretched to touch one silvery spear to the fiery bounds. A million hornets buzzed in rage, and lightnings flashed along the candent boundary, ceasing only when the spear point was withdrawn.

"Why do you still seek escape, Masrok?" Naipal demanded. "You cannot break our bargain so easily. Only lifeless matter can cross through that boundary from the outside, and nothing, not even you, can pass it from the inside. As you well know."

"If you make foolish errors, O man, there is no need for bargains." The booming words were pronounced stiffly around teeth that seemed designed for rending flesh, but a touch of arrogance came through. "Still, I will keep our pact."

"Most assuredly you will, and should from gratitude if for no other reason. Did I not free you from a prison that had held you for centuries?"

"Freedom, O man? I leave that prison only when summoned to this place by you, and here I am constrained to remain until commanded by you to return once more to that same prison. For this and promises, I aid you? I sent the demons to bear away your former master so that you could rise to what you consider power as the court wizard. I shield the eyes of the Black Seers of Yimsha while you attempt that which would draw their wrath upon your head. I do these things at your command, O man, and you dare speak to me of freedom?"

"Continue to obey me," Naipal said coldly, "and you will have your freedom entire. Refuse . . ." He flung open the golden coffer. From it he snatched a silvery dagger like the one the demon carried, even to the glow, and thrust it toward the demon. "When we made our pact, I demanded a token of you, and you gave me this with warnings as to the danger of its merest touch to human flesh. Did you think with a demon-weapon in my grasp I would not seek the secret of its powers? You hold human knowledge in contempt, Masrok, though it was mortal men who chained you in your adamantine prison. And in the knowledge of mere humans, in the ancient writings of human wizards, I found mention of weapons borne by demons, weapons of glowing silver, weapons that cannot miss what they strike at and slay whatever they strike. Even demons, Masrok. Even you!"

"Strike at me then," the demon snarled. "I marched to war beside gods, and against gods, when the highest achievement of man was to turn over a rock to eat the grubs beneath. Strike!"

Smiling thinly, Naipal returned the dagger to the coffer.

"You are of no use to me dead, Masrok. I simply want you aware that there is worse I can do to you than leave you in your prison. Even for a demon, imprisonment is to be preferred to death."

The demon's rubescent eyes fixed malevolently on the mage. "What do you wish of me this time, O man? There are limits to what I can do unless you remove the constraints on my journeying."

"There is no need for that." Naipal drew a deep breath; the moment of danger was at hand. "You were imprisoned to guard the tomb of King Orissa beneath the lost city of Maharashtra."

"You have asked before, O man, and I will not tell you the location of tomb or city. I will not betray that if I am bound for all of time."

"I know well the limits of your aid to me. Listen to my command. You will return to that tomb, Masrok, and bring to me one of the warriors buried with King Orissa. Bring me one man of the army that formed his bodyguard in death."

For a moment Naipal thought the demon would accept the command without demur, but abruptly Masrok screamed, and as it screamed, it spun. Faster and faster it whirled until it was an ebon blur streaked with silver. No part of that blur touched the boundaries of its cage, but the hornets screamed and lightnings slashed walls of fiery lace. The chamber vibrated with the penetrating shriek and a blue-white glare filled the air.

Calm did not desert Naipal's face, yet sweat beaded his brow. He knew well the forces contained in that barrier and the power necessary to make it cry out and flare as it did. It was almost to the point of shattering; almost to the point of unleashing Masrok. Through the thousand deaths he would die when that happened, the greatest pain would be the failure of all his grand designs.

As abruptly as the tempest had begun, it ended. Masrok stood as truly carved from obsidian, crimson eyes glaring at the wizard. "You ask betrayal!"

"A small betrayal," Naipal said blandly, though it took all his reserves to manage it. "Not the location of the tomb. Merely a single warrior out of thousands."

"To escape two millennia of bondage is one thing, to betray what I was set to guard is another!"

"I offer freedom, Masrok."

"Freedom," was all the demon said.

Naipal nodded. "Freedom, after two thousand years."

"Two thousand years, O man? The span of a human life is but a moment's dreaming to me. What are years to one such as I?"

"Two thousand years," the mage repeated. For a long moment there was silence.

"Three others guard as I do," Masrok said slowly. "My other selves, all of us created from the same swirl of chaos in the very instant time itself was born. Three to my one. It will take time, O man."

By the barest margin was Naipal able to mask his exhaltation. "Do it as quickly as possible. And remember that when your service to me is done, you will have your freedom. I await your sign that the task is done. Now go, Masrok! I command it!"

Once more thunder smote the chamber, and the fiery cage stood empty.

With an unsteady hand, Naipal wiped the sweat from his brow, then hastily scrubbed it on his dark robes as though denying its existence. It was done. Another thread had been placed in a tapestry of great complexity. There were a thousand such threads, many being placed by men—and women—who had no idea of what they truly did or why, but when the pattern had finally been woven. . . . A small smile touched his face. When it was woven, the world would bow to Vendhya, and Vendhya, unknowing, would bow to Naipal.

CHAPTER 9

From a distance the city seemed jeweled, ivory and gold beside a sea of sapphire, justifying the name of Golden Queen of the Vilayet Sea. A closer view showed why others gave Sultanapur's byname as "the Gilded Bitch of the Vilayet."

The broad mole-protected harbor was crowded with the ships that gave Sultanapur cause to call itself Queen to Aghrapur's King, but for every roundship filled to the gunwales with silks from Khitai, for every galley that carried the scent of cinnamon and cloves from Vendhya, another vessel, out of Khoraf or Khawarism, reeked of stale sweat and despair, the odiferous brand of the slaver.

Gold-leafed domes proliferated on palaces of pale marble, it was true, and alabaster spires stretched toward the azure sky, but the streets were cramped and crooked in the best of quarters, for Sultanapur had grown haphazardly over centuries beyond counting. Half a score of times in those numberless years had the city died, its gilded palaces and temples to now-nameless gods gone to ruin. At each

11

death, however, new palaces and new temples to new gods had grown like mushrooms on the rubble of the old, and like mushrooms, they crowded together where they would, leaving only rambling ways between for streets.

The city was dusty in a land that might know rain once in a year, and it, too, had as distinct a smell as the harbor. Without rain to wash the streets, the stenches of years hung in the hot air, a blend of spices and sweat, perfume and offal, a thousand aromas melded together till the parts could no longer be told one from the other. The whole was an ever-present miasma, as much a part of the city as any building.

Baths proliferated in Sultanapur: ornate marble structures with mosaicked pools, served by nubile wenches in naught but their sleek skins; wooden tubs behind taverns, where a serving girl might scrub a back for the price of a drink. It was the constant heat, however, and not the smell that made them a tradition. The wrinkled nose and the perfumed pomander were signs of the newcomer to Sultanapur, for those who dwelt there for any time no longer noticed the smell.

Newcomers there always were, for the Gilded Bitch of the Vilayet drew certain sorts of men from all corners of the known world. In a cool, fig-tree-shaded court or a shadowy tavern, an ebon-faced merchant from Punt might discuss with an almond-eyed Khitan the disposition of wines from Zingara, or a pale-cheeked Corinthian might speak with a turbaned Vendhyan of the ivory routes to Iranistan. The streets were a polyglot kaleidoscope of multi-hued garb in a hundred cuts from a score of lands, and the languages and accents to be heard among the babble of the marketplaces were too numerous for counting. In some instances the goods were honestly purchased. In others the purchase had been from the pirates who plagued the sea lanes, or coin had been passed to raiders of caravans or to smugglers on a dark coast. However obtained, on no more than half of what passed through Sultanapur was the King's custom paid. Sultanapur was a queen that took pride in her infidelity to her king.

For all that he was head and shoulders taller than most of those he passed, the muscular young man drew no special notice for his size as he made his way through streets filled with high-wheeled, ox-drawn wains squeaking on ungreased axles toward the docks. His tunic of white linen was tight across the breadth of his shoulders, and a broadsword swung at his side in a worn leather scabbard, but neither sword nor breadth of shoulders was enough to pick him out in Sultanapur. Big men, men who carried swords, were always sure of hire in a city where there was never a lack of goods or lives to guard.

Beneath a thick mane of black hair, held back from his face by a leather cord, were eyes as blue as the Vilayet and as hard as agates. Those eyes did cause stares from the few who noticed them. Some made a sign to ward off the evil eye as he passed, but those who did so did it surreptitiously. It was all very well to avoid the curse of those strange eyes, but to anger their possessor was another matter entirely when the leather wrappings of his sword-hilt were worn smooth with use and his bearing and face showed him little loath to add to that wear.

Aware of those who stared and made the sign of the horns, the youth ignored them. Two months in Sultanapur had made him used to such. Sometimes he wondered how those men would take it if they found themselves in his native mountains of Cimmeria, where eyes of any shade but blue or gray were as rare as his own were in this southern land of Turan. As often since coming to this place where the blue Vilayet mocked with its wetness the dry air, he thought longingly of the wind-swept, snowy crags of his homeland. Longingly, but briefly. Before coming to Turan he had been a thief, but he found that the gold that came from thievery had a way of trickling through his fingers as fast as he got it. He meant to return to Cimmeria—someday—but with gold enough to scatter like drops of water. And in Sultanapur he had found an old friend and a new trade.

At a stone-walled tavern with a crescent moon roughly daubed in yellow on its front, the Cimmerian went in, cutting off much of the noise of the street as he pulled the heavy door shut behind him. The Golden Crescent was cool inside, for its thick walls kept out the heat of the sun as well as the clatter. Tables were scattered across the stone floor so that talk at one could not easily be heard at another, and the interior was lighted poorly apurpose, for here whom a man talked to or what he said was considered no one's business but his own. The patrons were mainly Turanians, though they seemed a mixed lot. Their garments ranged from threadbare once-white cotton to costly velvets and silks in gaudy shades of scarlet and yellow. Not even the most ragged of them lacked coin, though, as evidenced by the number of doxies seated on men's knees or displaying their wares among the tables in narrow strips of brightly colored silk.

Some of the men nodded to the Cimmerian, or spoke. He knew them by name—Junio and Valash and Emilius—for they followed the same trade as he, but he did no more than acknowledge their greeting for he had no interest in them this day. He peered into the dimness, searching for one woman in particular. He saw her at the same moment she saw him.

"Conan!" she squealed, and he found his arms full of satiny olive flesh. A length of red silk two fingers in width encircled her rounded breasts, and another twice as wide was tucked through a narrow girdle of gilded brass set low on sweetly curving hips. Black hair cascaded down her back to all but bare buttocks, and her eyes shone darkly. "I hoped you would come to see me. I have missed you sorely."

"Missed me?" he laughed. "It has been but four days, Tasha. But to mend your loneliness . . ." He freed a hand to delve into the leather purse at his belt and held up a blue topaz on a fine golden chain. For the next few minutes he was busy being kissed, fastening the chain about her neck, then being kissed again. And being kissed by Tasha, he thought, was more definite than a night in some women's arms.

Lifting the clear azure stone from its nest between her breasts, she admired it again, then gazed up at him through long lashes. "You must have had good luck with your fishing," she smiled.

Conan grinned. "We fishermen must work very hard for our coin, casting nets out, hauling them in. Luckily, the price of fish is very high right now." To gales of laughter from men close enough to hear, he led Tasha to an empty table.

All of the men who frequented the Golden Crescent called themselves fishermen, and it was even possible that some few actually were, upon occasion. For the vast majority, however, their "catches" were landed at night on deserted stretches of the coast where none of King Yildiz's excisemen were about to see whether it was fish or bales of silk and casks of wine that were offloaded. It was said that if all of the so-called fishermen in Sultanapur actually brought fish to market, the city would be buried to the tops of the tallest tower, and the Vilayet would be stripped of its finny denizens.

At a table near the back of the room, Conan dropped to a bench and pulled Tasha on to his lap. A sloe-eyed serving girl appeared at his elbow, wearing little more than the doxies, though in cotton rather than silk. She was as available as the other women, for those who could not or would not pay the trulls' prices, and the smile she beamed at the broad-shouldered Cimmerian said she would take Tasha's place in an instant.

"Wine," he said and watched the rhythmic sway of her almost-covered hips as she left.

"You did come to see me, did you not?" Tasha asked acidly. "Or is that why you did not come yesterday? You said you would return yesterday. Were you off comforting some thick-ankled serving wench?"

"I did not think her ankles were thick," Conan said blandly. His hand barely caught Tasha's wrist before her slap reached his face. She squirmed on his lap as though to rise, and he tightened his arm around her waist. "Who is sitting on my knee?" he asked. "That should tell you whom I want."

"Perhaps," she pouted, but at least she had stopped trying to get up.

He released her arm carefully. He had been made aware of her temper early on. She was quite capable of trying to rake his eyes out with her nails. But the passion that went into her rages she put into other things as well, and so he continued to seek her out.

The serving girl returned with a clay pitcher of wine and two battered metal cups, taking away the coins he gave her. This time Tasha watched her depart, with a glare that boded ill. It had been Conan's experience that women, whatever they said, preferred men who were not easily bullied, but now he thought a little oiling of the waters might be in order.

"Now look you," he said. "We did not return to Sultanapur until this very morning, for the wind turned against us. From the boat to here I took only a few hours to find that bauble for you. If need be, I will fetch Hordo to vouch for it."

"He would lie for you." She took the cup he filled for her, but instead of drinking she bit her lower lip, then said, "He came looking for you. Hordo, I mean. I forgot, before. He wants to see you right away. Something about a load of 'fish.' "

Conan hid a smile. It was a transparent attempt to make him leave on a fool's errand. On leaving their vessel, the one-eyed smuggler had spoken of his intentions to seek out a certain merchant's wife whose husband was in Akif. The Cimmerian saw no reason to share that knowledge, however.

"Hordo can wait."

"But—"

"You, Tasha, I prize above any silk or gems. I will stay here. With you."

She gave him a sidelong glance with bright eyes. "You hold me so dear?" Lithely she snuggled closer to him and bent to murmur into his ear between teasing nips with small white teeth. "I like your present very much, Conan."

The sounds of the street intruded momentarily, indicating the entrance of another patron. With a gasp, Tasha crouched as though trying to use him as a shield. Even for the Golden Crescent, he realized suddenly, it had become too quiet. The constant low murmur of conversation was gone. The Cimmerian looked at the door. In the dimness he could barely make out the shape of a man, tall for a Turanian. One thing was plain, however, even in the shadows by the door. The man wore the tall pointed helmet of the City Guard.

The intruder walked slowly into the silent tavern, head

swiveling as if searching for someone, the fingers of one hand tapping on the hilt of the curved sword at his hip. None of the men at the scattered tables met his eyes, but he did not appear interested in any of them. He was an officer, Conan could now see, a narrow-faced man, tall for a Turanian, with a thin mustache and a small beard waxed to a point.

The officer's fingers stopped tapping as his gaze lit on Conan's table, then began again as he drew closer. "Ah, Tasha," he said smoothly, "did you forget I said I would come to you today?"

Tasha kept her eyes down and answered in a near whisper, "Forgive me, Captain Murad. You see that I have a patron. I cannot . . . I . . . please."

"Find another woman," Conan growled.

The captain's face froze, but he did not take his eyes from Tasha. "I did not speak to you . . . fisherman. Tasha, I do not want to hurt you again, but you must learn to obey."

Conan sneered. "Only a fool needs fear in his dealings with women. If you prefer cringing curs, find yourself a dog to beat."

The guardsman's face paled beneath its swarthiness. Abruptly he seized Tasha's arm, jerking her from the Cimmerian's lap. "Leave my sight, scum, before I—"

The threat cut off as Conan leaped to his feet with a snarl. The narrow-faced man's eyes widened in surprise, as though he had expected the girl to be given up without a fight, and his hand darted for his sword hilt, but Conan moved faster. Not toward his own blade, however. Killing guardsmen was considered bad business for smugglers unless it was absolutely necessary, and in truth usually even then. Soldiers who palmed a coin and looked the other way could become tigers in defense of the King's laws when one of their own was slain. The Cimmerian's fist smashed into the other's chin before a fingerwidth of steel was bared. The officer seemed to attempt a tumbler's back flip and fell against a table, toppling it as he dropped to the floor. His helmet spun across the floor, but the Turanian lay where he had fallen like a sack of rags.

The tavernkeeper, a plump Kothian with small gold rings in the lobe of each ear, bent to peer at the officer. He scrubbed his fat hands nervously on his wine-stained apron as he straightened. "You've ruined my custom for a tenday, northlander. *If* I'm lucky. Mitra, man! You've killed the perfumed buffoon! His neck's snapped."

Before anyone else could speak or move the door to the street slammed open, and two more guardsmen strode through. They marched into the common room sneering as though it were a barracks square filled with peasant conscripts. The unnatural stillness of the tavern was disturbed by tiny shiftings and rustlings as men marked escape routes.

Conan quietly cursed under his breath. He was all but standing over the accursed fool's body. To move would only draw attention more quickly than it would come already. As for running, he had no intention of dying with a sword in his back. With a small gesture he motioned Tasha from him. He found the alacrity with which she obeyed a trifle disappointing.

"We seek Captain Murad," one of the guardsmen shouted into the silence. An oft-broken nose gave him a brawler's face. The other tugged at a straggly mustache and stared superciliously about the room. The Kothian tried to scuttle into the deeper shadows, but the broken-nosed soldier froze him with a glare. "You, innkeeper! This smuggling scum you serve seem to have no tongues. Where is Captain Murad? I know he came in here."

The Kothian's mouth worked soundlessly, and he scrubbed his hands all the harder in his apron.

"Find your tongue, fool, before I slit it! If the captain's with a wench, still he must hear the word I bring without delay. Speak, or I'll have your hide for boots!"

Abruptly the straggly-mustached soldier caught the speaker's tunic sleeve. "It's Murad, Tavik!" he exclaimed, pointing.

From the still form of the officer the guards' eyes rose inexorably to Conan, their faces hard. The Cimmerian waited calmly, seemingly unaffected by their stares. What would happen, would happen.

"Your work, big man?" Tavik asked coldly. "Striking an officer of the City Guard will cost you the bastinado. Abdul, see to waking the captain."

They had rested too long under the protection of their position with regard to the smugglers, the big youth thought. Tavik drew his curved sword, but held it casually, lowered by his side, as though he did not believe anyone there would actually make him use it. The other did not even reach for his weapon.

Abdul squatted beside Captain Murad's body, grasped the officer's arms, and stiffened. "He's dead," he breathed, then shouted it. "He's dead, Tavik!"

Conan kicked the bench he had been sitting on at Abdul, who was attempting to leap to his feet and unsheathe his sword at the same time. As the scraggly-mustached man danced awkwardly to avoid falling over the impediment, the Cimmerian's own blade was bared. At his companion's cry, Tavik had raised his blade high to slash, which might have been all very well had his opponent been unarmed. Now he paid for his error as Conan's steel sliced across his exposed belly. With a shrill scream, Tavik dropped his sword, fingers clutching in a vain attempt to keep in the thick ropes of his intestines as he followed the weapon to the stone floor.

Conan leaped back as he recovered from the killing stroke, his broadsword arcking down barely in time to block Abdul's thrust at his side. The force of the blow knocked the guardsman's tulwar wide, and doomed desperation filled his dark eyes in the moment before the Cimmerian's blade pierced his throat to stand out a handspan from the back of his neck. As Conan jerked his sword free from the collapsing corpse, Tavik gave one last kick and died.

Grimly the Cimmerian wiped his sword on Abdul's tunic and sheathed it. The common room, he realized, now held but half those it had at the beginning of his fight, and more were disappearing every moment through the doors that led to alleys beside and behind the building. No man or wench in the tavern but would want to be able to deny being in the Golden Crescent on the day three of the City Guard died there.

The Kothian tavernkeeper cracked the door to the street enough to peer out, then closed it with a groan. "Guardsmen," he muttered. "Half a score of them. And they look impatient. They'll be in here in a trice to see what's keeping those two. How am I to explain this happening in my tavern? What am I to tell them?" His hand snatched the gold coin Conan tossed him, and he was not too despondent to bite it before making it disappear beneath his apron.

"Tell them, Banaric," Conan said, "of the slavers from Khoraf who killed the captain in a quarrel, and then the guardsmen. A dozen slavers. Too many for you to interfere."

Banaric nodded reluctantly. ''They might believe it. Maybe.''

They were the last two in the tavern, Conan saw. Even Tasha had gone. And without a word, he thought sourly. In a matter of moments the entire day had gone rotten. At least he would not have to worry about being hounded by the City Guard. Or he would not if the Kothian told the story he had been paid to tell.

''Remember, Banaric,'' he said. ''A dozen Khorafi slavers.'' He waited for the innkeeper's nod, then slipped out the back.

CHAPTER II

Conan hurried away from the Golden Crescent by the network of alleys, barely as wide as his shoulders and stinking of urine and offal, that crisscrossed the area of the tavern. His plans had been for a day in Tasha's arms, but that had certainly gone aglimmering. He slipped in the slime underfoot, barely caught himself, and cursed. Even if he managed to find the jade again, he was not sure he wanted to spend time with a woman who would take his gift and then run away—without so much as a kiss—just because of a little trouble. There were other women, and other uses for his time. Even after buying the topaz for her and tossing a gold piece to Banaric, Conan's purse was far from empty. The "fish" unloaded the night before on a secluded beach had been Khitan silks and the famed Basralla laces from Vendhya, and the prices paid for them were generous. He would spend a little coin on himself.

Deep into the heart of the sprawling city he went, far from the harbor district, yet all parts of Sultanapur had their share of bustling commerce. There were no ox-drawn

23

carts here, but still the narrow streets were filled with humanity, for coppersmith's shop and bawdy house might lie cheek by jowl with rich merchant's dwelling, and tavern and potter's shop with temple. Buyers, sellers and worshipers were all jumbled in the throng.

Sleek ladies in veils of lace, trailed by servants to carry their purchases, jostled with apprentices bearing rolled rugs or stacked bolts of cloth on their shoulders. Filthy urchins with greedy fingers stalked the purses of fat men with velvet tunics and even greedier eyes. In a small square a juggler kept six lighted brands in the air at the same time while shouting curses at trulls in girdles of coin and little else who solicited those who paused to watch.

At every street crossing, fruit peddlers sold pomegranates, oranges and figs, some from trays held before them by a strap about the neck, some from wicker panniers on donkeys. From time to time the donkeys added their braying to the general tumult. Geese and chickens in reed cages honked and cackled, pigs tethered by a leg grunted disconsolately. Hawkers cried a hundred varied wares, and merchants bargained at the top of their lungs, shouting that such a price would ruin them, then going lower still.

A copper bought a large handful of figs that Conan ate as he strolled and looked, and occasionally made a purchase. From a swordsmith, working his forge beneath a striped awning with the ring of hammer on white-hot metal, the Cimmerian purchased a straight-bladed dagger and sheath that he tucked through his sword-belt in the small of his back. Finely carved amber beads went into his pouch with the thought that they would grace the neck of some other wench than Tasha. Unless, of course, she apologized prettily for running away as she had.

A narrow, shadowed shop, presided over by a skinny man with an unctuous manner and oily countenance, yielded a white hooded cloak of the thinnest wool, not for the cold that never came in Sultanapur, but to keep off the sun. He had looked for such a cloak for some time, but most men in Sultanapur wore turbans, and few cloaks with hoods were sold, not to mention cloaks large enough to fit across his shoulders.

A ragged man passed Conan, bearing on his back a large clay jar wrapped in damp cloths. The handle of a ladle protruded from the mouth of the jar, and brass cups clinked against each other as they dangled on chains along the jar's sides. The sight of him awoke in Conan the thirst that came from eating so many sweetly ripe figs, for the ragged man was a water seller. In a city so hot and so dry as Sultanapur, water had a price as surely as did wine.

Conan motioned the man aside and squatted against a wall while the water seller set down his jar. The chains reached far enough for a Turanian to stand and drink, but Conan must needs either squat or stoop. A copper passed into the water seller's bony hand, and Conan took his cup of water.

Not so cool by far as a mountain stream in Cimmeria, he thought, freshened by the runoff of the spring thaws. But such thoughts were worse than useless, serving only to make the heat seem to suck moisture from a man even faster. He drew up the hood of his new cloak to give himself a little shade. As he drank, fragments of talk drifted to him through the cacophony of the street. Tasha occupied his mind, and but fragments of fragments registered on his ear.

". . . Forty coppers the cask is outrageous . . ."

". . . At least ten dead, they say, and one a general . . ."

". . . A prince, I heard . . ."

". . . If my husband finds out, Mahmoud . . ."

". . . A Vendhyan plot . . ."

". . . While the *wazam* of Vendhya is in Aghrapur talking peace . . ."

". . . So I seduced his daughter to even the bargain . . ."

". . . The assassin was a northland giant . . ."

Conan froze with the brass cup at his lips. Slowly he raised his eyes to the water seller's face. The man, staring idly at the wall against which the Cimmerian crouched, seemed merely to await the return of his cup, but sweat beaded his dark forehead where there had been none before, and his feet shuffled as though he would be away quickly.

"What did you hear, water seller?"

The ragged man jumped, rocking his jar. He had to catch it to keep it from toppling. "Master? I . . . I hear nothing." A nervous laugh punctuated his words. "There are always rumors, master. Always rumors, but I listen only to the babblings of my own head."

Conan slid a silver piece into the man's calloused palm. "What did you hear just now?" He asked in a milder tone. "About a northlander."

"Master, I sell water. Nothing else." Conan merely continued looking at him, but the man blinked and swallowed as though at a snarl. "Master, they say . . . they say there are soldiers dead, City Guardsmen, and perhaps a general or a prince. They say Vendhyans hired it done, and that one of the slayers . . ."

"Yes?"

The water seller swallowed again. "Master, they say one of the slayers was a . . . a giant. A . . . a northlander."

Conan nodded. The tale obviously had its roots in the occurrence at the Golden Crescent. And if so much were common knowledge, in however distorted a fashion, how much else was known also? His name perhaps? He did not worry about the how of the story spreading. Smugglers did not usually turn against their own, but perhaps one in the tavern that morning had been caught and put to the question by the guardsmen who had been in the street. Mayhap Banaric had not felt a gold piece enough for a lie in the face of the guardsmen's certain anger at what they found. At the moment he had quite enough worry in how to avoid capture in a city where he stood out like a camel in a zenanna. His eyes searched the street, and a possibility came to him. At least there were no guardsmen. Yet.

He emptied the cup with a gulp, but held it a moment longer. "It is a good thing to sell, water," he said. "Water and nothing else. Men who sell water and nothing else never have to look over their shoulders for fear of who might be there."

"I understand, master," the water seller gasped. "I sell water and nothing else. Nothing else, master."

Conan nodded and released the cup. The water seller heaved his jar onto his back so quickly that water slopped over the sides, and hurried into the streaming crowd. Before he was out of sight, Conan had already dismissed the ragged fellow from his mind. There would be a reward, likely as distorted as the numbers of guardsmen slain, and the water seller would sooner or later try for part of it, but with luck, he would remain silent for perhaps as much as an hour. In truth, the Cimmerian would settle for a tenth of that.

Drawing the hood of his cloak farther forward, Conan strode hurriedly down the street, searching for a vendor of a particular sort. A sort of vendor who did not seem to be present, he thought angrily. There were sellers of brass bowls and wicker baskets, of tunics and sandals and gilded jewelry, but not of what he sought. But he had seen apprentices carrying. . . . There it was. A rug merchant's stall, filled with carpets in all sizes and colors, stacked, rolled and hanging on the walls.

As Conan entered, the plump merchant hurried forward, hands rubbing in anticipation and a professional smile on his face. "Welcome, master. Welcome. Here you may see the finest carpets in all of Sultanapur. Nay, in all of Turan. Carpets to grace the palace of King Yildiz himself, may Mitra bless him thrice daily. Carpets from Iranistan, from—"

"That one," Conan cut him off, pointing to a rug that lay near the front of the stall in a roll thicker than a man's head. He was careful to keep his face down. The sight of blue eyes would bring more than a sign for warding off the evil eye now.

"Indeed, master, you are truly a connoisseur. Without even the bother of unrolling it, you chose the finest carpet in my shop. For the trifle of one gold piece—"

This time the rug merchant's jaw dropped, for Conan immediately thrust a gold piece into the man's hands. It left him with little in his purse, but he had no time for bargaining, however odd that might strike the merchant.

The plump man's mouth worked as he attempted to regain his equilibrium. "Uh, yes, master. Of course. I will fetch apprentices to bear your purchase. Two should be enough. They are strong lads."

"No need," Conan told him. Sword and swordbelt were hastily stored just inside the folds of the rug. "I will carry it myself."

"But it is too heavy for one. . . ."

The merchant faded into astounded silence as Conan easily hoisted the rolled carpet to his left shoulder, then casually shifted it to a more comfortable position. The thick tube on his shoulder would give him an excuse to walk with back bent and head down, and thus seem not quite so tall. So long as he kept the hood of his cloak well forward, he might be able to pass as just one more of the scores of men bearing carpets through the streets for weavers or rug sellers.

He noticed the open-mouthed merchant staring at him. "A wager," Conan explained, and as he could not think of the possible terms of such a bet, he hurried from the shop. As he left, he could feel the man's popping eyes on his back.

Once out in the narrow street there was a temptation to walk as swiftly as he could, but he forced himself to move slowly. Few laborers or apprentices in Sultanapur moved more quickly than a slow stroll unless under the eyes of their master. Conan gritted his teeth and matched his pace to that of the real laborers he saw. Even so, he impatiently used the rug to fend his way through the streams of people. Most moved from his path with no more than a muttered curse. A growl from beneath his hood answered the few who shouted their curses and shook a fist or caught at his sleeve. Having gotten a closer look at him, each of the latter decided they were needed urgently elsewhere. Surreptitious glances under the edge of his hood told Conan he was almost halfway to the harbor.

A change in the noise of the street slowly came to the Cimmerian's awareness. Leg-tied pigs and tethered sheep still grunted and bleated unabated, and the cackling from high-stacked wicker cages filled with chickens continued unaltered. But a woman bargaining loudly for a shawl of Vendhyan lace paused, then turned her back to the throng and continued more quietly. A peddler of pins and ribbons faltered in his cry and drew back to the mouth of an alley before giving voice again. Others started or stuttered in their tradings, or cast nervous eyes about.

It was not he who excited them. Of that Conan was sure. There was something behind him, but he could not turn to look. He strained his ears to penetrate the wall of the farmyard babble and market chatter. Yes. Among the many feet that walked that street were some number that moved to a silent cadence. Marching feet. Soldiers' feet. The Cimmerian moved his right hand to the rolled carpet as though to balance it. The hand rested not a fingerwidth from the hilt of his sword, hidden in those folds.

"I tell you, Gamel," came a harsh voice at Conan's rear, "this big oaf is naught but a laborer. A weaver's man. Let us not waste our time with him."

A second speaker answered in tones smoother and touched with mockery. "And I say he is big enough, if he stood straight. This could well be the giant barbar the Vendhyans hired. Will you forget the reward, Alsan? Can you forget a thousand gold pieces?"

"Gamel, I still say—"

"You there! Big fellow! Stand and turn!"

Conan stopped in his tracks. A thousand gold pieces, he thought. Surely Captain Murad could not be worth so much. But these men said he fit the description of the one for whom that amount would be paid, and he could not imagine that it could be someone else. Matters were occurring in Sultanapur of which he had no knowledge, but it seemed they concerned him all the same.

Slowly the Cimmerian turned, keeping the thick roll between the guardsmen and his face, making no effort this time to hurry people from the path of the swinging rug. The soldiers had continued to approach, apparently satisfied that he obeyed. By the time he was sideways to them, they had reached him.

A hand grabbed his arm. "All right, you," the harsh voice said. "Let's see your face."

Conan let the hand pull him around a handspan farther. Then, jerking his scabbarded broadsword from the rug, he dropped the heavy roll against the man who tugged. He

was only vaguely aware of the thin-mustached guardsman
falling with a scream and the snap of a broken leg. His
eyes were all for the twenty more filling the narrow street
behind the first.

For the merest instant all were frozen; Conan was the
first to move. His hand swept out to topple wicker cages of
wildly squawking chickens into the soldiers' midst. Chickens exploded from burst cages. Peddlers and shoppers,
shrieking as mindlessly as the birds, fled in all directions,
some even trying to trample a way through the soldiers,
who in turn attempted to club people from their way. The
pigs' grunts had become desperate squeals and sheep leaped
and jerked at their bonds.

Conan jerked his blade free of its sheath as a guardsman
burst out of the confusion and hurdled the downed man as
he drew his tulwar. Sidestepping, the Cimmerian struck.
The Turanian gagged loudly as he doubled over the steel
that bit deep into his middle. Before the man could fall,
Conan had freed his blade to slash at the cords binding the
nearest sheep. Fleeing the flashing blade, the wooly animals darted toward the jumble of soldiers shouting for the
way to be cleared and shoppers screaming for mercy, the
whole spiced with scores of fluttering, squawking chickens.
Two more soldiers struggled clear of the pack only to fall
over the sheep. Conan waited no longer. He ran, pulling
over more cages of chickens behind him as he did.

At the first corner he turned right, at the next, left.
Startled eyes, already turned in the direction of the tumult,
followed his flight. He had gained only moments, he
knew. Most of those who saw him would deny everything
when asked by the City Guard, for such was the way of
life in Sultanapur, but some would talk. Enough to make a
trail for the soldiers to follow. Ahead of him an ox-drawn,
two-wheeled cart, piled high with lashed bales to a height

greater than a man, passed his line of sight on a crossing street. Another high-wheeled cart followed behind, the ox-driver walking beside his animal with a goad, then another.

Abruptly Conan stopped before the stall of a potter. Before the potter's goggling eyes, he calmly reached up and wiped the blood from his sword on the man's yellow awning. Hurriedly resheathing his blade, Conan fastened the belt around his waist as he ran on. At the next crossing street he looked back. The potter, staring after him and pointing, stopped his shouting when he saw Conan's gaze on him. This man would certainly talk, even before the guardsmen asked. It was a risk he took, the Cimmerian knew, but if it failed, he would be no worse off than before. But it would work, he told himself. He had the same feeling that he had when the dice were going to fall his way.

Sure that the potter marked his direction, Conan turned in the direction from which the carts had come. As he started down the street, he let out a breath he had not been aware of holding. The feeling of certainty was assuredly working better than it usually did with dice. Still another ox-cart rumbled down the narrow street toward him.

Moving back against a wall to let the cart pass, he stepped around it to the far side as soon as it was by. When his legs were in line with the tall wheels, he slowed his pace to the trudge of the ox. The potter would tell the guardsmen of the direction he had gone, while he went off the opposite way. It was but another moment gained, but enough moments such as these could add up to a man's life.

As soon as the cart had crossed the street where the potter stood, Conan hurried on ahead. He had to get to the harbor and the jumble of docks, warehouses, and taverns, where he could find safety among the smugglers. And he had to find out why there was a reward of a thousand pieces of gold being offered for him. The first was the most urgent, yet it would not be so easy as simply walking there. He was far from inconspicuous, and the white cloak would soon be added to the description of the man for whom the reward was offered. Without the hood, though, his blue eyes would leave a trail easily followed by guardsmen seeking a big northlander. The question, then, was how to exchange the cloak for one of another color, but also with a hood, while not letting his eyes be seen.

He watched for a cloak he might buy or steal, but saw few with hoods and none large enough to avoid looking ludicrous on his broad shoulders. There was no point in drawing eyes by looking the clown when the purpose was to avoid them. As quickly as he could without gaining attention for his speed, pausing at every street crossing to look for guardsmen, he moved toward the harbor. Or tried to. Three times he was forced to turn aside by the sight of City Guardsmen, and once he barely had time to duck into a shop selling cheap gilded jewelry before half a score of guardsmen strode by. He was going north, he realized, parallel to the harbor district, and certainly not toward it.

Guardsmen's spears above the heads of the crowd before him turned him down a side street packed with humanity. Away from the harbor, he thought with a curse as he pushed through the crowd, then cursed again when shouts for the way to be cleared indicated the soldiers had entered the same street. They gave no sign that they had seen him, but that could not last for long, not with him standing a head taller than the next tallest man on the street. He lengthened his stride, then almost immediately slowed again. A score of spear points, glittering in the sunlight, approached from ahead.

This time he did not waste breath on curses. An alley, smelling strongly of offal and chamber pots, offered the only escape. As he ducked into it, he realized that he had been there before, in company with Hordo during his first days with the one-eyed man's band of smugglers. Stairs of crumbling brown brick, narrow yet, even so, all but filling the width of the alley, led to the floor above a fruit vendor's stall. Conan took them two at a time. A stooped man in robes of brown camel's hair jumped as the Cimmerian pushed open the rough wooden door without knocking.

The small room was sparsely furnished, with a cot against one wall and an upright chest with many small drawers against another. A table that leaned on a badly mended leg sat in the middle of the bare wooden floor, a single stool beside it. A few garments hung on pegs in the walls. All seemed old and weathered, and the stooped man was a match for his possessions. Sparse white hair and olive skin blotched with age and wrinkled like often-folded parchment made the fellow seem able to claim a century. His hands were like knobby claws as they clutched a packet of oilskin, and his dark eyes, hooded and glaring, were the only part of him that showed any spark of vitality.

"My apologies," Conan said quickly. He wracked his brain for the old man's name. "I did not mean to enter so abruptly, Ghurran." That was it. "I fish with Hordo."

Ghurran grunted and bent to peer fussily at the packets and twists of parchment atop the rickety table. "Hordo, eh? His joints aching again? He should find another trade. The sea does not suit his bones. Or perhaps you come for yourself? A love philtre, perhaps?"

"No." Half of Conan's mind was on listening for the soldiers below. Not until they were gone could he risk putting his nose outside. "What I truly need," he muttered, "is a way to become invisible until I reach the harbor."

The old man remained bent over the table, but his head swiveled toward the big youth. "I compound herbs, and occasionally read the stars," he said dryly. "You want a wizard. Why not try the love philtre? Guaranteed to put a woman helpless in your arms for the night. Of course, perhaps a handsome young man like you does not need such."

Conan shook his head distractedly. The parties of guardsmen had met at the mouth of the alley. A thin murmuring floated to him, but he could not make out any words. They seemed in no hurry to move on. All of this trouble, and he did not even know why. A Vendhyan plot, those he had overheard had said. "May their sisters sell for a small price," he muttered in Vendhyan.

"Katar!" Ghurran grunted. The old man lowered himself jerkily to his knees and fumbled under the table for a dropped packet. "My old fingers do not hold as once they did. What was that language you spoke?"

"Vendhyan," Conan replied without taking his mind from the soldiers. "I learned a little of the tongue, since we buy so much fish from Vendhyans." Most of the smugglers could speak three or four languages after a fashion, and his quick ear had already picked up considerable Vendhyan as well as smatterings of several others. "What do you know of Vendhya?" he went on.

"Vendhya? How should I know of Vendhya. Ask me of herbs. I know something of herbs."

"It is said that you will pay for herbs and seeds from far lands, and that you ask many questions of these lands when you buy. Surely you have purchased some herbs from Vendhya."

"All plants have uses, but the men who bring them to

me rarely know those uses. I must try to draw the information from them, asking all they know of the country from which the herbs or seeds came in order to sift out a few grains that are useful to me.'' The old man got to his feet and paused for breath, dusting his bony hands on his robes. ''I have bought some trifles from Vendhya, and I am told it is a land full of intrigue, a dangerous land for the unwary, for those who too easily believe the promises of a man or the flattery of a woman. Why do you wish to know of Vendhya?''

''It is said in the streets that a prince has been slain, or perhaps a general, and that Vendhyans hired the killing done.''

''I see. I have not been out the entire day.'' Ghurran chewed at a gnarled knuckle. ''Such a thing is unlikely at this time, for it is said that *wazam* of Vendhya, the chief advisor to King Bhandarkar, visits Aghrapur to conclude a treaty, and many nobles of the royal court at Ayodhya visit as well. Yet remember the intrigues. Who can say? You still have not told me why you are so interested in this.''

Conan hesitated. The old man provided poultices and infusions for half the smugglers in Sultanapur. That so many continued to trust him was in his favor. ''The rumor is that the assassin was a northlander, and the City Guard seems to think I am the man.''

The parchment-skinned man tucked his hands into the sleeves of his robe and peered at Conan with his head tilted. ''Are you? Did you take Vendhyan gold?''

''I did not,'' Conan replied. ''Nor did I kill a prince, or a general.'' Assuredly no man he had faced that day had been either.

''Very well,'' Ghurran said. His lips tightened reluctantly. Then he sighed and took a dusty dark-blue cloak from the wall. "Here. This will make you somewhat less conspicuous than the one you wear now."

Surprised, Conan nonetheless quickly exchanged his white cloak for the other. Despite the dust and folds of hanging, perhaps for years, the dark-blue wool was finely woven and showed little wear. It was tight across the Cimmerian's shoulders, yet had obviously been made for a man bigger than Ghurran.

"Age shrinks all men," the stooped herbalist said as though he had read Conan's mind.

Conan nodded. "I thank you, and I will remember this." The sound of the soldiers had faded away while he was talking. He cracked the door and peered out. The narrow street was jammed with people, but none were guardsmen. "Fare you well, Ghurran. And again, my thanks."

Without waiting for the other man to speak again, Conan slipped out, descended the stairs and melded into the crowd. The harbor district, he thought. Once he reached that, there would be time to consider other matters.

CHAPTER III

The patrols of guardsmen were a nuisance to the young Turanian who made his way out of the harbor district and into an area that seemed favored, as nearly as he could tell, solely by beggars, bawds and cutpurses. He avoided the soldiers deftly, and none of the area's denizens favored him with a second glance.

A Corinthian mother had given him features that were neither Corinthian nor Turanian, but rather simply dark-eyed and not quite handsome. Clean-shaven at the moment, he could pass as a native of any one of a half a score of countries and had done so more than once. He was above medium height, with a rawboned lanky build that often fooled men into underestimating his strength, several times to the saving of his life. His garb was motley, a patched Corinthian doublet that had once been red, baggy Zamoran breeches of pale cotton, well-worn boots from Iranistan.

Only the tulwar at his side and his turban, none too clean and none too neatly wrapped, were Turanian, he thought sourly. Four years gone from his own country and before he was back a tenday, he found himself skulking about the dusty streets of Sultanapur trying to avoid the City Guard. Not for the first time since leaving home at nineteen, he regretted his decision not to follow in his father's footsteps as a spice merchant. As always, though, the regret lasted only until he could remind himself of how boring a spice merchant's life was, but of late that reminding took longer than it once had.

Turning into an alley, he paused to see if anyone took notice. A single footsore trull began to flash a smile at him, then valued his garb in her mind and trudged on. The rest of the throng streamed by without an eye turning his way. He backed down the stench-filled alley, keeping a watch on the street, until he felt a rough wooden door under his fingers. Satisfied that he was still unobserved, he ducked through the doorway into darkness.

Instantly a knife at his throat stopped him in his tracks, but all he did was say quietly, "I am Jelal. I come from the West." Anything else, he knew, and the knife wielder would have used his blade, not to mention the two other men he was sure were in the pitch-black room.

Flint struck steel, light flared, and a lamp that smoked and reeked of rancid oil was held to his face. Two, he saw, beside the one who still held a razor edge to his throat, and even the man with the lamp, a thick half-moon scar curling around his right eye, clutched a bared dagger.

The scar-faced man stepped aside and jerked his head toward a door leading deeper into the building. "Go on," he said. Only then was the knife lowered from Jelal's throat.

Jelal did not say anything. This was not the first such meeting for him, nor even the twentieth. He went on through the second door.

The windowless room he entered was what was to be

expected in this quarter of the city, rough walls of clay brick, a dirt floor, a crude table tilted on a cracked leg. What was not to be expected were the beeswax candles giving light, the white linen cloth spread on the table top, or the crystal flagon of wine sitting on the cloth beside two cups of hammered gold. Nor was the man seated behind the table one to be expected in such a place. A plain dark cloak, nondescript yet of quality too fine for that region of Sultanapur, covered much of his garb. His narrow thin-nosed face, with mustaches and small beard neatly waxed to points, seemed more suited to a palace than a district of beggars. He spoke as soon as Jelal entered.

"It is well you come today, Jelal. Each time I must come out into the city increases the risk I will be seen and identified. You have made contact?" He waved a soft-skinned hand with a heavy gold seal-ring on the forefinger toward the crystal flagon. "Have some wine for the heat."

"I have made contact," Jelal replied carefully, "but—"

"Good, my boy. I knew that you would, even in so short a time. Four years in Corinthia and Koth and Khauran, posing as every sort of merchant and peddler, legal and otherwise, and never once caught or even suspected. You are perhaps the best man I have ever had. But I fear your task in Sultanapur has changed."

Jelal drew himself up. "My lord, I request to be reposted to the Ibari Scouts."

Lord Khalid, the man who ordered and controlled all the spies of King Yildiz of Turan, stared in amazement. "Mitra strike me, why?"

"My lord, you say I was never once suspected in four years, and it is true. But it is true because I not only acted the part, I *was* a merchant, or a peddler as the instant demanded, spending most of my days buying and selling, talking of markets and prices. My lord, I became a soldier in part to avoid becoming a merchant like my father. I was a good soldier, and I ask to serve Turan and the King where I can serve them best, as a soldier once more in the Ibari Mountains.''

The spy master drummed his fingers on the table. ''My boy, you were chosen for the very reasons you cite. Your service was all in the southern mountains, so no western foreigner is likely to ever have seen you as a soldier. Your boyhood training to be a merchant not only prepared you to play that part to perfection, but also, because of a merchant's need to winnow fact from rumor to find the proper market and price, it made sure that you could do the same with other kinds of rumors and give reports of great value. As you have. You serve Turan best where you are.''

''But, my lord—''

''Enough, Jelal. There is no time. What do you know of events in Sultanapur this day?''

Jelal sighed. ''There are many rumors,'' he began slowly, ''reporting everything but an invasion. Piecing together the most likely, I should say that Prince Tureg Amal was killed this morning. Beyond that I should say the strongest rumor is that a northlander was involved. As it was not what I came to Sultanapur for, I put no more than half my mind to it, I fear.''

''Half your mind, and you get one of two right.'' The older man nodded approvingly. ''You are indeed the best of my men. I do not know where the rumor of a northlander was born. Perhaps someone saw such a man in the street.''

''But the guardsmen, my lord. They seek—''

''Yes, yes. The rumors have spread even to them, and I've done nothing to change that state of affairs for the moment. Let the true culprits think they have escaped notice. It is not the first time soldiers have been sent

chasing shadows, nor will it be the last. And a few innocent foreigners—if any of them can truly be called
innocent—a few such put to the question, or even killed, is
a small price to pay if it helps us take the true villains
unaware. Believe me when I say the throne of Turan
could be at stake."

Jelal managed a nod. He was aware from experience
just how coldly practical this soft-appearing man could be,
even if the stakes were considerably less than the Turanian
throne. "And the prince, my lord? You said I was half
right."

"Tureg Amal," Kalid sighed, "drunkard, wastrel, lecher,
and High Admiral of Turan, died this morning of a poisoned needle thrust into his neck. Not by a northern giant,
as the rumors say, but by a woman. A Vendhyan assassin,
according to reports."

"An assassin?" Jelal said. "My lord, the prince's ways
with women are well know. Could he not perhaps simply
have driven some wench to murder?"

The spy master shook his head. "As much as I should
prefer it so, no. The servants at Tureg Amal's palace have
been questioned thoroughly. A Vendhyan woman was delivered to the palace this morning, supposedly a gift from a
merchant of that country seeking added protection for his
cargoes on the Vilayet. Within the hour the prince was
dead, the keeper of his zenanna drugged, and the woman
had disappeared unseen from a heavily guarded palace."

"It certainly sounds the work of an assassin," Jelal
agreed, "but—"

"There could be worse," the older man cut him off.
"The commander of the prince's bodyguard, one Captain
Murad, was also slain this morning, along with two of his
men, apparently in a tavern brawl. I do not like such
coincidences. Perhaps it was unrelated, and perhaps they

were silenced after effecting the woman's escape. And if men of the High Admiral's bodyguard took gold to aid in his death . . . well, that scandal could do more harm than the old fool's murder.''

"Be that as it may, my lord, the other does not make sense. I understand that the *wazam* of Vendhya is in Aghrapur to negotiate a treaty with King Yildiz. Surely the King of Vendhya would not countenance an assassination while his chief counselor was in our capital, in our very hands. And if he did, why the High Admiral? The King's death would create turmoil, while the prince's creates only anger toward Vendhya.''

"The King's death by a Vendhyan assassin would also create war with Vendhya," Khalid said dryly, "while Tureg Amal's . . .'' He shrugged. "I do not know the why of it, my boy, but Vendhyans suck intrigue with their mothers' milk and do nothing without a purpose, usually nefarious. As for the *wazam*, Karim Singh sailed from Aghrapur yesterday. And the treaty? I was suspicious of it before, now I am doubly so. Less than five years ago they nearly went to war with us over their claims to Secunderam. Now, without a protest, the *wazam* puts his seal on a treaty that does not so much as mention that city. And one that favors Turan on several other points, as well. I had thought they sought to lull us while they prepared some stroke. Now I no longer know what to think.'' He began to roll the tip of his beard between his thumb and forefinger, the greatest outward sign of inner turmoil that he ever showed.

Reluctantly Jelal felt the puzzle catching at him, as it so often had before. The desire to return to soldiering was still there but pushed to the back of his mind. For the moment. "What can I do, my lord?" he asked at last. "The Vendhyan assassin is surely no longer in the city.''

"That is true," the spy master replied, and his voice

hardened as he spoke. "But I want answers. I need them. The King depends on me for them. What is Vendhya up to? Are we to expect a war? Captain Murad's death may lead to some answers. Use the contacts you have made with the lawless underside of Sultanapur. Find a trail to the answers I need and follow it all the way to Vendhya if you must. But bring me the answers."

"I will, my lord," Jelal promised. But to himself he promised that this was the last time. Whether he was returned to the Ibari Scouts or not, after this one last puzzle, he would be a spy no more.

CHAPTER IV

Despite the cloak Ghurran had given him, Conan kept close to the sides of the narrow, bustling streets, on the edges of the continuous flow of people. It was true that the dark-blue cloak would not bring a moment's glance from a guardsman looking for one of white linen, and the hood did hide his face and damning blue eyes, but the sheer size of him was difficult to miss. Few men in Sultanapur came close to his height or breadth of shoulder, and certainly none of them was among the crowds thronging the streets he traveled this day. The big Cimmerian stood out like a Remaira stallion among mules.

Five times after leaving the herbalist Conan was forced to turn aside for patrols of guardsmen, their precisely slanted spears glinting in the bright sun as though to give warning of their coming, but luck seemed at last to be with him. His progress toward the harbor was constant, if zig-zag. High-wheeled ox-carts began once more to be almost as numerous as people. The long stone shapes of warehouses rose about him, and the tall white towers of the city granaries.

Men with the calloused hands and sweat-stained tunics of dockers and roustabouts outnumbered all but those with the rolling walk and forked queues of seafarers. Half the women were trulls in narrow girdles of jingling coin and thin silk or less, while most of the rest cast a sharp eye for a purse to cut or a bolt of silk or lace that could be snatched from a cart. Here, too, were people who knew him.

"An hour's pleasure, big man?" cooed a buxom doxy with hennaed hair piled high on her head and gilded brass hoops in her ears. She moved closer and pressed nearly bare breasts against his arm, dropping her voice for his ear alone. "You fool, the City Guard has already taken up three dockers just for being tall. And they are questioning outlanders, so you're doubly at risk. Now, put your arm around me, and we will go to my room. I can hide you till it all quiets. And I'll charge you but—oh, Mitra, I'll not charge you at all."

Conan grinned despite himself. "A generous offer, Zara. But I must find Hordo."

"I've not seen him, Conan. And you cannot risk looking. Come with me."

"Another time," he said, and she squealed as he pinched a plump buttock.

In short order a sailor in a tar-smeared tunic and a bearded warehouseman had repeated Zara's warning. A slender wench with a virgin's face and innocent eyes—and a cutpurse's curved blade with which she constantly toyed—echoed both warning and offer. None knew where Hordo was to be found, however. Conan almost accepted the slender woman's offer. The glass had been turned, he knew, and the sands were running out on him. Did he not find Hordo quickly, he must go to ground.

A short, wiry man, bent under the weight of a canvas

sack on his shoulder, suddenly caught the Cimmerian's eye. Conan snagged the man's bony arm with one hand and hauled him out of the stream of people.

"What are you doing?" the Cimmerian's captive whispered between teeth clenched in a wooden smile. His sunken eyes darted frantically above a pointed nose, giving him the image of a mouse searching for a hole. "Mitra, Cimmerian! I stole this not twenty paces from here, and they'll see it's gone in another moment. Let me go!"

"I am looking for Hordo, Tarek," Conan said softy.

"Hordo? He's at Kafar's warehouse, I think." Tarek stumbled a step as Conan released him, then rotated his shoulder in a broad gesture. "You should not grab a man so, Cimmerian. It could be dangerous. And don't you know the City Guard—"

"—is seeking a big outlander," Conan finished for him. "I know."

A shout rose from the direction Tarek had come, and the little man darted away like the rodent he resembled. Conan went the other way, soon passing by a stall where a salt peddler in voluminous robes seemed to dance with his helpers, they jumping about to dodge while he tugged at his beard and kicked at them and shouted that the gods were unmerciful to send the same man blind apprentices and thieves as well. While the salt vendor leaped and screamed, two girls of no more than sixteen years hefted one of his canvas sacks between them and disappeared, unseen by him, into the throng.

Twice more the Cimmerian was forced to turn aside for a patrol of the City Guard, but Kafar's warehouse was not far, and he reached it quickly. It was not one of the long stone structures owned by merchants, but rather a nondescript building of two stories, daubed in flaking white clay, that might once have held a tavern or a chandler's shop. In truth it was a warehouse of sorts. A smugglers' warehouse. Gold in the proper palms kept the guardsmen away, for the time at least. When the bribes failed, though, because higher authority decided an example must be made, or more likely because someone decided the reward for confiscated contraband outweighed the bribes, the smugglers of Sultanapur would not be slowed for an instant. Scores of such warehouses could be found near the harbor, and when Kafar's was no more, two others would spring up in its place.

The splintery wooden door from the street let into a windowless room dimly lit by rush torches in crude iron sconces. Two of the torches had guttered out, but no one seemed to notice. A small knot of men, dressed in mismatched garb from a dozen countries, squatted in a semicircle, casting dice against a wall. Others sat on casks at a table of boards laid on sawhorses, engrossed in whispered talk over clay mugs of wine. A Kothian in a red-striped tunic sat off by himself on a three-legged stool near a door at the back of the room, idly flipping a dagger to stick up in the rough-hewn planks of the floor. The air in the room was hot and close, not only because of the torches, but because few of the half-score men there ever made acquaintance with water and most thought soap a fine gift for a woman, if nicely perfumed, but not a thing to be used.

Only the Kothian looked up at Conan's entrance. "Do you not know—" he began.

"I know, Kafar," Conan said curtly. "Is Hordo here?"

The Kothian jerked his head at the door behind him and returned to flipping his dagger. "The cellar," he said as the blade quivered in the floor once more.

It was the custom in such places to store the goods of each smuggler in a separate room, for no man among them trusted those not of his band to the point of letting him know what kind of "fish" he carried or to where. Closed doors, iron-bound and held shut with massive iron locks, lined the corridor in the rear of the building. At the end of the corridor, beside a wide door leading to the alley behind the warehouse, were stone stairs leading down.

As the Cimmerian started down the stairs, Hordo opened the door at the bottom. "Where in Zandru's Nine Hells have you been?" the one-eyed smuggler roared. "And what in Mitra's name have you been doing?" He was nearly as big as Conan, though his muscles were overlaid with fat and the years had weathered his face. Large gold hoops hung from his ears and a jagged scar ran from under his eye-patch of rough leather down into the thick black thatch of his beard, pulling the left side of his mouth into a permanent sneer. "I leave word with Tasha and the next thing I hear. . . . Well, get on down here before the Guard seizes you right in front of me. If that fool wench failed to tell you I needed you, I'll have her hide."

Conan winced ruefully. So Tasha had been speaking the truth. If he had not thought she was lying from jealousy, he would have left the Golden Crescent before the captain arrived, and the City Guard would not be seeking his head. Well, it was far from the first time he had gotten into trouble from misreading a woman. And in any case, a man who used pain to frighten a woman to his bed deserved killing.

"It was not her fault, Hordo," he said, pushing past the bearded man into the cellar. "I had a trifle of trouble with—" He cut off at the sight of a stranger in the room, a tall, skinny man in a turban who stood beside a score of small wooden chests, like the tin-lined chests in which tea was shipped, stacked on the dirt floor against a dusty stone wall. Here, too, light came from rush torches. "Who is he?" the Cimmerian demanded.

"He's called Hasan," the one-eyed man replied impatiently. "A new 'fisherman.' Now! Is there any truth to these rumors, Cimmerian? I do not care if you've killed Tureg Amal; that old fool is no loss to the world. But if you have, you must get out of Sultanapur, perhaps out of Turan, and quickly. Even if you killed no one, you had best remain out of sight until they catch who did."

"The High Admiral?" Conan exclaimed. "I heard it was a general, though now that I think of it, someone did say a prince. Hordo, why would I kill the High Admiral of Turan?"

The lanky man spoke up suddenly. "The rumors say it was hired done. For enough gold I suppose a man might kill anyone."

Conan's face became stony. "You seem to be calling me liar," he said in a deadly quiet tone.

"Easy, Cimmerian," Hordo said, and added to the other man, "Are you trying to get yourself killed, Hasan? Offer this man coin for a killing, and 'twill be luck if you escape with no more than broken bones. And if he says he killed no one, then he killed no one."

"I did not say that exactly," Conan said uncomfortably. "There was a Guard captain, and two or three guardsmen." He glared at the turbaned man who had made a sound in his throat. "You have a comment about *that* as well?"

"You two fighting cocks settle your ruffs," Hordo snapped. "We have a load of 'fish' to carry. The man who wants it shipped will be here any instant, and I'll have no bloodshed, or snarling either, in front of him. He'll seek elsewhere if he thinks we will slay each other before delivering his chests." His bearded head swung like that of a bear. "I need my whole crew if we are to get the accursed things to the mouth of the Zaporoska in the time specified, and the only two who have heeded

my call squabble like dockers with their heads full of
wine.''

''You told me we'd not sail again for three or four
days,'' Conan said, walking over to examine the chests.
Hasan moved warily out of his way, but it was the finely
crafted boxes that interested him. ''The crew are scattered
among the taverns and bordellos,'' he went on, ''hip
deep in women, and with wine fumes where their wits
were four hours gone. I could enjoy a quick journey
out of Sultanapur now, but if we find all twenty by nightfall,
I'll become an Erlikite.''

''We must sail by dark,'' Hordo said. ''The gold is
more for being faster than agreed, but less for being
slower.'' The scar-faced smuggler moved Hasan farther
away from them with a look, then stepped closer to the
Cimmerian and dropped his voice. ''I do not doubt your
word, Conan, but *is* it you the guardsmen seek? For this
captain, perhaps?''

Conan shrugged, but did not stop his study of the chests.
''I do not know,'' he replied for Hordo's ears alone. ''The
rumors say nothing of Murad, and my name is not
mentioned.'' The largest dimension of the chests was the
length of a man's forearm. Their sides were smooth and
plain, and the flat, close-fitting lid of each was held by
eight leaden seals impressed with the image of a bird he
had never seen before. ''The tongues of the street speak of
Tureg Amal. Still, somewhere words have been spoken
concerning what occurred at the Golden Crescent, or there
would be no big northlander in the tale.'' He hefted one of
the boxes, trying its weight. To his surprise, it was light
enough to have been packed with feathers. ''Men from the
northern lands are not so common as visitors in Sultanapur
for that.''

''Aye,'' the one-eyed man agreed sagely. ''And it is

said that when two rumors meet, they exchange words. Also that a rumor changes on each journey from mouth to ear."

"Do you begin to quote aphorisms in your old age, Hordo?" Conan chuckled. "I know not the how or why of what has happened, but I do know that trouble sits on my shoulder until it is all made clear."

"I am not too old to try breaking your head," Hordo growled. "And when was the day trouble did not sit on your shoulder, Cimmerian?"

Conan ignored the question; he had long since decided a man could not live a free life and avoid trouble at the same time. "What is in these chests?" he asked.

"Spices," came an answer from the doorway.

The Cimmerian's hand went to his sword-hilt. The newcomer wore a dark gray cloak with a voluminous hood. As soon as he had closed the cellar door behind him, he threw back the hood to reveal a narrow, swarthy face topped by a turban twice as big around as was the fashion in Turan, fronted by heron feathers held by a pin of opal and silver. Rings covered his fingers with sapphires and amethysts.

"A Vendhyan!" Hasan burst out.

Hordo motioned him to silence. "I was afraid you were not coming, Patil."

"Not coming?" The Vendhyan's tone was puzzled, but then he smiled thinly. "Ah, you feared that I was involved with the events spoken of in the streets. No, I assure you I had nothing to do with the very unfortunate demise of the High Admiral. Such affairs are not for me. I am but a humble merchant who must avoid paying the custom both of your King Yildiz and of my King Bhandarkar if I am to make my poor profit."

"Of course, Patil," Hordo said. "And you have come to the proper men to see that Yildiz's excisemen take not a single coin of yours. The rest of my crew is even now preparing our boat for a swift passage. Conan, go see that all is in readiness." He half-turned his back to the Vendhyan and made small frantic gestures that only Conan and Hasan could see. "We must be ready to sail quickly."

Conan knew very well what the gestures meant. He was to go upstairs and intercept any of Hordo's crew who came staggering in with their brains half-pickled in wine. Five or six sots stumbling in and making it clear to this Patil that they were part of the crew would do little to convince him they could make good on Hordo's promise of sailing quickly. But Conan did not stir. Instead he hefted the chest again.

"Spices?" he said. "Saffron, pepper, and all the other spices I could name come across the Vilayet from the east. What spice crosses from the west?"

"Rare condiments from islands of the Western Sea," Patil replied smoothly. "They are considered great delicacies in my country."

Conan nodded. "Of course. Yet despite that, I've heard nothing of such being smuggled. Have you, Hordo?"

The bearded man shook his head doubtfully; worry that Conan was putting the arrangement in jeopardy creased his face. Patil's face did not change, but he wet his lips with the tip of his tongue. Conan let the box fall, and the Vendhyan winced as it thudded on the packed earth.

"Open it," Conan said. "I would see what we carry across the Vilayet."

Patil let out a squawk of protest directed at Hordo. "This is not a part of our agreement. Kafar told me that you were the most trustworthy of the smugglers, otherwise I would have gone elsewhere. I offer much gold for you to deliver my chests and myself to the mouth of the Zaporoska River, not for you to ask questions and make demands."

"He does offer a great deal of gold, Conan," Hordo said slowly.

"Enough to carry kanda leaf?" the Cimmerian asked. "Or red lotus? You have seen the wretches who would choose their pipes over wine, or a woman, or even over food. How much gold to carry that?"

Breathing heavily, Hordo scratched at his beard and grimaced. "Oh, all right. Open the chests, Patil. I care not what they contain so long as it is not kanda leaf or red lotus."

"I cannot!" the Vendhyan cried. Sweat made his dark face shine. "My master would be furious. I demand that—"

"Your master?" Hasan cut him off. "What kind of merchant has a master, Vendhyan? Or are you something else?"

Conan's voice hardened. "Open the chests."

Patil's eyes shifted in a hunted way. Suddenly he spun toward the door. Conan lunged to catch a handful of the Vendhyan's flaring cloak, and the swarthy man whirled back, his fist swinging at the Cimmerian's face. A tiny flicker of light warned Conan, and he leaped back from the blow. The leaf-shaped blade that projected from between Patil's fingers sliced lightly across Conan's cheek just below the eye. Conan's foot came down on the dropped chest, which turned and sent him sprawling on his back on the dirt floor.

The instant he was free of Conan's grasp, Patil darted to the door, flung it open and dashed through. Straight into three men who seemed each to be supporting the others as they walked, or rather staggered. All four went down in a thrashing, cursing heap.

Scrambling to his feet, Conan hauled the struggling men out of the tangle, heaving each aside as soon as he saw that it was one of Hordo's crew. The last was Patil, and the Vendhyan lay without moving. His large turban was knocked askew, and it came off completely as the Cimmerian rolled him onto his back. It was as Conan had feared. Patil's dark eyes stared at him emptily, twisted with pain, and the Vendhyan's teeth were bared in a frozen rictus. The would-be killer's fist was jammed against the center of his chest. Conan had no doubt the push-dagger's blade had been just long enough to reach the heart.

He brushed a hand across his cheek. The fingertips came away red, but the cut was little more than a scratch. It was luck, he thought, that the fellow had not simply stabbed at him. He might never have been aware of the small dagger until it found his own heart.

"Not the outcome you expected, is it?" he told the corpse. "But I would rather have you alive to talk."

Hordo pushed past him to grab the Vendhyan's robes. "Let us get this out of sight of anyone who wanders by the stairs, Cimmerian. No need to flaunt matters, especially as I'd not like anyone to think we killed this fool for his goods. Things like that can ruin a man's trade."

Together they dragged the body into the cellar and shut the iron-strapped door. The three smugglers who had inadvertently stopped the Vendhyan's escape lay sprawled against a wall, and two of them stared blearily at the corpse when it was dropped at their feet.

" 'S drunker 'n us," muttered an Iranistani wearing a stained and filthy headcloth.

" 'S not drunk," replied the man next to him, a Nemedian who might have been handsome had his nose not been slit for theft at some time in the past. " 'S dead."

The third man emitted a snore like a ripping sail.

"All three of you shut your teeth," Hordo growled.

Conan touched his cheek again. The blood was already congealing. He was more interested in the chest he had dropped, though. He set it upright on the floor and knelt to study the lead seals. The bird impressed in the gray metal was no more familiar now than before. Vendhyan, perhaps, though seemingly the chests went in the wrong direction for that. The seals could be simply a means of keeping the chests tightly closed or a way to tell if they had been opened. He had also seen such used as triggers to launch venom-tipped needles or poisonous vapors at those who pried where they were not wanted. Such were not usually found on smuggled goods, but then again, these were apparently no ordinary "fish."

"I'll take the chance," he muttered. His heart pounded as he pushed the point of his new dagger under one seal.

"Wait, you fool," Hordo began, but with a twist of his wrist, Conan sliced through the soft lead. "Some day your luck will be used up," the one-eyed man breathed.

Without replying, the Cimmerian quickly broke the other seals. The dagger served to lever up the tight-fitting lid. Both stared in disbelief at the contents of the chest. To the brim it was filled with small, dried leaves.

"Spices?" Hasan said doubtfully.

Conan cautiously stirred the leaves with his dagger, then scooped up a handful. They cracked brittlely in his grasp and gave off no aroma. "A man does not try to kill to hide spices," Conan said. "We'll see what is in the other chests."

He half-rose from his knees, swayed and sank back down. The heavy thumping in his chest continued unabated. He touched the cut on his face once more; it felt as though a piece of leather lay between fingers and cheek. "That blade." His tongue felt thick around the words. "There was something on it."

The blood drained from Hordo's face. "Poison," he breathed. "Fight it, Cimmerian. You must fight it! If you let your eyes close, you'll never open them again!"

Conan tried again to rise, to go over to the other chests, and again he almost fell. Hordo caught him, easing him to a sitting position against the wall.

"The chests," Conan said. "If I'm dying, I want to know why."

"Mitra curse the chests!" Hordo snapped. "And you're not dying! Not if we can get Ghurran here."

"I will go for him," Hasan said, then subsided under Hordo's glare.

"And how will you do that, who's never seen the man before? Prytanis!" Hordo stalked across the cellar, and with a hand the size of a small ham hauled the Nemedian to his feet by a fistful of tunic. His other hand slapped the slit-nosed fellow's face back and forth. "Grab your wits, Prytanis! Can you hear me? Listen, Erlik take you, or I'll break your skull!"

"I am listening," the Nemedian groaned. "By all the gods, do not hit my head so. It is breaking already."

"Then listen well if you do not want it shattered," Hordo growled, but he stopped his slapping. "Get you to Ghurran and fetch him here. Tell him it is poison and tell him there's a hundred gold pieces for him if he gets here in time. Do you understand that, you sotted spawn of a camel?"

"I understand," the Nemedian said unsteadily and staggered toward the door under the impetus of Hordo's shove.

"Then run, curse you! If you fail in this, I'll slit your belly and hang you with your own guts! Where do you think you're going?" the one-eyed man added as Hasan made to follow Prytanis from the cellar.

"With him," Hasan replied. "He's so drunk he will not remember what he's about beyond the first pitcher of wine he sees without someone to keep him to the task."

"He will remember," Hordo rumbled, "because he

knows I will do as I said. To the word. If you want to do
something, put a cloak over Patil so we do not have to
look at him.''

"You do not have a hundred pieces of gold, Hordo,"
Conan said.

"Then you can pay it," the smuggler replied. "And if
you die on me, I will sell your corpse for it."

Conan laughed, but the laughter quickly trailed off in
coughing, for he had no breath to spare. He felt as weak as
a child. Even if the others got him to his feet, he knew it
would be all he could do to stand. The fear and despair in
his friend's voice did not touch him, however. There was
an answer he must have, and it lay there in the chests
stacked against the wall. Or at least some clue to the
answer must. The question was simple, yet finding the
answer would keep him alive a while longer, for he would
not allow himself to die without it.

He would not die without knowing why.

CHAPTER V

One by one, five more of Hordo's crew staggered into Kafar's cellar, most as drunk as the first three. Decidedly sickly looks came over their faces as they heard what had happened. It was not the death of the Vendhyan, nor even his attempt on Conan, but rather the means of that attempt. They were used to an honest blade and could even understand the knife in the back, but poison was something a man could not defend against. Cups that changed color when poisoned wine was poured into them were in the realm of wizards, and of princes who could afford to pay wizards.

Their green faces did not bother Conan, but the funereal glances they cast at him did. "I am not dead yet," he muttered. The words came pantingly now.

"Where in Zandru's Nine Hells is Ghurran?" Hordo growled.

As though to punctuate his words, the iron-strapped door banged open, and Prytanis led Ghurran into the cellar by a firm grip on a bony arm. The slit-nosed Nemedian appeared to have sobered to a degree, whether from his exercise in fetching Ghurran or from Hordo's threats.

A leather strap crossed the stooped herbalist's heaving chest, supporting a small wooden case at his side. Freeing his arm with a jerk, he scowled about the room, at the swaying drankards and the still-snoring Iranistani and the cloak-shrouded mound that was the Vendhyan. "For this I was dragged through the streets like a goat going to market?" he grated breathlessly. "To treat men fool enough to drink tainted wine?"

"Tainted wine on a blade," Conan managed. He leaned forward and his head spun. "Once already today you helped me. Can you do it again, Ghurran?"

The old man brushed past Hordo and knelt to peer into the Cimmerian's eyes. "There may be time," he murmured, then in a firmer voice said, "You have the poisoned blade? Let me see it."

It was Hasan who lifted the cloak enough to tug the push-dagger from the corpse's chest. He wiped the leaf-shaped blade on the cloak before handing it to Ghurran.

The herbalist turned the small weapon over in scrawny fingers. A smooth ivory knob formed the hilt, carved to fit the palm while the blade projected between the fingers. "An assassin's weapon in Vendhya," he said. "Or so I have heard such described."

Conan kept his eyes on the old man's parchment-skinned face. "Well?" was all he said.

Instead of answering, Ghurran held the blade to his nostrils and sniffed lightly. Frowning, he wet a long-nailed finger at his mouth and touched it to the blade. With even greater caution than he had shown before, he brought the finger to his lips. Quickly he spat, scrubbing the finger on his robes.

"Do something!" Hordo demanded.

"Poisons are something I seldom deal with," Ghurran said calmly. He opened the wooden box hanging at his side and began to take out small parchment packets and stone vials. "But perhaps I can do something." A bronze mortar and pestle, no larger than a man's hand, came from the box. "Get me a goblet of wine, and quickly."

Hordo motioned to Prytanis, who hurried out. The herbalist set to work, dropping dried leaves and bits of powder into the mortar, grinding them together with the pestle. Prytanis returned with a rough clay goblet filled to the top with cheap wine. Ghurran took it and poured in the mixture from the mortar, stirring it vigorously with his finger.

"Here," the old man said, holding the wine to Conan's mouth. "Drink."

Conan looked at the offering. A few pieces of leaf floated on the wine's surface along with the sprinkling of varicolored powders. "This will rid me of the poison?"

Ghurran looked at him levelly. "In the time it would take you to reach the docks and return, you will either be able to walk from this room, or you will be dead." The listening smugglers stirred.

"If he dies—" Hordo began threateningly, but Conan cut him off.

"If I die, it will not be Ghurran's fault, will it, Ghurran?"

"Drink," the old man said, "or it will be your own fault."

Conan drank. With the first mouthful a grimace twisted his face, becoming worse with every swallow. As the goblet was taken from his mouth, he gasped. "Crom! It tastes as if a camel bathed in it!" A few of the listeners, those sober enough, laughed.

Ghurran grunted. "Do you want sweetness on the tongue, or the poison counteracted?" His eye fell on the opened chest. Face made even more hollow by a frown, he took some of the leaves, stirring them on his palm with a bony finger.

"Do you know the leaf?" Conan asked. He was not sure if his breathing was easier, or if he just imagined it so. "The man who did this told us they were spices."

"Spices?" Ghurran said absently. "No, I do not think they are spices. But then," he added, letting the leaves fall back into the chest, "I do not know all plants. I would like to look in the other chests. If there are herbs unknown to me in those also, perhaps I will take some of them in payment."

"Look all you want," Hordo said eagerly. "Prytanis, help him open the chests." The Nemedian and the herbalist moved toward the stacked chests, and Hordo dropped his voice to a whisper ranged for Conan's ears. "If he will take herbs rather than a hundred gold pieces, then well enough, I say."

Conan drew a breath; they *were* coming easier. "Help me to my feet, Hordo," he urged. "He said I would walk or die, and by Mitra's bones, I intend to walk."

The two of them exchanged a long look; then the one-eyed man reached down. Conan pulled himself up, putting a hand against the wall to steady himself. Leaning against a wall would not do, though. He took a tottering step. His bones felt ready to bend, but he forced himself to move the other foot forward.

"It is too late for that one," Prytanis' voice came loudly from where he stood beside the chests, dagger in hand. Three already had their lids pried open. "I found some more of those leaves."

Ghurran let the cloak fall back over the corpse's face. "I was curious as to the sort of man who uses a poisoned blade. But I suppose new herbs are more important than dead men. More of the leaves, you say?"

Conan made another step, and another. The weakness was still on him, but he felt firmer in some fashion, less like a figure made of reeds.

Hordo followed him, looking like an anxious bear. "Are you all right, Cimmerian?"

"Right enough," Conan told him, then laughed. "But moments ago I would have settled for living long enough to know the way of all this. Now I begin to think I may live a bit longer than that after all."

"This body is too frail," Ghurran said suddenly. "Too old!" He knelt, peering into one of the chests. All twenty had been opened, and some of their contents pulled out. There were more dried leaves, exactly like those in the first chest. There were saffron crystals that seemed, from the powder beneath the pile of them on the dirt floor, to crumble almost of their own weight, and tightly corded leather sacks, several of which had been sliced open to spill out what could have been salt except for its crimson color. Two of the chests contained clear vials filled with a verdant liquid and well-packed in linen bags of goose down.

"What ails you?" Conan asked. "I walk, as you said I would, and I will see that you get the gold Hordo promised you." The one-eyed smuggler made a muffled sound of pained protest.

"Gold," Ghurran snorted contemptuously.

"If not gold, then what?" Conan asked. "If any of the herbs or other substances in those chests can be of use to you, take them, leaving only a little for me. It seems we will be not be delivering them to the Zaporoska, but I still want to know why a man would try to kill to keep them hidden. A small portion of the leaves and the rest may help me find out."

"Yes," the herbalist said slowly, "you will want to

find out, won't you?" He hesitated. "I do not know exactly how to tell you this. If what I gave you had not been successful, there would have been no need to say anything. I hoped to find something in these chests, or more likely on the body. A man who carries a poisoned weapon will betimes also carry an antidote in case he himself is accidently wounded."

"What need is there of antidotes?" Hordo demanded. "You have already counteracted the poison."

Ghurran hesitated again, eying both Hordo and Conan in turn. "The treatment I have given you, northlander, has only masked the poison for a time."

"But I feel no more than a slight ache in the head," Conan said. "In an hour I will wrestle any man in Sultanapur."

"And you will continue to feel so for another day or two perhaps, then the poison will take hold again. A permanent cure requires herbs that I know, but that can be found only in Vendhya."

"Vendhya!" Hordo exclaimed. "Black Erlik's bowels and bladder!"

Conan motioned Ghurran to speak on, and the old man did so. "You must go to Vendhya, northlander, and I must go with you, for a daily infusion prepared by me will be necessary to keep you alive. The journey is not one I look forward to, for this old body is not suited to such travels. You, however, may find the answers you seek in Vendhya."

"Mayhap I will," Conan said. "It will not be the first time my life has been measured out a day at a time."

"But Vendhya," Hordo protested. "Conan, they do not much like folk from this side of the Vilayet in Vendhya. If you with your accursed eyes are thought strange here, how will they think you there? We'll lose our heads, like as not, and be lucky if we are not flayed first. Ghurran, are you sure there is nothing you can do here in Turan?''

"If he does not go to Vendhya," Ghurran said, "he dies."

"It is all right, my friend," Conan told the one-eyed man. "I will find the antidote there, and answers. Why are those chests worth killing for? Patil was Vendhyan, and I cannot think they were destined elsewhere. Besides, you know I have to leave Sultanapur for a time anyway, unless I want to hide from the City Guard until they find Tureg Amal's killer."

"The chests," Hasan said abruptly. "They can still be taken to the Zaporoska. Whoever was to meet Patil will not know he is dead. They will be waiting there, and they may have answers to our questions. They may even have an antidote."

" 'Tis better than Vendhya," Hordo said quickly. "For one thing, it is closer. No need to travel to the ends of the world if we do not need to."

"It cannot hurt to try," Conan agreed. "An easier trip for your bones, Ghurran." The old man shrugged his thin shoulders noncommitally.

"And if Patil's friends do not have what you need," Hordo added, "then we can think about Vendhya."

"Hold there!" Prytanis strode into the middle of the room, glaring angrily. The other smugglers were listening drunkenly, but he alone seemed sober enough to truly understand what had been said. "Take the chests to the Zaporoska, you say. How are we to find the men we seek? The mouth of the Zaporoska is wide, with dunes and hills to hide an army on both sides."

"When I agreed to carry Patil's goods," Hordo said, "I made sure he told me the signals that would be given by the men ashore, and the signs we must give in return."

"But what profit is there in it?" Prytanis insisted. "The Vendhyan cannot pay. Do you think his companions will when we arrive without him? I say forget these chests and find a load of 'fish' that will put gold in our purses."

"You spineless dog." Hordo's voice was low and seemed all the more deadly for it. "Conan is one of us and we stand together. How deep is the rot in you? Will you now throw goods over the side at the sight of a naval bireme, or abandon our wounded to the excisemen?"

"Call me not coward," the Nemedian snapped. "Many times I have risked having my head put on a pike above the Strangers' Gate, as you well know. If the Cimmerian wants to go, then let him. But do not ask the rest of us to tease the headsman's axe just for the pleasure of the trip."

The jagged scar down Hordo's left cheek went livid as he prepared a blast, but Conan spoke first.

"I do not ask you to come for the pleasure of the trip, Prytanis, nor even for the pleasure of my company. But answer me this. You say you want gold?"

"As any man does," Prytanis said cautiously.

"These chests are worth gold to the men waiting at the Zaporoska. Vendhyans, if Patil is a guide. You have seen other Vendhyans, men with rings on every finger and gems on their turbans. Did you ever see a Vendhyan without a purse full of gold?"

Prytanis' eyes widened as he suddenly realized that Conan spoke not only to him. "But—"

The big Cimmerian went on over the attempted interruption like an avalanche rolling over a hapless peasant. "The Vendhyans waiting on the Zaporoska will have plenty of gold, gold due us when we deliver the chests. And if they will not pay . . ." He grinned wolfishly and touched the hilt of his broadsword. "They'll not be the first to try refusing to pay for their 'fish.' But we did not let the others get away with it, and we'll not let the Vendhyans either."

Prytanis looked as though he wanted to protest further but one of the smugglers cried out drunkenly, "Aye! Cut 'em down and take it all!"

"Vendhyan gold for all of us!" another shouted. Others grunted agreement or laughingly repeated the words. The slit-nosed Nemedian sank into a scowling silence and withdrew sullenly to a corner by himself.

"You still have the gift of making men follow you," Hordo told Conan quietly, "but this time it would have been better to break Prytanis' head and be done with it. He will give trouble before this is done, and we'll have enough of that as it is. Mitra, the old man will likely heave his stomach up at every wave. He looks no happier at the prospect of this shorter journey than he did about traveling to Vendhya." Indeed, Ghurran sat slumped against the chests, staring glumly at nothing.

"I will deal with Prytanis if I must," Conan replied. "And Ghurran can no doubt concoct something to soothe his stomach. The problem now is to find more men." Hordo's vessel could be sailed by fewer than those in the cellar, but the winds would not always be favorable, and rowing against tides and currents would require twice so many at least. The Cimmerian surveyed the men sprawled about the floor and added, "Not to mention sobering this lot enough to walk without falling over their own feet."

"Salted wine," Hordo said grimly. Conan winced; he had personal experience of the one-eyed man's method of ridding a man of drunkenness. "And you cannot risk the streets in daylight," Hordo went on, "I will leave that part of it to you while I try to scrape some more crew out of the taverns. Prytanis! We've work to be done!''

Conan ran his eye over the drunken smugglers once more and grimaced. ''Hasan, tell Kafar we need ten pitchers of wine. And a large sack of salt.''

The next hour was not going to be pleasant.

CHAPTER VI

The harbor quays were quiet once night had fallen, inhabited only by shadows that transformed great casks of wine and bales of cloth and coiled hawsers into looming, fearsome shapes. Scudding clouds dappled a dull, distant moon. The seaward wind across the bay was as cold as it had been hot during the day, and the watchmen paid by the Merchants' Guild wrapped themselves in their cloaks and found shelter within the waterside warehouses with warming bottles of wine.

There were no eyes to see the men who worked around a trim vessel some sixteen paces long, with a single forward-raked mast stepped amidship. It was tied alongside a dock that leaned alarmingly and creaked at every step on its rough planks. But then the dock creaked whether there were steps or not. All the boats moored there were draped with nets, but few carried more than the faintest smell of fish. Actual fishermen sold small portions of their catch each day for the maintaining of that smell. King Yildiz's customs collectors would seize a fishing boat that did not smell of fish before they even bothered to search it.

Conan stood on the rickety dock with the dark cloak he had from Ghurran pulled about him so that he blended with the night. He was the only one there besides Hordo who knew that the one-eyed man privately called that boat *Karela*, after a woman he had not seen in two years, but looked for still. Conan had known her, too, and understood the smuggler's obsession.

While others loaded the ship, the Cimmerian kept an eye out for the rare watchman who might actually be trying to earn his coin or, more likely, for a chance patrol of the King's excisemen. A slight ache behind his eyes was the only remaining effect of the poison he could detect.

"The old man's potion works well," he said as Hordo climbed up beside him from the boat. "I could almost think the poison was gone completely."

"It had better work," his friend grunted. "You had to promise him those hundred gold pieces when he was ready to settle for herbs."

"My life is worth a hundred gold pieces to me," Conan said dryly. Muffled cursing and thumping rose from the boat. "Hordo, did you truly take on every blind fool you could find for this voyage?"

"We may wish we had twice as many blades before this is done. And with half my men vanished into wine pitchers, I had to take the best of what I could find. Or would you rather wait another day? I hear the City Guard cut an albino into dog meat just at twilight, mistaking him for a northlander. And they've set out to search every tavern and bordello in the city."

"That will take them a century," Conan laughed. A soft cooing caught his ear, and he stared in amazement as a wicker cage of doves was lowered onto the boat, followed by another cage of chickens and three live goats.

"One of the new men suggested it," Hordo said, "and I think it a good idea. I get tired of choosing between dried meat and salt meat when we are at sea."

"As long as they are not more of the crew, Hordo."

"The goats are no randier than some outlanders I know, and the—" The bearded man cut off as a light flared on the boat below. "What in Zandru's Nine Hells . . ."

Conan did not waste time on oaths. Leaping to the deck, he snatched a clay lamp from the hands of a tall, lanky Turanian and threw it over the side.

The man stared at him angrily. "How am I to see where to put anything in this dark?" He was a stranger to Conan, one of Hordo's new recruits, in the turban and leather vest that was the ubiquitous garb of the harbor district.

"What is your name?" the Cimmerian asked.

"I am called Shamil. Who are you?"

"Shamil," Conan said, "I will just assume you are too stupid to realize that a lamp could also be seen by others." His voice grew harder. "I will not even think you might be a spy for the excisemen, trying to draw their attention. But if you do that again, I will make you eat the lamp."

Hordo appeared beside him, testing his dagger on a horny thumb. "And after he does, I will slit your throat. You understand?" The lanky man nodded warily.

"Blind fools, Hordo," Conan said and turned away before his friend could speak.

The Cimmerian's earlier mirth had soured. Men such as this Shamil might well get them all killed before they ever saw the Zaporoska. And how many others like him were among the newcomers? Even if they were not done in by foolishness like lighting a lamp where stealth was required,

how many of the new could be trusted did matters come to
a fight on the other side of the Vilayet?

Muttering to himself, Ghurran stumbled his way down
the dark deck and thrust a battered pewter cup into Conan's
hands. "Drink this. I cannot be sure what effect the pitching of sea travel will have. It is best to have a double dose
and be safe."

Conan took a deep breath and emptied the cup in one
gulp. "It no longer tastes of camel," he said with a
grimace.

"The ingredients are slightly different," the herbalist
told him.

"Now it tastes as though a sheep was dipped in it."
Conan tossed the cup back to Ghurran as Hordo joined
them.

"The chests are lashed below," the smuggler said quietly,
"and we are as ready as we are likely to be. Take the
tiller, Cimmerian, while I get the men to the oars."

"See if they can keep from braining one another with
them," Conan said, but Hordo had already disappeared in
the dark, whispering muted commands.

The Cimmerian moved quickly aft, wincing at the clatter of oars as they were laid in the thole pins. As the craft
was pushed out from the dock, he threw his weight against
the thick wooden haft of the tiller, steering the boat toward
open water. The sounds of Hordo quietly calling the stroke
came over the creak of the oars. Phosphorescence swirled
around the oar blades and in the wake.

Scores of ships in all sizes were anchored in the harbor,
galleys and sailing craft from every port on the Vilayet.
Conan directed a zig-zag course that kept well clear of all
of them. The navy's biremes were berthed in the northern-
most part of the bay, but some of the merchantmen would
have a man standing watch. None would raise an alarm,

however, unless the smugglers' craft came too close. The watches were to guard against thieves or pirates—some of whom were bold enough to enter the harbor of Sultanapur, or even Aghrapur—not to draw unnecessary attention to ships whose captains often carried goods not listed on the manifest.

The offshore wind carried not only the smells of the city, but picked up the harbor's own stenches as well. The aromas of spice ships and the stink of slavers blended with the smell of the water. Slops and offal were tossed over the side whether a ship was at sea or in port, and the harbor of Sultanapur was a cesspool.

The vessel cleared the last of the anchored ships, but instead of relaxing, Conan stiffened and bit back a curse. "Hordo," he called hoarsely. "Hordo, the mole!"

The long stone barrier of the mole protected the harbor against the sharp, sudden storms of the Vilayet that could otherwise send waves crashing in to smash vessels against the quays. Two wide ship channels, separated by more than a thousand paces, were the only openings in the great breakwater, and on either side of each channel was a tall granite tower. The towers were not yet visible in the night and would usually be manned only in time of war. What was visible, however, was the gleam of torchlight through arrow slits.

Pounding a fist into his palm, Hordo slowly backed the length of the deck, staring all the while toward the slivers of light. They became less distant by the moment. He spoke quietly when close enough for Conan and no other to hear. "It must be this Mitra-forsaken assassination, Cimmerian. But if they've manned the towers . . ."

"The chains?" Conan said, and the bearded man nodded grimly.

The chains were another precaution for time of war, like

the manning of the towers. Of massive iron links capable of taking a ramming-stroke blow from the largest trireme without breaking, they could be stretched, almost on the surface of the water, to effectively bar the harbor entrances even to vessels as small as the one the smugglers rode.

Conan spoke slowly, letting his thoughts form on his tongue. "There is no reason for the towers to be manned unless the guard-chains have been raised. In the night they are little better than useless as watch posts. But there is no war, only the assassination." He nodded to himself. "Hordo, the chains are not to keep ships out, but to keep them in."

"Keep them in?"

"To try to keep the High Admiral's assassin from escaping," the Cimmerian said impatiently. "There are no city gates here to close and guard, only the chains."

"And if you are right, how does it aid us?" Hordo grunted sourly. "Chains or gates, we are trapped like hares in a cage."

"In war there would be a hundred men or more in each tower. But now. . . . They expect no attack, Hordo. And how many men are needed just to guard against someone trying to loose an end of the chain? As many as to guard a gate?"

The one-eyed man whistled tunelessly between his teeth. "A gamble, Cimmerian," he said finally. "You propose a deadly gamble."

"I have no choice. The dice will be tossed, one way or another, and my life is already wagered."

"As you say. But do not ask me to like it, for I do not. We will have to try one of the towers on the part separated from land. Otherwise we might have a few score guardsmen to contend with before our business is done."

"Not you," Conan said. "If we both go, how long do

you wager the ship will wait for us? The new men will not outstay the old, and the old are not overly eager for this voyage.''

''They all know I would follow any man who left me, and in my own ship,'' Hordo rumbled. ''Follow him to the end of the world, if need be, and rip out his throat with my bare hands.'' But he took the tiller from the Cimmerian. ''See who will go with you. You cannot do it alone.''

Conan moved forward to the mast and stood astride the yard on which the sail was furled, lying fore and aft on the deck. The pace of rowing, already ragged without Hordo to call a stroke, slowed further. Even in the dark he knew every eye was on him.

''The trouble in the city has given us a problem,'' he said quietly. ''The guard-chains are up. I intend to lower one and open a way out of the harbor for us. If it is not done, we have come this far for nothing. We will have a few chests of spices—or so I was told they were—that only the Vendhyans want, and the Vendhyans will keep their gold.'' He waited. Gold was always a good place to end, for the word then loomed large in the listeners' minds.

To his surprise, Hasan drew in his oar and stood silently. Ghurran shifted and wrapped his cloak tighter about himself. No one else moved.

Conan ran his gaze down the two shadowy lines of men, and some of those who had been with Hordo before his coming stirred uncomfortably on their rowing benches. It would not be easy convincing them. Outright cowards did not last long among the Brotherhood of the Coast, but neither did those too eager to seek battle. As well to start with the hardest to convince.

''You, Prytanis?''

The slit-nosed Nemedian's teeth showed white in what

could have been a smile or a snarl. "You want this journey, northlander? You lower the chain then. I'd as soon be back ashore with a mug of ale in my fist and a wench on my knee."

"A much safer place, it is true," Conan said dryly and there was a small laugh from the others. Prytanis hunched angrily over his oar.

Shamil, pulling an oar almost by Conan's side, had made no move to rise, but there was an air of watching and waiting about him that was plain even in the dim-mooned night.

"What of you, lighter of lamps?" the Cimmerian asked.

"I merely waited to be asked," the lanky man answered quietly. His oar rattled against the thole pins as it was pulled inboard.

Abruptly two men stood who had been with Hordo when Conan arrived in Sultanapur. "I would not have you think only the newlings are with you," said one, a Kothian named Baltis. Thick old scars were layered where his ears had been none too expertly removed in the distant past. The other, a hollow-faced Shemite who called himself Enam, did not speak but simply drew his tulwar and examined the blade's edge.

"Fools," Prytanis said, but he said it softly.

Conan waved his arm in signal to Hordo, only a gray blur in the stern, and the vessel curved toward the mole. The great breakwater reared before them, a granite wall rising from the dark waters, more than the height of a man, higher than the vessel's deck. Even the new men knew enough of boats to know what was needed now. They backed water smoothly; then those on the side next to the mole raised their oars to fend the craft off from the stone.

The big Cimmerian wasted no time on further words.

Putting a foot on the strake, he leaped. His outstretched hands caught the top of the mole, and he pulled himself smoothly up onto the rough granite surface. Grunts and muttered curses announced the arrival of the others, scrambling up beside him. There was no dearth of room, for the breakwater was nearly twenty paces wide.

"We kill them?" Hasan asked in a low voice.

"Perhaps we'll not need to," Conan replied. "Come."

The square, stone watch-tower occupied all of the end of the mole except for a narrow walkway around it. Its crenelated top was fifty feet above them, and only a single heavy wooden door broke the granite walls at the bottom. Arrow slits at the second level showed the yellow gleam of torchlight, but there were none higher.

Motioning the others into the shadows at the base of the tower, Conan drew his dagger and pressed himself flat against the stone wall beside the door. Carefully gauging distance, he tossed the dagger; it clattered on the granite two long paces from the door. For a moment he did not think the sound had carried to those inside. Then came the scrape of the bar being lifted. The door swung open, spilling out a pool of light, and a helmetless guardsman stuck his head through. Conan did not breathe but it was the dagger at the edge of the light that caught the Turanian's eye. Frowning, he stepped out.

Conan moved like a striking falcon. One hand closed over the guardsman's mouth. The other seized the man's sword-belt and heaved. A splash came from below, and then cries.

"Help! Help!"

"The fool's fallen in," someone shouted inside, and in a clatter of booted feet, four more guardsmen rushed from the tower.

Without helmets, one carrying a wooden mug, it was

clear they had no presentiment of danger. They skidded to a halt as they became aware of the young giant before them, and hands darted for sword-hilts, but it was too late. A nose crunched under Conan's fist, and even as that man crumpled, another blow took one of his companions in the jaw. The two fell almost one atop the other.

The rest were down as well, Conan saw, and no weapons had been drawn. "Throw their swords in the harbor," he ordered, retrieving his dagger, "and bind them." The cries for help still rose from the water, louder now, and more frantic. "Then make a rope of their belts and tunics, and haul that fool out before he wakes the entire city."

Sword in hand, he cautiously entered the tower. The lowest level was one large room lit by torches, with stone stairs against one wall, leading up. Almost the entire chamber was taken up by a monstrous windlass linked to a complex arrangement of great bronze gears that shone from the fresh grease on them. A long bar ran from the smallest gear to a bronze wheel mounted on the wall below the stairs. Massive iron chain was layered on the windlass drum, the metal of each round link as thick as a man's arm, and unrusted. It was said the ancient Turanian king who commanded that chain to be made had offered the weight in rubies of any smith who could produce iron that would not rust. It was said he had paid it, too, including the weight of the hands and tongue he took from the smith so the secret would not be gained by others.

From the windlass the chain led into a narrow, round hole in the stone floor. Conan ignored that, examining the gears for the means of loosing the chain. One bronze wedge seemed to be all that kept the gears from turning.

"Look out!"

At the shout Conan spun, broadsword leaping into his hand. Toppling from the stairs, a guardsman thudded to the stones at the Cimmerian's feet. A dagger hilt stood out from his chest and a still-drawn crossbow lay by his outstretched hand.

"He aimed at your back," Hasan said from the door.

"I will repay the debt," Conan said, sheathing his blade.

Quickly the Cimmerian worked the wedge free, tossed it aside, and then threw his weight against the bar. It could as well have been set in stone. By the length of the thick metal rod, five men at least were meant to work the windlass. Thick muscles knotted with effort, and the bar moved, slowly at first, then faster. Much more slowly the windlass turned, and huge links rattled into the hole in the floor. Conan strained to rotate the device faster. Suddenly Hasan was there beside him, adding more strength than his bony height suggested.

Baltis stuck his head in at the door. "The chain is below the water as far out as I can see, Cimmerian. And there is stirring on the far side of the channel. They must have heard the shouting for help."

Reluctantly Conan released the bar. A boat would be sent to investigate, and though it would not likely carry many men, the purpose was escape, not a fight. "Our craft draws little water," he said. "It will have to do."

As the three men hurried from the tower, Shamil and Enam straightened from laying the fifth guardsman, bound and gagged with strips torn from his own sopping-wet tunic, in a row with the four who were still unconscious. Without a word they followed Conan onto the narrow walkway that led around the tower. Hordo's one eye, the Cimmerian knew, was as sharp as Baltis's two. And the bearlike man would not waste precious moments.

Before they even reached the channel side of the tower, the soft creak and splash of oars was approaching. The vessel arrived at the same instant they did, backing water as it swung close to the breakwater.

"Jump," Conan commanded.

Waiting only to hear each man thump safely on deck, he leaped after them. He landed with knees flexed, yet staggered and had to catch hold of the mast to keep from falling. His head spun until it seemed as though the ship were pitching in a storm. Jaw clenched, he fought to remain upright.

Ghurran shuffled out of the darkness and peered at the Cimmerian. "Too much exertion brings out the poison," he said. "You must rest, for there is a limit to how much of the potion I can give you in one day."

"I will find the man responsible," Conan said through gritted teeth. "Even if there is no antidote, I will find him and kill him."

From the stern came Hordo's hoarse command. "Stroke! Erlik take the lot of you, stroke!"

Oars working, the slim craft crawled away from Sultanapur like a waterbug skittering over black water.

With a roar Naipal bolted upright on his huge round bed, staring fixedly into the darkness. Moonlight filtered into the chamber through gossamer hangings at arched windows, creating dim shadows. The two women who shared his bed—one Vendhyan, one Khitan, each sweetly rounded and unclothed—cowered away from him among the silken coverlets in fright at the yell. They were his favorites from his *purdhana*, skilled, passionate and eager to please, yet he did not so much as glance at them.

With the tips of his fingers he massaged his temples, trying to remember what it was that had wakened him. From a narrow golden chain about his neck a black opal dangled against his sweat-damp chest. Never was he without it, for that opal was the sole means by which Masrok could signal obedience or ask to be summoned. Now, however, it lay dark and cool against his skin. A dream, he decided. A dream of great portent to affect him so, but portent of what? Obviously it had come as a warning of some . . . *Warning*!

"Katar's teats!" he snapped, and the women cowered from him even farther.

Summoning servants would take too much time. He scrambled from the bed, still ignoring the now-whimpering women. They had many delightful uses, but none now. Hastily he donned his robes, a task he had not performed unaided for years. The narrow golden coffer stood on a table inlaid with turquoise and lapis lazuli. He reached for it, hesitated—no need now to summon Masrok; no need to threaten—then left the coffer and ran.

Desperate wondering filled his mind. What danger could threaten him now? Masrok shielded the eyes of the Black Seers of Yimsha. Zail Bal, the former court wizard and the one man he had ever truly feared, was dead, carried off by demons. If Bhandarkar divined his intent, he might summon other mages to oppose him, but he, Naipal, had men close to the throne, men the King did not know of. He knew what woman Bhandarkar had chosen for the night even before she reached the royal bedchamber. What could it be? What?

The darkness of the high-domed chamber far below the palace was lessened by an unearthly glow from the silver pattern in the floor. Naipal darted to the table where his sorcerous implements were laid out, crystal flasks and beakers, vials that gave off eerie light and others that seemed to draw darkness. His fingers itched to reach for the ebony chest, for the power of the *khorassani*, but he forced himself to lift the lid of the ornately carved ivory box instead. With shaking hands he thrust back the silken coverings.

A harsh breath rasped in his throat like a death rattle. A shadowed image floated on the polished surface, silvery no more. Reflected there was a small ship on a night-shrouded sea, a vessel with a single forward-raked mast, making its way by the rhythmic sweep of oars.

Strange devices of crystal and bone trembled as his fist pounded on the table. As it was meant to, the mirror showed him the source of his danger, yet he cursed its limits. What was the danger here? Across what sea did it come? There were seas to the south and far to the east was the Endless Ocean, said by some to end only at the brink of the world. To the west lay the Vilayet and even farther the great Western Sea. At least Mount Yimsha had been recognizable.

He ground his teeth, knowing it was to keep them from chattering and hating the fact. Like an inky cloud, terror coiled its tendrils around his soul. He had thought himself long beyond such, but now he knew that the years with the mirror standing watch had softened him. He had plotted and acted without fear, thinking he had conquered fear because the emptiness of the mirror had told him his plans were unthreatened. And now this ship! A tiny speck on the waters, by all the gods!

With tremendous effort he forced his features back to their normal outward calm. Forcefully he reminded himself that panic availed nothing. Less than nothing, for it hindered action. He had agents in many places and the means to communicate orders to them more swiftly than flights of eagles. His eyes marked the craft well and fingers that shook only slightly moved among the arcane implements on the table. From whatever direction that vessel came, on whatever shore it landed, there would be men to recognize it. Long before it ever reached him, the danger would be purged as though with fire.

CHAPTER VII

With his feet planted wide against the rise and fall of the deck and one hand on the stay supporting the mast, Conan peered through the night toward the blackness that was the eastern shore of the Vilayet. The vessel ran as close inshore as its shallow draft would allow. Not far to the west were islands of which the most pleasant thing said was that they were the lair of pirates. Other things were said as well, whispered in dark corners, but whatever lurked there, no one wanted to draw its attention.

The Cimmerian shared his vigil in the bow with only the two remaining goats and the wicker cage of pigeons. The chickens had gone the way of the other goat, into the smugglers' stomachs. Most of the crew were sprawled on the deck, heads pillowed on arms or coils of rope. Clouds covered the moon, and only through brief rents was there even a slight lessening of the darkness. The triangular sail was full-bellied with wind, and the rush of water along the hull competed with the occasional snore. But then, he thought, none of them had his reasons for eagerness to be

ashore, to find the men for whom the chests below were
bound. Keen as his eye was, however, he could make out
no details of the land. Worse, there was no sign of the
signals Hordo had told him of.

"They must be here," he muttered to himself.

"But will they have the antidote?" Ghurran asked,
handing Conan the goblet that had become a nightly
ritual.

Conan avoided looking at the muddy liquid in the battered pewter cup. It did not grow to look more appetizing
with repeated viewing. "They will have it." Holding his
breath, he emptied the goblet, trying to pour the mixture
down his throat rather than let it touch his tongue.

"But if they do not?" the old man persisted. "There
seems not even to be anyone there."

The Cimmerian's grimace from the taste of the potion
turned to a smile. "They are there." He pointed to three
pinpricks of light that had just sprung into being in the
blackness of the shoreline on the southern headland of
the river mouth. "And they *will* have the antidote."

The herbalist trailed after him as he made his way
down the deck. Hordo was kneeling beside a large, open
chest of iron-bound oak that was lashed to the mast.

"I saw," the one-eyed man muttered when the Cimmerian
appeared. "Now to see if they are the ones we seek." In
short order he had assembled a peculiar-looking apparatus,
three hooded brass lamps fastened to a long pole. There
were hooks for attaching more of the lamps if need be, and
pegs for crosspieces if other configurations were desired.
This was a not-unusual method of signaling among the
smugglers.

Once the lamps were alight, Hordo raised the pole high.
Those few of the crew not asleep stood to watch. Ashore,
the center light of the three disappeared as though sud-

denly extinguished. Thrice the bearded smuggler lowered and raised the pole of lamps.

The remaining lights ashore vanished and, with a grunt, Hordo lowered the pole and put out his own lamps. Almost with the breath that extinguished the last flame, he was roaring. "Up, you mangy curs! On your feet, you misbegotten camel spawn! Erlik blast your tainted souls, move!" The ship became an anthill as men lurched out of sleep, some aided by a boot from the one-eyed man.

Conan strode to the tiller and found Shamil manning it. He motioned the lanky newcomer aside and took his place. The lower edge of the sail was just high enough for him to watch the coastline ahead.

"What has happened?" Ghurran demanded. "Were the signals wrong? Are we to land or not?"

"It is a matter of trust," Conan explained without looking away from his task. "The men ashore see a ship, but is it the smuggler they expect? Signals are exchanged, but not with the place of landing. If a shipload of excisemen or pirates lands at the signal lights, they'd find no more than a single man, and that only if he is slow or stupid." Another tiny point of light appeared on the coast, separated from the location of the others by almost a league. "And if we had not given the proper signals in return," the Cimmerian went on, "that would not now be showing us where to come ashore."

Ghurran peered at the bustle among the smugglers. Some eased tulwars and daggers in their sheaths. Others loosed the strings of oilskin bags to check bowstrings and arrow fletchings. "And you trust them as much as they trust you," he said.

"Less," Conan grinned. "Even if those ashore haven't tortured the signals out of the men we are truly here to meet, they could still want what we have without the bother of paying for it.''

"I had no idea this could be so dangerous.'' The herbalist's voice was faint.

"Who lives without danger does not live at all,'' Conan quoted an old Cimmerian proverb. "Did you think to journey all the way to Vendhya by magic? I can think of no other way to travel so far without danger.''

Ghurran did not reply, and Conan turned his whole attention to the matter at hand. The wind carried them swiftly toward the waiting light, but a landing on a night shore was not made under sail. To the creaking of halyards in the blocks, the long yard was lowered and swung fore and aft on the deck, a few hasty lashings being made to keep the sail from billowing across the deck and hindering movement. Men moved to the rowing benches. The rasp of oarshafts on thole-pins, the slow swirl of blades dipping into the black water, and, incongruously, cooing from the cage of pigeons became the only sounds of the vessel.

Conan swung the tiller, and the smugglers' craft turned toward land and the guiding point of light. The vessel began to pitch with the swells rolling to shore, and the faint thrash of breakers drifted to his ear. That there was a safe beach ahead he did not doubt. Even excisemen wanted a smuggler's cargo undamaged for the portion of its value that was theirs in reward. Of what came after the prow had touched shore, however, there was always doubt.

Sand grated under the keel and without the need of orders, every man backed water. To be too firmly aground could mean death. A splash came from the bow as Hordo tossed a stone anchor over the side. It would help hold the lightly beached craft against the tide, but the rope could be cut in an instant.

Even as the shudder of grounding ran through the craft,

Conan joined the one-eyed man in the bow. The point of light that had brought them ashore was gone. Varying shades of darkness suggested high dunes and perhaps stunted trees.

Abruptly a click as of stone striking metal came from the beach. Almost directly before them a fire flared, a large fire, some thirty-odd paces from the water. A lone man stood beside the fire, hands outspread to show they were empty. His features could not be seen, but the turban on his head was large, like those favored by Vendhyans.

"We'll discover no more by looking," Conan said and jumped over the side. He landed to his calves in water and more splashed over him as Hordo landed.

The bearded man caught his arm. "Let me do the talking, Cimmerian. You've never been able to lie well, except to women. The truth may serve us here, but it must be used properly."

Conan nodded, and they moved up the beach together.

The waiting man was indeed a Vendhyan, with swarthy skin and a narrow nose. A large sapphire and a spray of pale plumes adorned his turban and a ring with a polished stone was on every finger. Rich brocades and silks made up his garments, though there were stout riding boots on his feet. His dark, deep-set eyes went past them to the boat. "Where is Patil?" he said in badly accented Hyrkanian. His tone was flat and unreadable.

"Patil left Sultanapur before us," Hordo replied, "and by a different way. He did not tell me his route, as you may understand."

"He was to come with you."

Hordo shrugged. "The High Admiral of Turan was slain, you see, and it was said the deed was done by a Vendhyan. The streets of Sultanapur are likely still not safe for one of your country."

The truth, Conan thought. Every word the truth, but handled, as Hordo would put it, properly.

A frown creased the Vendhyan's brow, though he nodded slowly. "Very well. You may call me Lord Sabah."

"You may call me King Yildiz if you need names," Hordo said.

The Vendhyan's face tightened. "Of course. You have the . . . goods—Yildiz?"

"You have the gold? Patil spoke of a great deal of gold."

"The gold is here," Sabah said impatiently. "What of the chests, O King of Turan?"

Hordo raised his right hand above his head, and from the vessel came the grate of the hatch being pushed back. "Let your men come on foot for them," he cautioned, "and no more than four at a time. And I will see the gold before a chest is taken."

Six of the smugglers appeared on the edge of the firelight, bows in hand and arrows nocked. The Vendhyan looked at them levelly, then bowed to Hordo with a dry smile. "It shall be as you wish, of course." Backing around the fire, he faded into the darkness up the beach.

"I mistrust him," Conan said as soon as he was gone.

"Why?" Hordo asked.

"He accepted the tale of Patil too easily. Would you not have asked at least a few more questions if you were he?"

The one-eyed man shook his shaggy head. "Perhaps. But keep your eyes open, and we will get out of this with whole skins whatever he intends."

A dark band of wet about the bottom of his robes, Ghurran puffed up the sandy shelf. "This mode of travel is uncomfortable, inconvenient and damp," he muttered, holding his bony hands out to the fire. "Have you spoken to that man about the antidote, Cimmerian?"

"Not yet."

"Do not. Hear me out," he went on when Conan opened his mouth. "They will be nervous of a man like you with a sword on his hip. And what reason would you give for asking? I have one, you see." To Conan's surprise, the herbalist produce Patil's push-dagger from his sleeve. "I purchased the weapon from Patil, but he said he had none of the antidote. If you said such a thing, they would assume you took the blade from his body. If I say it . . . well, they would sooner believe I had bedded one of their daughters than that these old arms had slain a man." He hastily made the small dagger disappear as Sabah walked into the circle of light.

Two obvious servants followed the Vendhyan, turbaned men in dull-colored cotton, without rings or gems. One carried a dark woolen blanket that he spread beside the fire at Sabah's gesture. The other bore a leather sack, which he upended over the blanket. A cascade of golden coins tumbled to the blanket, bouncing and ringing against each other till a hundred gleaming roundels lay in a scattered heap.

Conan stared in amazement. It was far from the first time he had seen so much gold in one place, but never before offered so casually. If those chests had been filled with saffron, they would not be worth so much. "What is in the chests?" he asked.

The Vendhyan's smile touched only his lips. "Spices."

The tension was broken by Hordo bending to scoop up five of the coins at random. He examined them closely, finally biting each before tossing it back to the blanket. "I will want the sack as well," he said, then shouted over his shoulder, "Bring up the chests!"

Half a score of smugglers appeared from the direction of the ship, each bearing one of the small chests. Hordo motioned, and they set their burdens down off to one side of the fire, then trotted back toward the water. Without a word, Sabah hurried to the chests, the servants at his heels, and two more men ran down the beach to join them. Conan saw Ghurran there as well, but he could not tell if the old man was speaking to anyone. Dropping to his knees, Hordo stuffed coins into the leather sack as fast as he could.

Abruptly a cry of rage rose from the men around the chests. Smugglers coming up the beach with the second load of chests froze where they stood. Conan's hand went to his sword-hilt as Sabah all but hurled himself back into the firelight.

"The seals!" the Vendhyan howled. "They have been broken and resealed!"

Hordo's hand twitched as though he wanted to drop the last coins he held and reach for a weapon. "Patil did it on the day he left," he said hastily. "I do not know why. Check the chests and you will see that we have taken nothing."

The Vendhyan's fists clenched and unclenched, and his eyes darted in furious uncertainty. "Very well," he rasped at last. "Very well. But I will examine each chest." His hands still worked convulsively as he stalked away.

"You were right, Cimmerian," Hordo said. "He should not have accepted that so easily."

"I am glad you agree," Conan said dryly. "Now have you considered that this fire makes us targets a child could hit?"

"I have." The one-eyed man jerked the drawstrings of the sack closed and knotted them to his belt. "Let us get everyone back aboard as quickly as possible."

Sabah was gone, Conan saw, as well as the first ten chests. Turbaned men waited warily for the rest. Ten, not the agreed-upon four, but the Cimmerian was not about to argue the point now. Ghurran was with them, and talking, by his gestures. Conan hoped the herbalist had found what they sought. There was certainly no more time for looking.

With seeming casualness, Conan drifted to the line of smugglers who still waited well down toward the water. Beyond them some of the archers had half-drawn their bows, but all still held their weapons down.

"What was that shouting?" Prytanis demanded.

"Trouble," Conan replied. "But I do not think they will attack until those chests are safely off the beach. Not unless they decide we are suspicious. So take the chests on up, then get back aboard as fast as you can without running. And bring Ghurran."

"And you go back to the ship now?" Prytanis sneered. A ripple of uneasiness ran through the others.

It was an effort for Conan to keep the anger out of his voice. "I stand right here until you get back, as if we trust them like brothers. They are getting impatient, Prytanis. Or do you not want a chance to leave this beach without fighting?"

The Nemedian still hesitated, but another man pushed by him, then another. With a last glare at the big Cimmerian, Prytanis fell in with the file.

Crossing his arms across his chest, Conan tried to give the image of a man at ease, all the while scanning the beach for the attack he was sure must come. The file of smugglers met the clustered Vendhyans, the chests changed hands, and the two groups parted, walking swiftly in opposite directions. The smugglers had the shorter distance to go. Even as the thought came to Conan, one of the Vendhyans looked back, then said something to his fellows, and they all broke into a run made awkward by the chests they carried.

"Run!" Conan shouted to the smugglers, and for once they obeyed with alacrity, two of them dragging Ghurran between them. A rhythmic pounding came to him as he drew his sword, and he stifled a curse to shout to the archers. "Ware horsemen!"

The archers had only time to raise their bows before half a score of mounted men in turbaned helmets and brigantine hauberks galloped out of the dunes with lowered lances. Bowstrings slapped against leather bracers, and five saddles were emptied. The others, one swaying, jerked at their reins and let the charge carry them back into the dark. There were bowmen among the Vendhyans as well, but their target was not men. Flaming arrows arched into the night to fall around the ship. Some hissed into the sea, but others struck wood.

Then Conan had time to worry neither about the ship nor about anyone else. Two horsemen pounded out of the night, bent low in their saddles, seeming to race shoulder to shoulder to see which would lance him first. Snarling, he leaped to the side, away from the long-bladed lances. The two riders tried to wheel on him together, but he closed with them, thrusting at the closer of them. His blade struck a metal plate in quilted brigantine, then slid off and between the plates. The movements of his attack were continuous. Even as his steel pierced ribs and heart, he was scrambling onto the dying man's horse, throwing both the corpse and himself against the second enemy.

The second Vendhyan's eyes bulged with disbelief behind the nasal of his turbaned helmet; he dropped the lance and struggled to reach his tulwar. Conan grappled the live man with one hand while trying to pull his broadsword from the dead one with the other, and the two horses, joined by three linked bodies, danced wildly on the sand. In the same instant, Conan's blade and the Vendhyan's came free. The dark-eyed man desperately raised his weapon to slash. Conan twisted and all three men fell. As they slammed into the ground, the Cimmerian sliced his sword across a dark neck as though he were wielding a dagger and rose from two corpses.

The horses' pavane had carried him well down the beach, and what he saw as he looked back did not appear good. Bodies dotted the sand, though he could not make out how many were smugglers, and neither a standing man nor a mounted one was to be seen. Worse, the stern of the ship was a bonfire. As he watched, a man with a bucket silhouetted himself against the flames. Almost as soon as he appeared, the man dropped the bucket, tried to claw at his back with both hands and toppled into the fire. Not Hordo, Conan thought. The one-eyed man was too smart to do something like that with bowmen about.

The fire had lessened the darkness on the beach considerably, Conan realized. He was not so well lit as the man on the boat but neither could he consider himself shielded by the night from the Vendhyan archers. It was always better to be the hunter than the hunted, and the Easterners were not to be found by staying where he was.

Bent almost double, he ran for the dunes . . . and threw himself flat against a slope of sand as nearly a score of riders appeared above him. This, he thought sourly, was a few more than he had hoped to find at once. He was considering whether or not he could slip away unnoticed when the Vendhyans began talking.

"Are the chests on the pack animals?" a harsh, rasping voice demanded.

"They are."

"And where is Sabah?"

"Dead. He wanted to take the one-eyed man alive to see

what he said about the seals under hot irons. The smuggler drowned him in the surf and escaped.''

Conan smiled at that, at both parts of it.

"Good riddance," the harsh voice snapped. "I said from the start that we should come down on them as soon as the chests were in sight. Sabah always had to complicate matters. I think he was beginning to believe he really was a lord, with his secrets and his plottings.''

"No matter. Sabah is dead, and we will soon hunt down the rest of the vermin.''

"You propose to wait that long?" the harsh voice said. "How long do you think the caravan will wait?''

"But Sabah said we must kill all of them. And there is the gold.''

"You think of a dead man's orders and a hundred gold pieces?" the harsh voice sneered. "Think instead of our reception if those chests fail to reach Ayodhya safely. Better we all join Sabah now than that.''

The silence was palpable. Conan could almost feel agreement radiating from the listeners. As if no further words were necessary, the Vendhyans reined their mounts around and galloped into the dark. Moments later Conan heard other hooves joining these, and all receded to the south.

There was much in what the Cimmerian had heard for him to consider. For one thing, the accursed chests seemed to take on greater importance every time someone spoke of them. For the moment, though, there were more immediate matters to be concerned with.

Half of the boat was burning by the time he reached it. In the light of the fire, Hordo and three others, waist-deep in the surf with buckets, were picked out clearly as they desperately threw water on the flames and watched the shore with equal desperation.

"The Vendhyans are gone!" Conan shouted. Grabbing

the strake, he vaulted to the deck. Rivulets of fire ran forward along the sail. "It is too late for that, Hordo!"

"Erlik blast you!" the one-eyed man howled. "This is my ship!"

One of the goats was dead, an arrow through its throat. Food might be in short supply, Conan thought, and tossed the carcass toward the beach. The live goat followed, almost dropping on Hordo's head.

"My ship!" the one-eyed man growled. "Karela!"

"There will be another." Conan lowered the cage of fluttering pigeons and met Hordo's glare over it. "There will be another, my friend, but this one is done."

With a groan, Hordo took the wicker cage. "Get off, Cimmerian, before you burn, too."

Instead, Conan began seizing everything he found loose and not burning—coils of rope, water bags, bundles of personal possessions—and hurled them shoreward. They were stranded in a strange land, which meant it was best to assume a hostile land, and all they would have by way of supplies was what was saved from the flames. The heat became blistering hot as the fire crept closer. Pitch caulking bubbled and fed the conflagration, giving off foul black smoke. Only when there was nothing left unburning within his grasp, however, did Conan leap from the fiery craft.

Splashing to shore, he sank coughing to his knees. After a time he became aware of Ghurran standing over him. The herbalist's parchment-skinned hands clutched a leather bag with a long strap.

"I regret," Ghurran said quietly, "that none of the Vendhyans had the antidote you seek. Though as they apparently planned to slay us, it may be they lied. I will search their dead in any case. You may be assured, however, that I have what is needed to keep you alive until we reach Vendhya."

Conan ran his eyes over the beach. Dead and wounded dotted the sand. A handful of smugglers were tottering hesitantly out of the dark. Behind him the boat was a pyre. "Until we reach Vendhya," he said bleakly.

As the last flames flickered out on the ruin of the smugglers' craft, Jelal slipped away into the dunes, a coarse-woven bag under his arm. The others were too tired to take notice, he knew, so long as he was quick.

By touch he found dead twigs on the stunted trees scattered in the low hills of sand, and in a spot well-sheltered from the beach, he built a tiny fire. Flint and steel went back into his pouch, and other things came out. A small brass bottle, tightly capped. A short length of goose quill. Strips of parchment, scraped thin. As rapidly as he could without tearing the parchment, he wrote.

My Lord, by chance I have perhaps stumbled on to a path to the answers you seek. To believe otherwise is to believe in too great a coincidence. I have no answers as yet, only more questions. As you fear, the path leads to Vendhya, and I will follow it there.

Something rustled in the night, and Jelal hastily pushed a handful of sand over the tiny fire, quenching the light. A faint aroma of burned wood lingered in the air but that could easily be mistaken for the smell of the charred remains of the ship. For a long moment he listened, holding his breath. Nothing. But there was no reason to take chances at this point. Signing the message by feel, he stowed his paraphernalia and rolled the strip of parchment into a thin tube.

From the coarse-woven sack he took a pigeon. It had been sheer luck, getting the birds brought along, and greater

luck that they were not all eaten. Deftly he tied the parchment tube to the pigeon's leg, then tossed the bird aloft. In
a flutter of wings it was gone, carrying all he was really
sure of thus far to Lord Khalid in Sultanapur. It was little
enough, he knew. But if the indications he had seen so far
grew much stronger, he vowed to see that this Conan and
this Hordo returned to a Turan ready to put their heads on
pikes.

CHAPTER VIII

Dawn south of the Zaporoska was gray and dull, for heavy clouds filtered the light of the rising sun to lifelessness. From where he crouched in the dunes behind a twisted scrub oak, Conan watched the Bhalkhana stallion cropping scattered tufts of tough grass and wondered if the animal had settled enough for another try. The tall black's high-pommeled saddle was worked with silver studs and a fringe of red silk dangled from the reins.

Carefully the Cimmerian straightened. The horse flicked an ear but munched in seeming unconcern at another clump of grass. Sand crunched underfoot as Conan approached with slow steps. His hand touched the reins . . . and the stallion seemed to explode.

Fingers tangled in the bridle, Conan was jerked into the air as the ebon animal reared. Like a cat he twisted, throwing his legs around the horse's neck, clutching its mane with his free hand. The stallion dropped, and the added weight of the man pulled it to its knees. Scrambling back to its feet, the horse shook its head furiously. With wild snorts and whinnies, the animal leaped and plunged but Conan clung tenaciously. And as he knew it must, his presence in such an unaccustomed place began to take a toll. The leaps became shorter, the rearings farther apart. Then the stallion was still, nostrils flared and blowing hard.

The animal was not beaten, Conan knew. He was all but staring it in the eye, and that eye was filled with spirit. The question was whether or not it had decided to accept a strange rider. He knew better than to let go of the beast. With infinite caution he pulled himself onto its back, then lifted himself over the high pommel and into the saddle. The stallion only shifted as he took up the red-fringed reins. Finally letting himself relax, Conan patted the glossy arched neck and gently kneed the animal into a trot toward the beach.

The charred ribs of the smugglers' craft, awash in the frothy surf, yet with tendrils of gray smoke still rising, spoke eloquently of the previous night's attack. Some three hundred paces to the north, gray kites screamed and circled above the dunes as they contended with the larger vultures for the pickings below. No one among among the smugglers had considered digging graves for the Vendhyan dead, not after digging three for their own.

The situation on the beach had changed since Conan's leave-taking that morning. Then the smugglers had been gathered around the fire, where the last of the arrow-slain goat still decorated a spit. Now they were in three well-separated knots. The seven survivors of those who had previously sailed with Hordo formed one group, huddled and muttering among themselves, while the men who had joined on the night they left Sultanapur made a second group. All were bedraggled and sooty-faced, and many sported bandages.

The third group consisted of Hordo and Ghurran, standing by the eight Vendhyan horses the smugglers had spent the morning gathering. Hordo glared indiscriminately at newcomers and oldsters alike, while the herbalist looked as though he wished he knew the location of a soft bed.

As Conan swung down from his saddle beside Hordo, Prytanis limped from the cluster of old crew members.

"Nine horses," the Nemedian announced. His tone was loud and ranting but directed only to his six fellows. "Nine horses for three and twenty men."

The newer men stirred uneasily, for the numbers were plain when considered the way Prytanis obviously intended. If they were left out of the calculation, there were horses to go around.

"What happened to his foot?" Conan said softly.

Hordo snorted. "He tried to catch a horse, and it stepped on him. The horse got away."

"Look at us," Prytanis shouted, spinning to face Conan and Hordo. "We came for gold, at your urging, and here we stand, our boat in ashes, three of our number dead, and the width of the Vilayet between us and Sultanapur."

"We came for gold and we have it," Hordo shouted back. He slapped the bulging sack tied at his wide belt; the clinking weight of it pulled the belt halfway down his hip. "As for the dead, a man who joins the Brotherhood of the Coast expecting no danger would do better to become a real fisherman. Or have you forgotten other times we have had to bury comrades?"

The Nemedian seemed taken aback at the reminder that the gold was still with them. It would be difficult to work up much opposition to Hordo among the smugglers as long as the one-eyed man had gold to hand out. Mouth working, Prytanis cast his eyes about angrily until they landed on Ghurran. "The old man is to blame," he cried. "I saw him among the Vendhyans, talking to them. What did he say to stir them up against us?"

"Fool!" Ghurran spat, and the coldness of that bony face was startling. "Why should I bring them down on us? A sword can split my head as easily as yours, and my desire to live is easily as great as yours. You are a fool, Nemedian, and you rant your foolishness because seeking to blame others for your troubles is easier than seeking solutions to those troubles."

Every man there stared at the unexpected outburst, Prytanis the hardest of all. Face pale with rage, the Nemedian stretched a clawed hand toward the scrawny old man, who stared at him disdainfully.

Conan drew his sword, not threatening anyone, just letting it hang at his side. Prytanis' hand stopped short of the herbalist's coarse brown robes. "If you have something to say," Conan said calmly, "then say it. Touch him, though, and I will cut your head off." The Nemedian jerked his hand back and muttered something under his breath. "Louder," Conan said. "Let everyone hear."

Prytanis took a deep breath. "How are nine horses going to carry three and twenty men back to Sultanapur?"

"They are not," Conan said. "One horse goes to Vendhya with me, and another for Ghurran."

"A horse each for the two of you, while the rest of us—" The Nemedian took a step back as Conan raised his blade.

"If you want the horses badly enough," Conan said grimly, "then take them. Myself, I want the animals very much indeed."

Prytanis' hand moved slowly in the direction of his sword, but his eyes shifted as though he wished he could gauge the support of those behind him without being so obvious as looking over his shoulder.

"Four horses go to Vendhya," Hordo said quickly. "At least. I will ride one, and we will need one for supplies.

Anyone else going with us gets a horse, as well, for we have the longer way to go, and the harder. What are left over go to those returning to Sultanapur. I'll give each man his share of the Vendhyan gold before we part. That should buy all the horses you need before you reach Khawarism—"

"Khawarism!" Prytanis exclaimed.

"—Perhaps sooner," Hordo went on as though there had been no interruption. "There should be caravans in the passes of the Colchians."

The Nemedian seemed ready for further argument, but Baltis pushed by him.

"That is fair enough, Hordo," the earless man said. "I speak for the others as well. At least for those of us who have been with you before. It is only Prytanis here who wants all this crying and pulling of hair. As for Enam and myself, we have it in mind to go with you."

"Aye," the cadaverous Shemite agreed. His voice matched his face. "Prytanis can go his own way and take his wailing with him. Straight to Zandru's Ninth Hell for all I care."

The other group, the newcomers, had been stirring and murmuring among themselves all this time. Now Hasan growled, "Enough!" at his fellows and moved away from them. "I want to go with you, too," he said to Hordo. "I will likely never get another chance to see Vendhya."

Shamil was almost on Hasan's heels. "I, also, should like to see Vendhya. I joined you for gold and adventure, and there seems little of either in trudging back to Sultanapur. In Vendhya, though . . . well, we have all heard that in Vendhya even beggars wear gold. Perhaps," he laughed, "some of it will stick to my fingers."

None of the rest of the newlings seemed tempted by tales of Vendhyan wealth and when it came to them that but a single horse was left for those returning to Sultanapur, they lapsed into glum silence, slumping like half-empty sacks on the sand. The experienced smugglers were already seeing to their boots and sandals for the long walk around the Vilayet.

Prytanis seemed stunned by the turn of events. He glared about him at the men, at the ruins of the ship, at the horses, then sighed heavily. "Very well then. I will go as well, Hordo."

Conan opened his mouth to refuse the Nemedian but Hordo rushed in.

"And welcome, Prytanis. You are a good man in tight places. The rest of you see to dividing the supplies. The sooner we travel, the sooner we all reach our destinations. You come with me, Cimmerian. We have plans to make."

Conan let himself be drawn away from the others, but as soon as they were out of earshot, he spoke. "You were right in Sultanapur. I should have broken his head or slit his throat. All he wants is that last horse to himself instead of having to share it. And mayhap a chance to steal the rest of the gold."

"No doubt you speak the truth," Hordo replied. "At least about the horse. But credit me with the one eye I have. While you and Prytanis stared at each other, I was watching the newlings."

"What do they have to do with the Nemedian? I doubt they trust him as much as I do."

"Less, of a certainty. But they are none too sure of setting out afoot either. It would not take much spark—say you and Prytanis attempting to slay each other—for half of them to try for the horses. Then instead of going to Vendhya, we can all kill each other on this Mitra-forsaken bit of coast."

Conan shook his head ruefully. "You see a great deal

with that one eye, my old friend. Karela would be proud of you.''

The bearded man scrubbed at his nose and sniffed. ''Perhaps she would. Come. They will be wanting their gold and likely thinking they should have twice as much.''

The gold—three pieces laid in each man's calloused palm—caused no squabble at all, though there were a few sharp looks at the leather bag Hordo tied to his sword-belt. The way it tugged the broad belt down less was clear the proof that he had shared out most of the contents. The division of the supplies was the source of greater friction.

Conan was surprised at how many arguments could arise over dried fruit ruined by heat and immersion, or coils of rope for which no one could think of any use at present. Eventually, however, water bags, blankets and such were parceled out in proportion to numbers. The live goat and the remains of the cooked one would go with the men afoot. The cage of pigeons was lashed to the spare horse, along with a sack of grain for feed.

''Better to give the grain to the horses,'' Conan grumbled, ''and feed ourselves what we can catch.'' He tossed a stirrup leather up over the silver-studded saddle on the big black and bent to check the girth strap. The two parties had truly become separate now. Those who would ride to Vendhya checked their horses while a short distance away, the men who were returning to Sultanapur bundled and lashed their share of the supplies into backpacks, murmuring doubtfully among themselves.

''Mitra's Mercies, Cimmerian,'' Hordo told him, ''but there are times I think you do your best just to avoid a few comforts. I look forward to a spitted pigeon or two roasting over the fire tonight.''

Conan grunted. ''If we put less attention to our bellies and more to riding hard, we could catch that caravan by

nightfall. The Vendhyans spoke as if it were not far
off.''

"That," said Ghurran, leading his horse awkwardly by
the reins with both hands, "would be a good way to travel
to Vendhya. We could journey in safety and in comfort."
As though realizing that he intruded on a private conversation, he gave an apologetic smile and tugged his
horse on.

"That old man," Hordo muttered, "begins to fray my
patience. The Vendhyans nearly kill us, my boat is burned,
and through it all nothing seems to matter to him except
reaching Vendhya."

"His single-mindedness does not bother me," Conan
said, "though I should be glad to be able to do without his
potions."

The one-eyed man scratched at his beard. "You know it
would be best to forget this caravan, do you not? If the
men we fought last night have gone to join it, there will
certainly be trouble there for us. We will be strangers,
and they members of the caravan already."

"I know," Conan said quietly. "But you must know
the antidote is not enough for me. A man has tried to kill
me, and perhaps succeeded, over chests that look to be
worth more than their contents. I will know the why of it,
and the answer lies with those chests."

"But be a little careful, Conan. It will profit you little to
be spitted on a Vendhyan lance."

"We tried to be careful last night. From now on, let
them be careful of me." Conan swung up into the saddle
and had to catch hold of the high pommel as his head
spun. Grimly he forced himself erect.

"Let them be careful of me," he repeated and kicked
the Bhalkhana stallion into motion.

CHAPTER IX

Sand dunes quickly gave way to plains of tough, sparse grass and low, isolated hills. Scrub growth and thorn bushes dotted the land, though to the east taller trees could be seen along the banks of the Zaporoska. To the south the grayness of mountains, the Colchians, rose on the horizon. The sun climbed swiftly, a blazing yellow ball in a cloudless sky, with a baking heat that sucked moisture from man and ground. A puff of dust marked each hoof-fall.

Throughout the day Conan kept a steady pace, one the horses could maintain until nightfall. And he intended to maintain it that long and longer, if need be, despite the heat. His sharp eyes had easily located the tracks left by the Vendhyans and their pack mules. No effort had been made to conceal them. The harsh-voiced man had been concerned with swiftness, not with the unlikely possibility that someone might follow his trail. Enam and Shamil proved to be good hands with a bow, making forays from the line of travel that soon had half a score of lean brown hares hanging from their saddles.

107

The Cimmerian ignored suggestions that they should stop at midday to cook the hares. Stops to give the horses a drink from cupped hands he tolerated, but no sooner had he pushed the plug back into his water bag than he was mounted again and moving. Always to the south, though drifting slightly to the east as if not to get too far from the Zaporoska. Always following the tracks of two score of mounted men with pack horses.

The sun dropped toward the west, showing a display of gold and purple on the mountains, and still Conan kept on, though the sky darkened rapidly overhead and the faint glimmerings of stars were appearing. Prytanis was no longer the only one muttering. Hordo, and even Ghurran, joined in.

"We will not reach Vendhya by riding ourselves to death," the old herbalist groaned. He shifted on his saddle, wincing. "And it will do you no good if I am too stiff and sore to mix the potion that keeps you alive."

"Listen to him, Cimmerian," Hordo said. "We cannot make the journey in a single day."

"Has one day's riding done you in?" Conan laughed. "You who were once the scourge of the Zamoran plains?"

"I have become more suited to a deck than a saddle," the one-eyed man admitted ruefully. "But, Erlik blast us all, even you can no longer see the tracks you claim to follow. I'll believe much of those accursed northern eyes of yours, but not that."

"I've no need to see the tracks," Conan replied, "while I can see that." He pointed ahead where tiny lights were barely visible through the thickening twilight. "Have you gotten so old you can no longer tell stars from campfires?"

Hordo stared, tugging at his beard, then finally grunted, "A league, perhaps more. 'Tis all but full dark now.

Caravan guards will not look with kindness on strangers approaching in the night.''

"I will at least be sure it is the right caravan," Conan said.

"You will get us all killed," Prytanis grumbled loudly. "I said it from the first. This is a fool's errand, and you will get us all killed."

Conan ignored him, but he did slow the stallion to a walk as they drew closer to the fires. Those fires spread out like the lights of a small city, and indeed he had seen many respectable towns that covered a lesser expanse. A caravan so large would have many guards. He began to sing, somewhat off tune, a tavern song of Sultanapur, relating the improbable exploits of a wench of even more improbable endowments.

"What in Mitra's name?" Hordo growled perplexedly.

"Sing," Conan urged, pausing in his effort. "Men of ill intent do not announce themselves half a league off. You would not wish a guard to put an arrow in you just because you came on him suddenly in the night. Sing." He took up the song again, and after a moment the others joined in raggedly, all save Ghurran, who sniffed loudly in disapproval of the lyrics.

The bawdy words were ringing through the night when, with a jingle of mail, a score of horsemen burst out of the darkness to surround them with couched lances and aimed crossbows. They wore Turanian armor for the most part, but mismatched. Conan saw a Corinthian breastplate and helmets from three other lands. He let the song trail off— the others had ceased in mid-word—and folded his hands on the pommel of his saddle.

"An interesting song," one of the lancers growled, "but who in Zandru's Nine Hells are you to be singing it here?" He was a tall man, his features hidden in the dark by a nasaled Zamoran helm. At least his voice was not a harsh rasp.

"Wayfarers," Conan replied, "journeying to Vendhya. If you also travel in that direction, perhaps you could use a few extra swords."

The tall lancer laughed. "We have more swords than we can use, stranger. A few days past Karim Singh himself, the *wazam* of Vendhya, joined this caravan with five hundred Vendhyan cavalry sent to escort him from the shores of the Vilayet."

"A great many Vendhyans," Conan said, "to be this close to Turan. I thought they stayed beyond Secunderam."

"I will tell Yildiz of it the next time I speak with him," the lancer replied dryly. A few of his men laughed, but none of the weapons was lowered.

"Do you have other latecomers in your caravan?" Conan asked.

"A strange question. Do you seek someone?"

Conan shook his head as though he had not noticed the creak of leather and mail as the caravan guards tensed. In the long and often lawless passages between cities, caravans protected all of their members against outsiders, no matter the claims or charges. "I seek to travel to Vendhya," he said. "But if there are other latecomers, perhaps some of them need guards. Possibly some of your merchants feel less safe, not more, for the presence of five hundred Vendhyans. Soldiers have been known to have their own ideas of what taxes are due, and how they should be collected."

The lancer's long drawn-out breath told that the idea was not a new one to him. Caravans had paid one tax to the customs men before, and then another to the soldiers supposedly sent to protect them. "Eight swords," he muttered, shaking his head. "Two score and three parties of merchants make up this caravan, stranger, including seven who have joined us since we rounded the southern end of the Vilayet. There are always those—no offense intended—who think to make the journey alone until they see the wastes of the Zaporoska before them and realize the Himelias are yet ahead. Then they are eager to join the first caravan that appears, if they are lucky enough that one does. I will pass the word of your presence, but you must understand that I can allow you to come no closer in the night. How shall I tell them you are called, stranger?''

''Tell them to call me Patil,'' Conan replied. Hordo groaned through his teeth.

''I am Torio,'' the lancer said, ''captain of the caravan guard. Remember, Patil, keep your men well clear of the caravan until first light.'' Raising his lance sharply, he wheeled his mount and led the guards away at a gallop toward the caravan's fires.

''I expect this is as good a spot to camp as any,'' Conan said, dismounting. ''Baltis, if you can find something to burn, we can make a good meal on roast hare before sleeping. I could wish we had saved some wine from the ship.''

''He is mad,'' Prytanis announced to the ebon sky. ''He gives a name that will bring men after us with blades in their fists, then wishes he had some wine to go with the hare.''

''As much as I hate to agree with Prytanis,'' Hordo rumbled, ''he is right this time. If you had to give a name other than your own—though, by Mitra's bones, I cannot see why—could you not have chosen another than that?''

''The Cimmerian is wily,'' Baltis laughed. ''When you hunt rats, you set out cheese. This is cheese our Vendhyan rats cannot fail to sniff.''

Conan nodded. ''He has the right of it, Hordo. There

must be more than a thousand people in that caravan. Now I do not have to search for the men I seek. They will search me out instead."

"And if they search you out with a dagger in the back? Or a few score swordsmen falling on us in the night?" The one-eyed man threw up his hands in exasperation.

"You still do not see," Conan said. "They will want to know who I am, and what I do here, especially using Patil's name. Think of the pains to which they have gone to keep those chests secret. What do I know, and who have I told? They can learn nothing if I am dead."

"You begin to sound as devious as a Stygian," Hordo muttered into his beard.

"For myself," Ghurran said, lowering himself unsteadily to the ground, "I do not care at this moment if Bhandarkar's Lion Guard descends on us." He knuckled the small of his back and stretched, grunting. "After I find myself on the outside of one of those hares, I may feel different, but not now."

"Well?" Conan said, eying the others. "Even if the first man Torio speaks to is one of those I seek, you still have time to be away before they get here."

One by one they got down, Prytanis last of all, and he still muttering. By the time the horses were relieved of their saddles and hobbled, Baltis had a fire going, and Enam and Shamil were skinning and spitting hares. Water, Conan discovered, went very well with roast hare when nothing else was available.

The fire burned low, clean-picked bones were tossed aside, and silence replaced the talk that had prevailed while they ate. Conan offered to take the first watch, but no one seemed to have any interest in wrapping himself in his blankets. One by one all but Conan and Ghurran took out oil and stone to tend their blades. Each tried to act as though this had nothing to do with any possible attack but every man turned his back to the dying fire as he worked. There would be less adjustment for the eyes to the dark that way.

Ghurran fussed about his leather sack, at last thrusting the too-familiar pewter goblet at the big Cimmerian. A anticipatory grimace formed on Conan's face as he took it. As he steeled himself to drink, a clatter of hooves sounded in the night. He leaped to his feet, slopping some of the foul-tasting potion over the rim of the cup, and his free hand went to his sword.

"I thought you were sure there would be no attack," Hordo said, holding his own blade at the ready. Every man around the fire was on his feet, even Ghurran, who twisted his head about as though looking for a place to hide.

"If I was always right," Conan said, "I should be the wealthiest man in Zamora instead of being here." Some-one—he was not sure who—sighed painfully.

Seven horses halted well beyond the firelight, and three of the riders dismounted and came forward. Two of them stopped at the very edge of the darkness while the third approached the fire. Dark eyes, seeming tilted because of an epicanthic fold, surveyed the smugglers from a bony, saffron-skinned face.

"I hope that your swords are not for me," the man said in fluent, if overly melodious, Hyrkanian as he tucked his hands into the broad sleeves of a pale-blue velvet tunic embroidered on the chest with a heron. A round cap of red silk topped with a gold button sat on his shaven head. "I am but a humble merchant of Khitai, intending harm to no man."

"They are not for you," Conan said, motioning the others to put up their weapons. "It is just that a man must be on guard when strangers approach in the night."

"A wise precaution," the Khitan agreed. "I am Kang Hou, and I seek one called Patil."

"I am called Patil," Conan said.

The merchant arched a thin eyebrow. "A strange name for a *cheng-li*. Your pardon. It means simply a person with pale skin, one from the lands of the distant west. Such men are considered mythical by many in my land."

"I am no myth," Conan snorted. "And the name suffices me."

"As you say," Kang Hou said blandly. He gave no signal that Conan could see, but the other two figures came forward. "My nieces," the merchant said, "Chin Kou and Kuie Hsi. They accompany me everywhere, caring for an aging man in his dotage."

Conan found himself gaping at two of the most exquisite women he had ever seen. They had oval faces and delicate features that could have been carved by a master striving to show the beauty of Eastern women. Neither looked at all like their uncle, for which the Cimmerian was grateful. Chin Kou seemed a flower fashioned of aged ivory, with downcast almond eyes and a shy smile. Kuie Hsi's dark eyes were lowered, too, but she watched with a twinkle through her lashes, and her skin was like sandalwood-hued satin.

He was not the only one struck by the women, Conan realized. Baltis and Enam appeared to be mentally stripping them of their silken robes, while Prytanis all but drooled with lust. Hasan and Shamil merely stared as if hit in the head. Even Hordo had a gleam in his eye that spoke of calculation as to how to separate one or both of the women from the company of their uncle. As usual, only Ghurran seemed unaffected.

"You are welcome here," the Cimmerian said loudly. "You and your nieces both. The man who offends *any* of you offends me." That got everyone's attention, he noted with approval, and dimmed a few amatory fires by the sour looks he saw on their faces.

"I am honored by your welcome," the merchant said, making a small bow.

Conan returned the bow and smothered a curse as he spilled more of the potion over his hand. Emptying the goblet in one long gulp, he tossed the cup to Ghurran, not quite hurling it at his head. "Filthy stuff," he spat.

"Men doubt the efficacy of medicine without a vile taste," Ghurran said, and Kang Hou turned his expressionless gaze on the herbalist.

"That is an old Khitan proverb. You have journeyed to my land?"

Ghurran shook his head. "No. I had it from the man who taught me herbs. Perhaps he went there, though he never spoke of it to me. Do you know much of herbs? I am always interested in discovering plants new to me, and the uses of them."

"Regrettably, I do not," the merchant replied. "And now, Patil, if I may rush matters unconscionably, I would speak of business."

"Speak of what you will," Conan said when he realized the other man was going to await permission.

"I thank you. I am a poor merchant, a dealer in whatever I can. On this trip, velvets from Corinthia, carpets from Iranistan, and tapestries from Turan. I joined the caravan but two days ago and would not have done so save for necessity. The captain of the vessel that brought me across the Vilayet Sea, a rogue called Valash, had promised to provide ten men as guards. After putting my goods and my animals ashore, however, he refused to honor his agreement. My nieces and I thus must try to tend half a score of camels with only the aid of three servants who, I fear, are of no use at all as protection against brigands.''

"I know of Valash," Hordo said, spitting after the name. " 'Tis Hanuman's own luck he did not slit your throat and sell your goods—and your nieces—in Khawarism.''

"He attempted no such," the Khitan said. "I was not aware that you were men of the sea.''

"We have all been many things in our time," Conan replied. "At the moment we are men with swords who might be hired as guards if enough coin is offered.''

Kang Hou tilted his head as though considering. "I think," he said at last, "that two silver coins for each man would be equitable. And a gold coin each if I and my goods reach Ayodhya in safety.''

Conan exchanged a look with Hordo, then said, "Done.''

"Very good. Until you are ready to ride to the caravan, I will wait with the guards Captain Torio was good enough to lend me. Come, nieces.''

As soon as the Khitans were gone, Baltis let out a low laugh. "A gold and two silvers to make a journey we were making for free. The Khitan must have a king's wealth to pay so. There's luck in you, Cimmerian. Take that sour look off your face, Prytanis.''

"That," Hasan announced, "was the most beautiful woman I have ever seen.''

"Kuie Hsi?" Shamil said jealously.

"The other. Chin Kou.''

"That is all we need," Hordo grumbled as he began rolling his blankets, "for those two to lose their heads over this Khitan's nieces. You realize he was lying, do you not? Unless there are two men called Valash captaining ships on the Vilayet, he never got those wenches off that vessel as easily as he makes out.''

"I know," Conan said. "I did not hear you refusing him because of it though." The one-eyed man muttered something. "What, Hordo?"

"I said, at least this time you've not gotten us involved with a wizard. You have a bad habit of making wizards annoyed with you."

Shouldering his saddle, Conan laughed. "This time I will not come within a league of a wizard."

CHAPTER X

The music of cithern, flute and tambour sounded softly in the alabaster-columned chamber, the musicians hidden behind a lacy screen carved of ivory. Golden lamps, hanging on silver chains from the vaulted ceiling, cast a sheen on the olive skins of six veiled, supple women, clothed in naught else but tinkling golden bells at their ankles, who danced with finger-cymbals. The smell of incense and attar of roses suffused the air. Other women, as lovely as the dancers and garbed as they, scurried with dainty steps to proffer silver trays of sweetmeats, figs and candied delicacies to Naipal, reclining at his ease on cushions of brocaded silk. Two of their sisters worked long fans of pale ostrich plumes to cool him. The mage merely picked at the offerings and toyed with his goblet of Shirakman wine. He gave as little heed to the women, for his mind was distant from his surroundings.

Near Naipal's head knelt a soft, round-faced man whose tunic of scarlet silk and turban of gold and blue seemed gaudy beside the wizard's soft grays. He, too, gave no eye to the women as he reported in a soft voice on how the day had seen his master's wishes carried out. "And one thousand *pice* were handed out in your name, lord, to the beggars of Ayodhya. An additional one thousand *pice* were . . ."

Naipal stared into his wine, as heedless of its exquisite bouquet as of the eunuch's voice. Five times as the tortuous days passed he had gone to the hidden chamber; twice he actually put his hand on the ornate ivory case. But each time he convinced himself to wait, each time with a new reason. The canker in his bosom was that he well knew the true cause of his hesitancy. To open the case, to gaze on the mirror within, perhaps to see that danger to all his plans was yet reflected there, this was more than he could bear. The fear he had fought off in that night of frenzy was returned a hundredfold to paralyze him. Something whispered in the back of his mind, *wait*. Wait a little longer, and surely the mirror would again be empty, the danger dealt with by his far-flung minions. He knew the whisper was false, yet even as he castigated himself for listening, he waited.

To take his mind from doubts and self-flagellation, he tried to listen to the eunuch. The fat man now murmured of the day's happenings in Ayodhya, such as he thought might interest his master.

". . . And finding his favorite wife in the embrace of her two lovers, each a groom from his own stables, Jharim Kar slew the men and flogged his wife. He slew as well three servants who were witness, but the tale is already laughed at in the bazaars, lord. In the forenoon Shahal Amir was slain on the outskirts of the city, by bandits it is said, but two of his wives . . ."

Sighing, Naipal let the man's continued burblings pass his ears unheard. Another time the matter of Jharim Kar would have been pleasing, though not of prime importance. A score of deft manipulations to lead a woman to folly and a husband to discovery of that folly, with the result that a man who once gathered other lords around him was now laughed at. A man could not be at once a leader and the butt of bawdy laughter. It was not that Naipal bore Jharim Kar any animus. The nobleman had simply attracted too many others to his side, creating what could have grown into a island of stability in a sea of shifting loyalties and intrigues. The wizard could not allow that. Greater intrigues and increasing turmoil were necessary to his plans. Bhandarkar guarded himself well against his wizard; kings who trusted too much did not long rule, and this king's toenail parings or hair clippings were burned as soon as cut. But Bhandarkar would die, if not from so esoteric a means as he feared, and without his strong hand, turmoil would become chaos, a chaos on which Naipal would impose a new order. Not in his own name, of course. But he would pull the strings, and the king he put on the throne would not even know he danced at another's will.

Lost in dreams of the future, Naipal was startled by the sudden throbbing warmth on his chest. Not quite believing, he clutched at the black opal beneath his robes. Through layers of silk the stone pulsed against his palm. Masrok signaled!

"Be silent!" he roared, throwing the goblet at the eunuch's head for emphasis. The round-faced man snapped his mouth shut as though fearing for his tongue. "Go to Ashok," Naipal ordered. "Tell him that all I have commanded is to be readied at once. At once!"

"I run to obey, lord." The eunuch began shuffling backward on his knees, bumping his forehead to the floor.

"Then run, Katar take you!" Naipal shouted. "Or you will find there is more than can be taken from a man than you have lost!'' Babbling terrified compliance, the eunuch scrambled to his feet, still genuflecting, and fled. Naipal's glare swept from the sleek nudity of the dancers to the ivory screen hiding the musicians. At his command for silence, all had frozen, hardly daring to breathe. ''Play!'' he barked. ''Dance! You will all be beaten for laziness!''

The music burst forth desperately, and the dancers writhed in a frenzy to please, but Naipal dismissed them from his awareness and waved away the serving girls. His heart seemed to beat in time with the throbbing of the opal against his hand. The stone was all his mind had room for, the sign from Masrok that the demon should be summoned, and what that must mean. Ashok, chief among the tongue-less ones, would quickly prepare the chamber below. In such terror was the wizard held by those who served the gray chambers that he knew they would literally run themselves to death to obey his slightest wish, let alone a command. It could not be done quickly enough to suit him, however. Impatience bubbled in him like the surface of a geyser before eruption.

Able to wait no longer, Naipal flung himself to his feet and stalked from the chamber. Behind him dancers and musicians continued their vain strivings, fearful now to cease without his express command.

To his bedchamber Naipal went first, to fetch the golden coffer containing the demon-wrought dagger. That must be in Masrok's view, not mentioned this time, but no less a reminder that even a demon could be slain.

When he reached the gray-domed chamber beneath the palace, the wizard nodded in satisfaction without even realizing that he had done so. A large, tightly woven basket, its lid lashed firmly in place, stood near his worktable. A bronze gong with a padded mallet hanging from its teakwood frame had been placed near the iron latticework set in one wall.

Naipal paused by the bars. From the door that was part of the iron mesh a ramp led down into a round pit lit by rush torches set high on the walls. On the sand-covered floor of the pit a score of swords in various patterns made an untidy heap. Directly opposite the ramp a massive iron-bound door let into the pit.

For a single test he had used the fires of the *khorassani* to carve out the pit and the cells and connecting corridors beyond. A single test but most necessary, for he had to test the truth of the ancient writings. He did not believe they lied, but none knew better than he that there were degrees of truth, and he must know the exact degree of this truth. But other things must be done first. Beneath his robes the black opal still pulsed against his chest.

Denying his own need for haste, Naipal took greater care than ever before in setting the nine *khorassani* on their golden tripods. Anticipation burned in him like fanned coals as the tenth stone, blacker than midnight, was placed. He settled on the cushions before it, and once more the ancient incantation rolled against the canescent walls.

"*E'las eloyhim! Maraath savinday! Khora mar! Khora mar!*"

Once more bars of fire leaped up. The stones blazed like imprisoned suns, and a pathway was opened to realms unknowable to mortal man.

"Masrok," Naipal called, "I summon you!"

The winds of infinity blew. Thunder roared and the huge obsidian demon floated within the fiery cage. And with it floated another figure, that of a man in armor of studded leather and a spiked helm of a kind unseen in Vendhya for more than a thousand years. Two swords of unbelievable antiquity—one long and straight, one shorter and curved—hung at the armored figure's sides. Almost did Naipal laugh with joy. Success! He did not realize he had spoken aloud until the demon replied in tones like a storm.

"Success you call it, O man? I call it betrayal! Betrayal heaped upon betrayal!"

"Surely a small betrayal only," Naipal said. "And freedom is your eventual reward." A shudder passed through the demon, and its eight arms shook until the wizard feared it might attempt to hurl one of its weapons at him, or even try to fling itself through the flaming barrier. He laid a nervous hand on the golden coffer.

"You speak of what you do not know, O man! A small betrayal? To do your bidding I was forced to slay one of my other selves! For the first time since time itself began, one of the Sivani is slain, and by my hand!"

"And you fear the vengeance of the other two? But surely they do not know, or you would not be here."

"And how long before they discover the deed, O man?"

"Fear not," the mage said. "I will find a way to protect you." Before the demon could speak again, Naipal shouted. "Go, Masrok! I command it!"

With a deafening roar the demon was gone, and only the ancient warrior floated within the bars of the fire.

Now Naipal did permit himself to laugh. Demons, it seemed, could indeed be enmeshed as easily as men.

Swiftly he set about lowering the sorcerous barrier, a task more difficult in some ways than erecting it had been. At last it was done, and he hurried to examine the figure that now stood precisely centered on the arcane pattern in the floor. No breath stirred the ancient warrior's chest, and no light shone in his dark, staring eyes, yet his dusky skin seemed to glow with life. Curious, Naipal touched the warrior's cheek and grunted. Despite what seemed living suppleness to the eye, it was like touching leather stretched tight over wood.

"Now," Naipal murmured to himself.

From the myriad of crystal beakers and vials on his worktable, he chose out five, pouring small, precisely measured portions of their contents into a mortar wrought from the skull of a virgin murdered by her mother. Four of those ingredients were so rare that he begrudged even the tiny amounts needed. With the thigh bone of the virgin's mother for a pestle, he ground and mixed until he had a black paste.

The mage hesitated before turning to the large wicker basket. Then, steeling himself, he tore open the lashings that held its lid. Pity rose in him as he looked down on the ragged boy within, bound and gagged, frozen with fear. Forcefully he stifled emotion and lifted the child from the basket. The small form trembled as he laid it before the shape of the warrior. He could feel the child's eyes on him, though he tried to ignore them.

Hastily now, as if to be done with the thing, Naipal fetched the foul-made mortar. Dipping the little finger of his left hand into the black paste, he drew a symbol on the forehead of the bound child, then again on that of the warrior. The residue he scrubbed carefully from his finger with a cloth.

The warrior, the child and the largest of the *khorassani* lay in a straight line. Naipal lowered himself to the cushions to invoke powers not summoned before.

"*Mon'draal un'tar, maran vi'endar!*"

The words were softly spoken, yet the walls of the chamber chimed in resonance with them. Thrice Naipal repeated the chant and at the third speaking, rays of light, cold and pale as mountain snow, lanced from the ebon stone, one to strike the dark symbol on the warrior's forehead, the other that on the child's. On and on Naipal spoke the incantation. A third icy beam sprang into being, linking the two symbols directly. The child arched his back and screamed, unable to move his head from beneath the glittering point of that sorcerous triangle. Naipal cried the words loudly to drown out the scream. A whine shimmered from the light like the string of a zither drawn too tight.

Abruptly all was silence; the rays of light vanished. Naipal expelled a long breath. It was done. Getting to his feet, he approached the lifeless body of the child. He had eyes only for that small form.

"You have been freed from a life of misery, pain and hunger," he said. "Your spirit has gone to dwell in a purer realm. Only life was taken from you. It had to be a young life, not yet fully formed." He paused, then added, "I would use the children of nobles and of the wealthy if I could." Funeral fires fit for a lord, he decided. Such would he give this nameless waif.

Slowly his gaze rose to the leather-armored figure. Still no breath stirred in that body. Was there light in the eyes? "Can you hear me?" he demanded. There was no reply. "Step forward!" Obediently the warrior took one pace forward and stood again as a statue. "Of course," Naipal mused. "You are without volition of your own. You obey me, who gave you life again, and only me, unless I command you to heed another. Good. It is as the writings said. So far. Follow me!"

Maintaining the exact distance between them, the warrior obeyed. Naipal unlocked the door in the iron latticework and motioned. The other stepped through, and the wizard closed and relocked the barred door. It was good, Naipal thought, that spoken commands were not necessary. The writings had been unclear.

A hollow tone boomed as Naipal struck the gong with the padded mallet. In the pit the iron-bound door swung open. Moving cautiously, twenty men appeared, eyes going immediately to Naipal and the motionless figure at the head of the ramp. Behind them the door closed silently. When they saw the swords piled on the sand, there was but a moment's hesitation before they rushed for the weapons. The men were as varied as the blades they seized, wearing garb ranging from filthy rags to some noble's cast-off silken finery. They had not been randomly chosen. The test would not be complete then. In that pit were brigands, bandits, deserters from the army, each one familiar with a sword. Freedom and gold had been promised to those who survived. Naipal thought he might even honor the promise.

"Kill them," he commanded.

Even as the words left his mouth, six of the ruffians charged howling up the ramp, blades swinging. His face an expressionless mask, the leather-clad warrior drew his archaic swords and moved smoothly to meet them. The six attacked with a frenzy driven by the promise of freedom; the warrior fought with lightning precision. When the form in ancient armor moved on, a single head rolling down the ramp before it, six corpses littered the way behind.

In the pit two of the deserters hastily chivvied those remaining into two lines as though they were infantry on a battlefield. The warrior neither slowed his approach nor altered his stride. The two ranks of desperate men tensed to meet him. But a pace short of them, the warrior suddenly leaped to his right, attacking. The rogues Naipal had gathered may have thought their formation made them infantry, but they had no shields to protect them. Two fell, bloodied and twitching, before the ranks could wheel under the deserters' shouted instructions. The resurrected warrior did not wait for them, however. As the lines pivoted, he leaped back the other way and dashed into their midst from the flank. The deserters' small order dissolved in a melee of hacking steel, welling blood and screaming men, each fighting frantically for himself alone, each dying as the ancient warrior's flashing blade reached him.

When the leather-armored figure slit the throat of the last kicking wretch, Naipal breathed deep in wondering satisfaction. Twenty corpses littered the crimson-splashed sand, and the reborn warrior stood unharmed. In truth there were rents in the studded leather of his armor, and his teeth could be seen through a gash that laid open his cheek, but not a drop of blood fell from him. He moved among the bodies, making sure that each was actually dead, as though no blade had ever touched him.

Turning his back on the scene below, the wizard sagged against the bars, laughing until he wheezed for breath. Everything the ancient writings had claimed was true. The wounds would heal quickly. Nothing could slay the warrior he had resurrected.

More than two thousand years earlier, a conqueror called Orissa had carved a score of small nations and city-states into the kingdom of Vendhya, with himself as its first king. And when King Orissa died, an army of twenty thousand warriors was entombed with him, a royal bodyguard for the afterlife, preserved so perfectly by intricate thaumaturgies that though they no longer lived, neither were they dead as ordinary men died. With the proper rituals, life could be restored after a fashion, and an army that could not die would march again. All that was necessary was to find the centuries-lost tomb.

"And that," Naipal laughed, loud and mocking, "is all but done, is it not, Masrok, my faithful servant?"

Success so filled him with ebullience that the stupefying

fear of the past few days was swept away. Certainly enough time had passed. On whatever waters that vessel rode, if it was near enough to threaten him when he was so close to his goals, it must have made shore by now. And if it had, surely whatever danger it carried had been dealt with by his myrmidons. He would admit no other thought, not when so many victories were already his on this day.

With a firm hand he raised the carven ivory lid and brushed back the silken coverings. Black was the surface of the mirror, and dotted with tiny points of light. It took a moment for Naipal to realize that he saw a vast array of campfires, viewed from a great height. If one small ship had threatened him before, now it seemed that an army did. For his days of fear he was repaid with more fear, and with uncertainty. Had the danger of the ship been disposed of, or had it been transmogrified to this? Was this a new threat, surpassing the old?

Long into the night Naipal's howls of rage echoed in the vast dome.

CHAPTER XI

When the first paleness of dawn appeared on the horizon, Conan was already up and saddling the stallion. The hollow thunk of axes chopping wood drifted to him from the bank of the Zaporoska, not half a league off and lined with tall trees. He shook his head at the Khitan merchant's camels, sharing the picket line with the smugglers' horses. Camels were filthy beasts, to his mind, both in habits and smell, and untrustworthy besides. He would rather have a horse at any time, or even a mule.

"Stinking beast," Hordo grumbled, slapping a camel's flank to make it move aside. Coughing from the cloud of dust he had raised, the one-eyed man edged into the space created to reach his own mount. "And dirty, too."

"Have you looked at the goods they carry?" Conan asked quietly.

"I saw no chests, if that's what you mean. We cross the river this morning, you know."

"Pay attention, Hordo. It is all carpets and velvet and tapestries, as the Khitan said. But the value of it, Hordo."

129

The big Cimmerian had been a thief in his youth, and his eye could still gauge the price of anything worth stealing. " 'Tis mainly of the third quality, with only a little of the second. I should not think it worth carrying to Arenjun, much less all the way to Vendhya."

"Distance and rarity increase value," Kang Hou said, approaching silently on felt-slippered feet. His hands were tucked into the sleeves of a pale-blue velvet tunic, this one embroidered with swallows in flight. "It is clear you are no merchant, Patil. The Iranistani carpet that will barely procure a profit in Turan will bring fifty times as much in Vendhya. Do you think the finest Vendhyan carpets go to Turan? Those grace the floors of Vendhyan nobles, yet a far greater price may be obtained by taking a carpet of the second quality to Aghrapur than by selling one of the first quality in Ayodhya."

"I am no merchant," Conan agreed, backing the black Bhalkhana away from the picket line, "nor wish to be. Yet I am as eager to reach Vendhya as you. If you will excuse me, Kang Hou, I will see when the caravan is to move on. And what else I can discover," he added for Hordo's ears.

Conan rode through the encampment slowly, for though he was indeed eager to travel onward, also did he wish to give his eyes a chance to roam, to see if they might perchance light on some chests like those used for shipping tea.

The caravan was in fact three encampments, though the three camps butting one against the other, and even larger than Conan had supposed. Three and forty merchants, with their servants, attendants and animal tenders, made up nearly the thousand people he thought the entire caravan contained, numbering among them Vendhyans and Khitans,

Zamorans and Turanians, Kothians and Iranistanis. Men scurried to collapse and fold tents, to load bales and bundles and wicker panniers on camels and mules under the watchful eyes of finely-clad merchants, who eyed each other as well with surreptitious suspicion, wondering if some other had cut a sharper bargain or aimed for the same markets. Conan received his own share of speculative glances, and more than one merchant called nervously for his guards as the tall Cimmerian rode past.

Vendhyan nobles who had accompanied the *wazam* to Aghrapur had the second encampment, and it was odd enough for a second glance even if the chests were not there. Conan's first thought was that he had stumbled onto a traveling fair, for well over half a thousand people surrounded those gaily striped and pennoned pavilions, being lowered now by turbaned servants. Here, too, were men from many lands, but these were jugglers keeping a dozen balls in the air at once, and acrobats balancing atop limber poles. A bear danced to a flute, tumblers leaped and twisted, and strolling players plucked lute and zither. Skull-capped men in flowing robes and long beards moved through the seeming carnival as if it did not exist, talking in twos and threes, though in truth two of them, screaming insults, were being held from each other's throats by one who, stripped to the waist and with bulging muscles oiled, appeared to be a strongman.

The third encampment had already been struck and taken to the river, where axemen were building rafts for the crossing, but Conan had no intention of approaching that one in any case. It was not that he could imagine no way the chests might have ended up in the baggage of Karim Singh, *wazam* of Vendhya, but five hundred hard-eyed Vendhyan cavalry provided steep odds. Their brigantine hauberks and turbaned helms with mail neck guards were much like those of the Vendhyans on the beach, but these men were very obviously aware of just how far into disputed territory they were. They rode like cats, ready to jump at a sound, and their long-bladed lances swung down if anyone came within a hundred paces.

Abruptly something whistled past Conan's face, close enough for him to feel the breeze. Crossbow bolt, a part of his mind told him even as he instinctively dropped as low as the high pommel would permit and dug his heels into the big black's flanks. The stallion bounded forward and was at a dead run in three strides. Conan sensed rather than saw other quarrels streak by, and once his saddle was jolted by a hit.

As the river drew closer, he finally pulled up and looked back. Nothing in the breaking camp appeared out of the ordinary. No crossbows were in evidence; no one even looked in his direction. Dismounting, he checked the black over. The animal was uninjured and eager to run farther, but in the high cantle of the saddle there was a quarrel thicker than his finger. Conan felt a grim chill. A handbreadth higher and it would have been in his back. At least there could no longer be any doubt that the chests were in the caravan.

"You there!" came a shout from the direction of the river. "You, Patil!"

Conan looked up and saw Torio, the caravan guard captain, riding toward him. A quick tug pulled the quarrel free. Letting it fall to the ground, he mounted and rode to meet the other man, who began to speak immediately.

"Twice each year for ten years I have made the journey from Aghrapur to Ayodhya and back, and every time there is something new. Now comes something in its own way stranger than any I have seen before."

"And what is this strange thing?"

"His Most Puissant Excellency, Karim Singh, *wazam* of Vendhya, Adviser to the Elephant, wishes your presence, Patil. I mean no offense, but you are obviously no noble, and Karim Singh rarely admits the existence of anyone lower. Why should he suddenly wish to see you, of whom it is most unlikely he has ever heard before?"

"Adviser to the Elephant?" Conan said, partly because he could think of no possible answer to the question and partly from amusement. He had heard of the great gray beasts and hoped to see one on this journey.

"One of the King of Vendhya's titles is the Elephant," Torio replied. "It is no more foolish than Yildiz being called the Golden Eagle, I suppose, or any of the other things kings call themselves."

"Where is this Adviser to the Elephant?"

"Across the river already, and I would watch my tongue around him if I did not want to lose it. That is his pavilion." Torio pointed to a large sprawling tent of golden silk on the opposite bank, encircled by a hundred Vendhyan lancers facing outward. "He cares not at all if we are held up because he wants to talk to you, but his party must be the first in line of march. Karim Singh will breathe no man's dust." The guard captain paused, frowning at nothing, occasionally seeming to study Conan from the corner of his eye. "Mine is a difficult position, Patil. I am responsible for the safety of all in the caravan but must offend no one. What who has said to whom, who seeks advantage and where, these things become important. All the dangers do not come from outside, from Kuigars or Zuagirs. A man can earn silver, and as the sums are not so large as others might offer, only silence as to who was told is required, not total loyalty. Do you understand?"

"No," Conan replied truthfully, and the other man stiffened as though struck.

"Very well then, Patil. Play the game alone if you wish, but remember that only the very powerful can play alone and survive." Jerking the reins viciously, Torio trotted away.

The man belonged with the Vendhyan nobles and the jugglers, Conan thought. He spouted gibberish and was offended when he was not understood.

The tree-lined riverbank was a scene of sweating and shouting. With a crash another thick bole toppled, and laborers rushed with their axes to hew away limbs so it could be lashed to the large raft half-finished at the water's edge. A complement of Vendhyan lancers was leading the horses onto another raft, some fifty feet in length, while a third was in mid-river, making its way along one or a pair of thick cables bowed by the slow current of the Zaporoska. Another heavy cable was already being fastened in place for the raft under construction. Ropes attached to the rafts led to the motive power for the journey in both directions: two score of ragged slaves on either bank for each raft.

The Vendhyan cavalrymen stared at Conan, black eyes unblinking and expressionless, as he led the stallion among them onto the raft. They were tall men, but he was half a head taller than the biggest. Some tried to stand straighter. The only sound on the raft was the occasional stamp of a hoof. Conan could feel the tension in the soldiers. Any one of them would take a direct look as a challenge and being obviously ignored as an insult. As he was not looking for a fight before he even got across the river, the Cimmerian involved himself with pretending to check his saddle girth.

The raft lurched and swayed, swinging out into the

current as a strain was taken on the two ropes. It was then that Conan found something to look at in earnest, something on the shore behind them. Well away from the water, Torio rode slowly, peering at the ground. Looking for what he had thrown down, Conan realized. He watched the guard captain until the raft touched the far bank.

CHAPTER XII

Seen close, the huge tent of golden silk was impressive, supported by more than a score of tent poles. The hundred Vendhyan lancers could have fit inside easily, and their horses as well.

The circle of mounted men opened before Conan, seemingly without command. As he rode through, it closed again. He wished he did not feel that those steel-tipped lances were the bars of a cage.

Turbaned servants rushed to meet the Cimmerian, one to take the stallion's bridle, another to hold his stirrup. At the entrance to the pavilion stood a servant with cool, damp towels on a silver tray, to wipe his hands and face. Still another knelt and tried to lave his sandaled feet.

"Enough," Conan growled, tossing back a crumpled towel. "Where is your master?"

A plump man appeared in the entrance, a spray of egret plumes on his large turban of gold and green. Beneath the edge of his gold-brocade tunic peeked the pointed, curling toes of silken slippers. Conan thought this was the *wazam* until the man bowed deeply and said, "Pray follow me, master."

Within, a large chamber had been created by hangings of cloth of gold and floors of Vendhyan carpets fit for the palace of a king. Incense lay thick and heavy in the air. Hidden musicians began to play on flute and cithern as Conan entered, and five women, so heavily veiled and swathed in silk that he could see nothing but their dark eyes, began to dance.

Reclining on a rainbow of silken cushions was a tall man, his narrow olive face topped by a turban of scarlet silk. The servant's snowy plumes were duplicated here in diamonds and pearls. About his neck hung a thick necklace of gold set with emeralds as large as pigeon's eggs, and every finger wore a ring of rubies and sapphires. His dark eyes were deep-set and harder than any of the gems he wore.

"Are *you* Karim Singh?" Conan asked.

"I am." The seated man's deep voice held a note of shock, but he said, "Your lack of the proper forms is strange, but amusing. You may continue it. You are the one called Patil. It is a name of my country and seems odd on one so obviously from distant lands."

"There are many lands," Conan said, "and many names. The name Patil serves me."

The *wazam* smiled as though the Cimmerian had said something clever. "Sit. One must endure the deprivations of travel, but the wine, at least, is tolerable."

Seating himself cross-legged on the cushions, Conan ignored silver trays of candied dates and pickled quail eggs proffered by servants who seemed to appear and vanish by magic, so obsequiously silent were they. He did accept a goblet of heavy gold, ringed by a wide band of amethysts. The wine had a smell of perfume and tasted of honey.

"Word travels quickly," Karim Singh went on. "I soon heard about you, a pale-skinned giant with eyes like. . . . Most disconcerting, those eyes." He did not sound in the least disconcerted. "I know much of the western world, you see, though it is a veiled land to many of my countrymen. Before journeying to Aghrapur to make treaty with King Yildiz, I studied what has been written. While there, I listened. I know of the pale barbarians of the distant north, fierce warriors, stark slayers, ruthless. Such men can be useful."

For the first time in what seemed a very great while, Conan felt he was on ground he knew, if ground he did not particularly like. "I have taken service as far as Ayodhya," he said. "After that my plans are uncertain."

"Ah, yes. The Khitan. He is a spy, of course."

Conan almost choked on the wine. "The merchant?"

"In Vendhya all foreigners are considered spies. It is safer that way." The intent look in Karim Singh's eyes made the Cimmerian wonder for whom he himself was considered to be spying. "But there are spies, and there are spies. One who spies on a spy, for instance. Not all in my land have Vendhya's best interests in their hearts. It might be of interest to me to know to whom in Vendhya the Khitan speaks, and what he says. It might interest me enough to be worth gold."

"I am not a spy," Conan said tightly. "Not for anyone." He felt a moment's confusion as the *wazam* gave a pleased smile.

"Very good, Patil. It is seldom one finds a man faithful to the first buyer."

There was a patronizing tone to his words that made Conan's eyes grow cold. He thought of explaining, but he did not think this man would recognize the concept of honor if it were thrust in his face. As he cast about for a way to change the subject, the Cimmerian's gaze fell on the dancers and his jaw dropped. Opaque veils still covered the faces of the five women to the eyes, but the other swathings of silk now littered the carpets beneath their feet. All of them. Supple curves of rounded olive flesh spun across the chamber, now leaping like gazelles with stretching legs, now writhing as though their bones had been replaced with serpents.

"You appreciate my trinkets?" Karim Singh asked. "They are trophies, after a fashion. Certain powerful lords long opposed me. Then each discovered he was not so powerful as he thought, discovered, too, that even for a lord, life itself could have a price. A favorite daughter, for instance. Each personally laid that price at my feet. Are they not lovely?"

"Lovely," Conan agreed hoarsely. He strove for a smoother tone, lest the other take his surprise for a lack of sophistication. "And I have no doubt their faces will be equally as lovely when the final veil is dropped."

Karim Singh stiffened momentarily. "I forget that you are an outlander. These women are of my *purdhana*. For them to unveil their faces before anyone other than myself would shame them greatly, and me as well."

Considering the soft nudities before him, Conan nodded. "I see," he said slowly. He did not see at all. Different lands, different customs, but this tended toward madness. Taking a deep breath, he set down the goblet and rose to his feet. "I must go now. Kang Hou will soon be crossing the river."

"Of course. And when you reach Ayodhya and no longer serve him, I will send for you. There is always need for a man of loyalty, for a ruthless slayer untroubled by civilized restraints."

Conan did not trust himself to speak. He jerked his

head in what he hoped might pass for a bow and stalked out.

Outside the tent the plump man with the egret plumes on his turban was waiting, a silver tray in his hands. "A token from my master," he said, bowing.

There was a leather purse on the tray. It was soft and buttery in Conan's palm and he could feel the coins within. He did not open it to count them or to see if they were gold or silver.

"Thank your master for his generosity," he said, then tossed the purse back to the startled man. "A token from me. Distribute it among the other servants."

He could feel the plump fellow's eyes on his back as he strode to his horse—the two servants were still there; one to hold the bridle, one to hold the stirrup for him to mount—but he did not care. If Karim Singh was insulted by the gesture, so be it. He had had all of His Puissant Excellency, the Adviser to the Elephant, that he could stomach.

The steel-tipped circle opened once more, and Conan rode toward the water. Cursing camel drivers used long switches to drive their laden charges from a raft held tightly against the bank by the slaves on the tow rope. All three of the rafts were in service now. One, loaded with Vendhyan nobles, was in mid-river, and the last, crammed with camels and merchants, was close behind. Two milling masses, merchants in one, nobles and their odd companions in the other, showed the crossings had begun soon after he had reached this side. The far bank was crowded with those waiting.

The Cimmerian did not see Kang Hou or any of the others. If he crossed back, however, it was just as possible as not that they would pass each other on the river. He drew rein where he could watch all three landing places.

As the black stood flicking its tail at flies, stamping its feet with impatience to run, a Vendhyan cavalryman rode up beside him. The silk and velvet of the Vendhyan's garb marked him as an officer, the gem-studded scabbard of his sword and the gilding of his turbaned helmet as an officer of rank. An arrogant sneer was on his face and his eyes were tinged with cruelty. He did not speak, only stared at the big Cimmerian in fierce silence.

He had sought to avoid a fight once this morning, Conan told himself. He could easily do so again. After all, the man but looked at him. Only that. Just looked. Lowering, Conan kept his own gaze on the approaching rafts. The Vendhyan was alone, therefore it had nothing to do with the incident of the purse. In his experience, men like the *wazam* did not reply to perceived insults in such small ways. But then again, this was beginning not to seem so small. Conan's jaw tightened.

"You are the man Patil," the Vendhyan barked suddenly. "You are not Vendhyan."

"I know who and what I am," Conan growled. "Who and what are you?"

"I am Prince Kandar, commanding the bodyguard of the *wazam* of Vendhya. And you will guard your tongue or lose it!"

"I have heard a warning much like that once already today," Conan replied flatly, "but my tongue is still mine, and I will not let go of it easily."

"Bold words," Kandar sneered, "for an outlander with the eyes of a *pan-kur*."

"The eyes of a what?"

"A *pan-kur*. The spawn of a human woman's mating with a demon. The more ignorant among my men believe such bring misfortune with their presence, and evil with

their touch. They would have slain you already had I
permitted it.''

There was a shifting in the Vendhyan's eyes as he
spoke. The more ignorant of his men? Conan smiled and
leaned toward him. ''As I said, I know who and what I
am.''

Kandar gave a start, and his horse danced a step sideways,
but he mastered his face and his mount quickly. ''Vendhya
is a dangerous land for a foreigner, whoever, or whatever,
he is. A foreigner who wished to have no fear of what lay
around the next turning or what might come in the night
would do well to seek a shielding hand, to cultivate a
patron in high places.''

''And what would this seeking and cultivating require?''
Conan asked dryly.

The Vendhyan moved his horse closer and dropped his
voice conspiratorially. ''That certain information, the contents of certain conversations, be passed on to the patron.''

''I told Karim Singh,'' Conan replied, biting off each
word, ''and now I tell you, I will not spy on Kang Hou.''

''The Khitan? What are you saying? The *wazam* has an
interest in *him?* Bah! I care nothing for merchants!''

The Cimmerian felt as though the other's confusion
were contagious. ''If not Kang Hou, then who in Zandru's
Nine Hells . . .'' He paused at a wild thought. ''Karim
Singh?''

''Aaah,'' said Kandar, suddenly all urbanity. ''That
might be pleasing.''

''I begin to believe it all,'' Conan muttered in tones far
from belief. ''I begin to believe you Vendhyans actually
could sign a treaty with Yildiz on one day and kill the
High Admiral of Turan the next.''

The smoothness that had come to the Vendhyan was as
suddenly swept away. He clutched Conan's arm with a

swordsman's iron grip, and his teeth were bared in a snarl. "Who says this? Who speaks this lie?"

"Everyone in Sultanapur," Conan said quietly. "I suspect, everyone in Turan. Now take your hand from my arm before I cut it off."

Behind Kandar the raft loaded with nobles had reached the bank, and men were streaming off. Two Vendhyan women riding sidesaddle walked their horses toward Conan and the prince. One was plainly garbed and veiled so that only her eyes showed. The other, riding in advance, had a scarf of sheer red silk over her raven hair, with pearls worked into her tresses, but she wore no veil. Necklaces and bracelets of gold and emeralds adorned her and there were rubies and sapphires on her fingers.

As Kandar, glaring at Conan, opened his mouth, the unveiled woman spoke in a low musical tone. "How pleasant to see you, Kandar. I had thought you avoided me of late."

The Vendhyan prince went rigid. For an instant his eyes stared through Conan, then he rasped, "We will speak again, you and I." Without ever once looking around or acknowledging the women's presence, Kandar kicked his horse to a gallop, spurring toward the *wazam*'s pavilion, which was already being taken down.

Conan was not sorry to see him go, especially not when he was replaced by so lovely a creature as the jewel-bedecked woman. Her skin was dusky satin, and her sloe eyes were large pools in which a man might willingly lose himself. And those dark, liquid eyes were studying him with as much interest as he studied their owner. He returned her smile.

"It seems Kandar does not like you," he said. "I think I like anyone he does not."

The woman's laugh was as musical as her voice. "On

the contrary, Kandar likes me much too much." She saw his confusion and laughed again. "He wants me for his *purdhana*. Once he went so far as to try to have me kidnapped."

"When I want a woman, I do not ride away without so much as looking at her." He kept his eyes on her face so she would know it was not of Kandar he spoke at all.

"He has cause. My tirewoman, Alyna," she waved a negligent hand toward the heavily veiled woman, "is his sister."

"His sister!" Conan exclaimed, and once more she laughed. The veiled woman stirred silently on her saddle.

"Ah, I see you are bewildered that the sister of a prince could be my slave. Alas, Alyna dabbled with spies and was to face the headsman's sword until I purchased her life. I then held a masque to which Kandar came, intending to press his suit yet again. For some reason, when he discovered Alyna among the dancing girls, he all but ran from my palace. Such a simple way to rid myself of the bother of him."

Conan stared at that beautiful, sweetly smiling face, appearing so open and even innocent, and only what he had already seen and heard that morning allowed him to credit her words. "You Vendhyans seem to have a liking for striking at your enemies through others. Do none of you ever confront an opponent?"

Her laughter was tinkling bells. "You Westerners are so direct, Patil. Those Turanians! They think themselves devious. They are childlike."

He blinked at that. Childlike? The Turanians? Then something else she had said struck him. "You know my name."

"I know that you call yourself Patil. One must needs be deaf not to hear of a man such as yourself, calling himself by a name of Vendhya. You interest me."

Her gaze was like a caress running over his broad shoulders and chest, even down to his lean hips and thick-muscled thighs. Many other women had looked at him in like fashion and betimes he enjoyed it. This time he felt like a stallion in the auction barns. "And do you want me to spy on someone, too?" he asked gruffly.

"As I said," she smiled. "Direct. And childlike."

"I am no child, woman," he growled. "And I want no more of Vendhyan deviousness."

"Do you know why so many of King Bhandarkar's court accompanied the *wazam* to Turan? Not as his retinue, as the Turanians seemed to think. For us it was a new land to be looted, in a manner of speaking. I found jugglers and acrobats who will seem new and fresh when they perform at my palace in Ayodhya. I bring a dancing bear with me and several scholars. Though I must say the philosophers of Turan do not compare with those of Khitai."

"Do none of you speak straight out? What has this to do with me?"

"In Vendhya," she said, "the enjoyment of life is a way of life. Men of the court give hunts and revels, though the last are often no more than drunken debauches. In any case, neither is proper for a woman of breeding. Yet for every decision made by men on horseback while lancing wild boars, two are made in the palace of a noblewoman. You may ask how mere women compete with the lords and princes. We gather about us scholars and men of ideas, the finest musicians, the most talented poets, the best artists, whether in stone or metal or paint. The newest plays are performed in our palaces and there may be found strange visitors from far-off, mysterious lands. Nor does it hurt that our serving wenches are chosen for their beauty, though unlike the men, we require discretion in their use."

Conan's face had become more and more grim as he

listened. Now he exploded. "That is your 'interest' in me? I am to be a dancing bear or a montebank?"

"I do not believe the women of the court will find you a dancing bear," she said, "although you are nearly as large as one." Suddenly she was looking at him through long kohled lashes, and the tip of her tongue touched a full lip. "Nor can I see you as a montebank," she added throatily.

"Co—Patil!" came a cry, and Conan saw Hordo leading his horse up from the river.

"I must go," the Cimmerian told her roughly, and she nodded as though in some manner she was satisfied.

"Seek my tent tonight, O giant who calls himself Patil. My 'interest' in you is not done with." A smile swept away the seductress to be replaced by the innocent again. "You have not asked my name. I am the Lady Vyndra." And a flick of her gold-mounted riding whip sent her horse leaping away, the veiled woman at her heels.

Behind Hordo, Kang Hou's servants were driving the merchant's camels ashore, aided by the smugglers. One of the humped beasts knelt on the bank while Hasan and Shamil solicitously helped Chin Kou and Kuie Hsi into tented *kajawahs,* conveyances that hung like panniers on the animal's sides.

"Pretty wench," Hordo commented, staring after the galloping Vyndra. "Rides well, too." He looked around to see if anyone was close by, then dropped his voice. "Did you find the chests?"

Conan shook his head. "But they are here. Someone tried to kill me."

"Always a good way to begin a day," Hordo said dryly. "Did you discover anything at all?"

"Three men tried to hire me as a spy and that 'pretty wench' wants to add me to her menagerie."

"Your humor is beyond me, Cimmerian."

"I also found out that my eyes are demon-spawned, and beyond that I learned that Vendhya is a madhouse."

The one-eyed man grunted as he swung into the saddle. "The first I've told you before myself. And the second is known to all. It looks as if we were finally moving."

The *wazam*'s party—Conan remembered Torio saying it had to be first in the line of march—was beginning to stretch out in a line somewhat east of due south, with Vendhyan lancers in two columns to either side. Karim Singh himself was in an ornate litter of ebony and gold, borne between four horses. An arched canopy of gleaming white silk stretched above the palanquin and hangings of golden gossamer draped the sides. Kandar rode beside the litter, bending low out of his saddle to speak urgently to the man within.

"If they tried to kill you," Hordo went on, "at least you have stirred them up."

"Perhaps I have," Conan said. He pulled his gaze away from the *wazam*'s litter. "Let us join Kang Hou and the others, Hordo. There are hours of light left for traveling yet today."

CHAPTER XIII

Night and the depths of the earth were necessary for some things. Some doings could not bear the light of day or exposure to witness of the open sky. As it did so often of late, night found Naipal in the gray-domed chamber far below his palace. The air had the very smell of necromancy, a faint, sickly-sweet taint of decay blended with the indefinable yet unmistakable hellish odor of evil. The smell hung about Naipal, a thing it had not done before his last deeds in that chamber, but he did not notice nor would he have cared had he.

He swung from contemplation of the resurrected warrior, standing as still as stone against the canescent wall in the same spot to which Naipal had at last commanded him on the previous night. The wizard's eyes went to his worktable, skipping quickly over the chest of carved ivory. There, in crystal-stoppered flasks, were the five ingredients necessary for the transfer of life, the total quantity of them that he possessed. In King Orissa's tomb beneath the lost city of Maharashtra stood twenty thousand deathless warriors.

An undying, ever-conquering army. And he could give life to perhaps twenty.

With a wordless snarl, he began to pace. The ancient mages who prepared Orissa's tomb had complied with the King's commands to set him an ever-lasting bodyguard. But those thaumaturges feared the uses to which that bodyguard could be put if ever it were wakened, and they planned well. Only one of the five ingredients could be obtained in Vendhya. The others, chosen partly because they were little-used in sorceries, could be found only in lands little more than legend in Vendhya even two thousand years later. He had made arrangements, of course, but of what use were they when disaster loomed over his head?

Forcing his eyes to the ornate ivory chest, he clenched his fists and glared as though he wished to smash it, and he was not sure that he did not. When finally he had dragged himself from the chamber on the night before, it had been as one fleeing. Creeping through the corridors of his own palace like a thief, he told himself that this was not the paralysis returning, not the fear. He had conquered that. Merely he needed to rest, to refresh himself. Musicians were summoned, and food and wine, but all tasted like sawdust, and the flutes and citherns clawed at his nerves. He ordered cooks and musicians both to be flogged. By twos and threes the women of his *purdhana* were brought to him and returned, weeping and welted for their failures to please. Five times in the course of the day he had commanded that ten thousand *pice* be distributed to the poor in his name, but even that produced no uplifting of his spirits. Now he was back in his sorcery-carved chambers in the earth's bowels. Here he would deal at last with the source of his danger, whatever or wherever it was.

His hands reached toward the flat ivory box . . . and stopped at the chime of a bell. Quizzically his head swiveled toward the sound. On one corner of the rosewood table, crowded amidst crystal beakers filled with noxious substances and oddly glowing vials sealed with lead, was another flat chest, this of polished satinwood with a silver bell, scribed about with arcane symbols, mounted atop it. Even as he looked, the bell sounded once more.

"So the fool finally found the courage to use it," Naipal muttered. He hesitated, wanting to see to his own problems, but the bell rang again. Breathing heavily, he moved around the table to the satinwood chest.

Its lid came off, and he set it aside to stare down at a mirror that showed his image and that of the chamber in quite ordinary fashion. The mirror slid within the box on rails and props so that it could be set at any angle. He raised it almost upright. Eight tiny bone trays came next, atop silver pegs that fitted into holes on the edge of the box, one at each corner, one in the precise middle of each side.

Again the bell chimed, and he cursed. Powders prepared long in advance and stored with the mirror were carefully ladled onto the tiny trays with a bone spatula. Last to come from the box was a small silver mallet, graven with minis-cule renderings of the symbols on the bell.

"*Sa'ar-el!*" Naipal intoned. A blue spark leaped from mallet to bell, and the bell rang. As it did, the powders at the four cardinal points flared in blue flame. Before those tiny berylline fires died in wisps of smoke, he spoke again. "*Ka'ar-el!*" Once more the bell sounded untouched, and blue flame leaped at the minor points. "*Ma'ar-el! Di-endar!*" For the third time the chime came and in the mirror Naipal's reflection swirled and dissolved into a mael-strom of color.

Slowly the polychrome whirling coalesced into the im-age of a narrow-faced man in turban of cloth-of-gold wrapped about with golden chains set with rubies. "Naipal?" the man said. "Asura be praised that it is you."

"Excellency," Naipal said, suppressing his irritation, "how may I serve the Adviser to the Elephant, soon to *be* the Elephant?"

Karim Singh started and stared about him as though fearing who might be behind him. The man could not be fool enough, Naipal thought, to have someone with him while he used the scrying mirror. Could he?

"You should not say such things," the *wazam* said. "Asura alone knows who might overhear. Another wizard perhaps, listening. And now, of all times."

"Excellency, I have explained that only those in the actual presence of these two mirrors . . ." Naipal stopped and drew a deep breath. Explaining to the fool for the hundredth time was useless. "I am Naipal, court wizard to King Bhandarkar of Vendhya. I plot the death of Bhandarkar and spit on his memory. I plot to place His Excellency Karim Singh on the throne of Vendhya. Your Excellency sees. I would not say these things if anyone could overhear."

Karim Singh nodded, though his face was pasty. "I suppose I must . . . trust you, Naipal. After all, you serve me faithfully. I also trust that you know it would be well to give more faithfulness to me than you have given Bhandarkar."

"I am Your Excellency's servant." Naipal wondered if the man had any inkling of how much of his rise to power was the wizard's doing. "And how may I serve Your Excellency now?"

"I . . . do not know exactly," the *wazam* said. "It could be disaster. The treaty is destroyed, without doubt. Our heads may roll. I warn you, Naipal, I will not go to the block alone."

Naipal sighed irritably. The treaty with Turan followed

the simple principles he had led Karim Singh to believe were his own. To seize the throne at Bhandarkar's death required a land in turmoil. Outside enemies tended to unify a country. Therefore all nations that might threaten Vendhya—Turan, Iranistan, the nations and city-states of Khitai and Uttara Koru and Kambuja—must be placated, made to feel neither threatened by nor threatening toward Vendhya. The wizard's preferred method was the manipulation of people in key positions, supplemented by sorcery where needed. It was Karim Singh who thought in terms of treaties. Still, the journey to Turan *had* kept him safely out of Naipal's way for a time.

"Excellency, if Yildiz would not sign, it is of no import. Assuredly, even if Bhandarkar holds the failure against Your Excellency, he has no time to—"

"Listen to me, fool!" Karim Singh's eyes bulged hysterically. "The treaty was signed! And perhaps within hours of that signing the High Admiral of Turan was dead! At the hands of Vendhyan assassins! Who else but Bhandarkar himself would dare such a thing? And if it is indeed him, then what game does he play? Do we move against him unseen, or does he merely toy with us?"

Sweat dampened Naipal's palms as he listened, but he would not wipe them while the other could see. His eyes flickered to the ivory chest. An army? With wizards perhaps? But how could such be mobilized without his knowing? "Bhandarkar cannot know," he said at last. "Is Your Excellency sure of all of the facts? Stories often become distorted."

"Kandar was convinced. And this Patil, who told him, is no man for intrigue. Why, he is as devious as a newborn infant."

"Describe . . . this Patil to me," the wizard said softly. Karim Singh frowned. "A barbarian. A pale-skinned giant with the eyes of a *pan-kur*. Where are you going? Naipal!''

Before the description was finished, the wizard leaped to the ivory chest. He threw back the lid, brushed aside the silken coverings and stared at exactly what he had seen the night before, a vast array of fires in the night. Not an army. A huge caravan. So many pieces suddenly fell into place, yet for every answer there was a new question. He became aware again of Karim Singh's shouting.

"Naipal! Katar take you! Where are you? Return instantly or by Asura . . .'' The wizard moved again in front of the mirror that contained Karim Singh's now-apoplectic visage. "Just in time to save your head! How dare you leave like that, without so much as craving permission or a word of explanation? I will not tolerate such—''

"Excellency. Please, Your Excellency must listen. This man calling himself Patil, this barbarian giant with the eyes of a *pan-kur*''—in spite of himself, Naipal shuddered at that; could it be an omen, or worse?—''he must die, and everyone with him. Tonight, Excellency.''

"Why?'' Karim Singh demanded.

"His description,'' the mage improvised. "Various divinations have brought it to me that a man of that description can bring ruin to all our plans. And as well there is another threat to us in the same caravan with Your Excellency, a threat of which I learned only a short time ago. There is a party of Vendhyan merchants. Their leader is a man called Sabah, though he may use another name. They have pack mules rather than camels, bearing what will appear to be bales of silk.''

"I suppose these men must die as well,'' Karim Singh said and Naipal nodded.

"Your Excellency understands well.'' Commands had

been given and apparently not obeyed. Naipal did not tolerate failure.

"Again, why?"

"The arts of divination are uncertain as to details, Excellency. All that I can say for certain is that every day, every hour that these men live, is a threat to Your Excellency's ascension to the throne." The wizard paused, choosing his words. "There is one other matter, Excellency. Within what appear to be the bales of silk of the Vendhyan merchants will be chests sealed with lead seals. These chests must be brought to me with the seals unbroken. And I must add that the last is more important to Your Excellency's gaining the throne than all the rest, than all we have done so far. The chests must be brought to me with the seals unbroken."

"My gaining the throne," Karim Singh said flatly, "depends on chests being brought to you? Chests that are with the very caravan in which I travel? Chests of which you knew nothing until a short time ago?"

"Before Asura, it is so," Naipal replied. "May my soul be forfeit." It was an easy oath to make; that forfeit had been made long since.

"Very well then. The men will be dead before the sun rises. And the chests will be brought to you. Peace be with you." The silver bell chimed in sympathy with the silver bell in the *wazam*'s tent so far away, and the image in the mirror leaped and was that of Naipal.

"And peace be with you, most excellent of fools," the wizard muttered.

He looked at his palms. The sweat was still there. So many new questions, but death would provide all the answers he needed. Smiling, he wiped his hands on his robes.

CHAPTER XIV

Absolute darkness was pushed back from the night-swathed encampment by hundreds of campfires scattered among a thousand tents. Many of those tents glowed with the light of lamps within, casting moving, mysterious shadows on walls, whether silk or cotton, made less than opaque. The thrum of citherns floated in the air, and the smell of cinnamon and saffron from meals not long consumed.

Conan approached Vyndra's tent with an uncertainty he was not used to. All during the day's march he had avoided her, and if that consisted mainly in staying with Kang Hou's camels rather than seeking her out, it had not been so easily done as it sounded. It was possible she wanted him only as an oddity for her noble friends in Ayodhya, a strange-eyed barbarian at which to gawk, but on the other hand, a woman did not look at an oddity coquettishly through lowered lashes. In any case, she was beautiful, he was young, and therefore he had come as she asked.

Ducking through the tent's entrance flap, he found him-

self staring Alyna in the eyes, which was still all he could
see of her for thick veils and heavy robes. "Your mistress,"
he began and cut off as a flash of murderous rage flickered
through the woman's eyes.

As quickly as it appeared, though, it was gone, and she
bowed him deeper into the tent, which, though smaller
than Karim Singh's, was divided within in much the same
fashion by silken hangings.

In a central chamber floored with exquisite Vendhyan
carpets and lit by golden lamps, Vyndra stood awaiting
him. "You came, Patil. I am glad."

Conan clamped his teeth firmly to keep from gaping.
Gold and rubies and emeralds still bedecked her, but the
robes she had worn earlier were now replaced by layers of
purest gossamer. She was covered from ankles to neck, yet
her position in front of a lamp cast shadows of tantalizing
mystery on rounded surfaces, and the scent of jasmine
floating from her seemed the very distillation of wickedness.

"If this were Turan," he said when he found his tongue,
"or Zamora or Nemedia, and there were two women in a
room dressed as the two of you, it would be Alyna who
was free, and you who were slave. To a man, without
doubt, and the delight of his eye."

Vyndra smiled, touching a finger to her lips. "How
foolish of those women to let their slaves outshine them.
But if you wish to see Alyna, I will have her dance for
you. I have no other dancing girls with me, I fear. Unlike
Karim Singh and the other men, I do not find them a
necessity."

"I would much rather see you dance," he told her, and
she laughed low in her throat.

"That is something no man will ever see." Yet she
twined her arms above her head and stretched in a motion
so supple it cried dancer, and one that dried Conan's

throat. That fabric was more than merely sheer when drawn tight.

"If I could have some wine?" he asked hoarsely.

"Of course. Wine, Alyna, and dates. But sit, Patil. Rest yourself."

She pressed him down onto piled cushions of silk and velvet. He was not sure of exactly how she managed this since she had to reach up to put her small hands on his shoulders, but he suspected the perfume had something to do with it.

He tried to put his arms around her then, while she bent over him so enticingly, but she slipped away like an eel and reclined on the cushions just an arm's length away. He settled for accepting a goblet of perfumed wine from Alyna. The cup was as heavy as the one in which the *wazam* had given him wine, though instead of amethysts, it was studded with coral beads.

"Vendhya seems to be a rich land," he said after he had drunk, "though I've not been there yet to see it."

"It is," Vyndra said. "And what else do you know of Vendhya before you have been there?"

"Vendhyans make carpets," he said, slapping the one beneath the cushions, "and they perfume their wine and their women alike."

"What else?" she giggled.

"Women from the *purdhana* are shamed by baring their faces but not by baring anything else." That brought an outright laugh, though the edges of a blush showed about Alyna's veil. Conan liked Vyndra's laughter, but he was already tired of the sport. "Beyond that, Vendhya seems to be famous for spies and assassins."

Both women gasped as one, and Vyndra's face paled. "I lost my father to the Katari. As did Alyna."

"The Katari?"

"The assassins for which Vendhya is so famous. You mean you did not even know the name?" Vyndra shook her head and shuddered. "They kill, sometimes for gold, sometimes for whim it seems, but always the death is dedicated to the vile goddess Katar."

"That name I have heard," he said, "somewhere."

Vyndra sniffed. "No doubt on the lips of a man. It is a favorite oath of Vendhyan men. No woman would be so foolish as to call on one dedicated to endless death and carnage."

She was clearly shaken, and he could sense her withdrawing into herself. Frantically he sought another topic, one fit for a woman's ears. One of her poets would no doubt compose a verse on the spot, he thought bitterly, but all the verse he knew was set to music, and most of it would made a trull blush.

"A man of your country did say something out of the ordinary to me today," he said slowly, and latched on to the one remark out of several that would bear repeating. "He thought my eyes marked me as demon-spawn. A *pan-kur,* he called it. You obviously do not believe it, else you'd have run screaming rather than inviting me to drink your wine."

"I might believe it," she said, "if I had not talked to learned men who told me of far-off lands where the men are all giants with eyes like sapphires. And I rarely run screaming from anything." A small smile had returned to play on her lips. "Of course, if you actually claim to be a *pan-kur,* I would never doubt the man who calls himself Patil."

Conan flushed slightly. Everyone seemed to know the name was not his, but he could not bring himself to say that he had lied about it. "I have fought demons," he said, "but I am none of their breed."

"You have fought demons?" Vyndra exclaimed. "Truly? I saw demons once, a score of them, but I cannot imagine anyone actually fighting one, no matter what the legends say."

"You saw a score of demons?" Despite his own experience seemingly to the contrary, Conan was aware that demons—and wizards, for that matter—were not so thick on the ground as most people imagined. It was just that he had bad luck in the matter, though Hordo insisted it was a curse. "A score in one place?"

Vyndra's dark eyes flashed. "You do not believe me? Many others were there. Five years ago in the palace of King Bhandarkar, he who was then the court wizard, Zail Bal, was carried off in full view of scores of people. The demons were *rajaie,* which drink the life from their victims. You see, I know whereof I speak."

"Did I say I did not believe you?" Conan asked. He would believe in twenty demons in one place—much less anyone escaping alive from that place—when he saw it, but he hoped devoutly that his luck was never quite that bad.

A small crease appeared between Vyndra's brows, as though she doubted his sincerity. "If you have truly fought demons—and you see I do not question *your* claim—then you must certainly stay at my palace in Ayodhya. Why, perhaps even Naipal would come to meet a man who has fought demons. What a triumph that would be!"

It might have sounded promising, he thought ruefully, if not for this other man. "Do you wish me there, or this Naipal?"

"I want both of you, of course. Think of the wonderment. You, a huge warrior, obviously from a land shrouded in distance and mystery, a fighter against demons. He, the court wizard of Vendhya, the—''

"A wizard," Conan breathed heavily. Hordo would believe he had done this apurpose, or else he would mutter about the curse.

"I said that," Vyndra said. "He is the most mysterious man in Vendhya. No more than a handful other than King Bhandarkar, and perhaps Karim Singh, know his face. Women have arranged assignations with him merely in the hope they might be able to say they could recognize him."

"I have never met the man," he said, "nor intend to, yet I do not like him."

Her laugh was low and wicked. "He keeps the assignations, too, with those women pretty enough. They are gone for days and return on the point of exhaustion with stories of passion beyond belief, but when they are asked of his features, they grow vague. The visage they describe could belong to any handsome man. Still, the transports of rapture they speak of are such that I myself have considered—''

With a curse Conan hurled the golden goblet aside. Vyndra squeaked as he pounced, catching her face between his hands. "I do not want you to attract some sorcerer," he told her heatedly. "I do not want you because you are from a country distant from mine or because you would seem strange to the people of my land. I want you because you are a beautiful woman and you make my blood burn." There was invitation on her face and when he kissed her, she tangled her hands in his hair as though it were she who held him, not the reverse.

When at last she snuggled against his chest with a sigh, there was a mischevious twinkle in her big dark eyes, and small white teeth indented her full lower lip. "Do you intend to take me now?" she asked softly and then added as he growled in his throat, "With Alyna watching?"

Conan did not take his eyes from her face. "She is still here?"

"Alyna is faithful to me in her fashion and rarely leaves my side."

"And you do not intend to send her away." It was not a question.

"Would you have me separated from my faithful tirewoman?" Vyndra asked with a wide-eyed smile.

Clearing his throat, Conan got to his feet. Alyna was there, bright eyes glinting with amusement above her veil. "I have half a mind," he said conversationally, "to switch both your rumps till you have to be tied across your saddles like bolts of silk. Instead, I think I will see if there is an honest trull in this caravan, for your games bore me."

He stalked out on that, thinking he had quieted her, but laughing words followed him before he let the tent flap fall. "You are a violent man, O one who calls himself Patil. You will be a wonderment to my friends."

CHAPTER XV

There were panderers on the outskirts of the encampment, as Conan had known there would be in a caravan so large and going so far. Two of them. Karim Singh might have his own women along, as would the Vendhyan noblemen and even many of the merchants, but for the rest— for guards and camel drivers and mule handlers—from Khawarism to Secunderam was a long way without a woman. Except for the panderers.

They had set out tables made of planks laid on barrels before their tents, with casks to sit on and drink while a man waited his turn for the use of the tents. Cheap wine they gave away to those who bought their other merchandise, sour wine served by sweet women, slender jades and voluptuous trulls, tall wenches and short. Soft, willing flesh. If the gilded brass girdles low on their hips and their strips of diaphanous silk were more than a *purdhana* dancer wore, all could be removed for a coin, for women were the goods sold here.

And yet, Conan realized, it was not a woman he wanted. He sat on an upended keg before the second panderer's

tents, a leathern jack of thin wine in his fist, a slender
wench wiggling on his knee as she bit at his neck with
small white teeth. He could not pretend disinterest in her,
but she seemed a distraction, if a pleasant one. A buxom
jade at the first panderer's tent had been the same. Though
he was not yet twenty, he had long since learned to curb
his anger when need be, but on that day he had held it in
check with Karim Singh and lashed it down with Kandar.
And then there had been Vyndra. Now he wanted to loose
the rage, to strike out at something. He wanted one of the
other men fondling a woman to challenge him for the doxy
on his lap, or two, or five. Hammering fists, even bloody
steel, would drain the anger coiled in his belly like a
serpent dripping venom from its fangs.

The slender trull snuggled against him contentedly as he
stood with her in his arms, then stared at him in consternation when he plopped her bottom onto the keg. "I am not
a Vendhyan," he told her, dropping coins in her hands. "I
do not take out my anger on others than those who have
earned it." Her look was one of total uncomprehension,
but he spoke for his own benefit as much as hers.

The raucous laughter of the panderers' tents followed
him into the encampment. Many of the merchants' tents
were darkened now, and silence lay even on the picket
lines of animals behind each, though the thin sounds of
zither and flute, cithern and tambor, drifted from the nobles'
portion of the camp. Sleep, he thought. Sleep, then journey on the morrow, then sleep again and journey again.
The antidote would be found in Vendhya, and the answers
he sought would come, but he would dissipate the tightness of anger with sleep.

The fire burned low in front of the lone tent shared by
Kang Hou and his nieces. A Khitan servant poking the
embers was all that moved among the blanket-wrapped

shapes of smugglers scattered about the merchant's tent. But Conan stopped short of the dim light of that fire, a jangling in the back of his head that he recognized as a warning that something was wrong.

His ears strained for sounds below normal hearing, and his eyes sought the shadows between the other tents. The sounds were all about him now that he listened. The rasp of leather on leather, the soft clink of metal, the pad of softly placed feet. Shadows shifted where they should be still.

"Hordo!" Conan roared, broadsword coming into his hand. "Up, or die in your blankets!" Before the warning was past his lips, smugglers were rolling to their feet with swords in hand. And Vendhyans as well, afoot and mounted, were upon them.

To attempt to make his way to his companions was madness, the Cimmerian knew. They did not fight to hold a piece of ground but to escape, and every man would be seeking to break through the ring of steel. He had no time for thought on the matter. He had killed one man and was crossing swords with a second by the time he shouted the last word.

Jerking his blade free of the second corpse, he all but decapitated another Vendhyan, searching all the while for his path to freedom, ignoring the screams and clanging steel around him as he fought his way away from the Khitan's tent. A turban-helmed horseman appeared in front of him, lance gone but tulwar lifted to slash. The Vendhyan's fierce, killing grin turned to shock as Conan leaped to grapple with him. Unable to use his sword so close, the horseman beat at Conan with the hilt as the horse danced in circles. The big Cimmerian could not use his broadsword either, merely wrapping that arm about the Vendhyan, but his dagger quickly slid between the metal plates of the

brigantine hauberk. The horseman screamed, and again as
he was toppled from the saddle. Then Conan was scrambling into the other's place, seizing the reins and slamming
his heels into the horse's flanks.

The calvary-trained animal burst into a gallop, and Conan,
lying low in the saddle, guided it between the tents. Merchants and their servants, roused by the tumult, jumped
shouting from the path of the speeding rider. Suddenly
there was a man who did not leap aside, a caravan guard
who dropped to one knee and planted the base of his spear.
The horse shrieked as the long blade thrust into its chest,
and abruptly Conan was flying over the crumpling animal's
head. All of the breath was driven from him by the fall,
yet the Cimmerian struggled to rise. The guard rushed in
for an easy kill of the man on his knees, tulwar raised
high. With what seemed his last particle of strength, Conan
drove his sword into the other's chest. The force of the
man's charge carried him into the big Cimmerian, knocking him over. Still fighting for breath, Conan pushed the
man away, extricated his blade, and staggered into the
shadows. Half-falling, he pressed his back against a tent.

Wakened merchants shouted on all sides.

"What happens?"

"Are we attacked?"

"Bandits!"

"My goods!"

Vendhyan soldiers shoved the merchants aside, beating
at them with the butts of their lances. "Go back to your
tents!" was their cry. "We seek spies! Go back to your
tents, and you will not be harmed! Anyone outside will be
arrested!"

Spies, Conan thought. He had found his fight, but there
was yet a trickle of his previous anger remaining, a trickle
growing stronger. Moments before, escape from the en-

campment had been paramount in his mind. Now he thought he would first visit the man who considered all foreigners spies.

Like a hunting leopard, the big Cimmerian flowed from shadow to shadow, blending with the dark. Curious eyes were easily avoided, for there were few abroad now. No one moved between the tents save soldiers, announcing their coming with creak of harness and clink of armor and curses that they must search when they would be sleeping. Silently Conan moved into deeper shadows as the Vendhyans appeared, watching with a feral grin as they marched or rode past him, sometimes within arm's reach, yet always unseeing.

Karim Singh's tent glowed with light within, and two fires blazed high before the canopied entrance. The fires made the dim light filtered through golden silk at the rear seem almost as dark as the surrounding light. A score of Vendhyan cavalry sat their horses like statues in a ring about the tent, facing outward, ten paces at least separating each man from the next.

Like statues they were in truth, or else thought they guarded against attack by an army, for on his belly Conan crawled unseen between two at the rear of the tent. As he prepared to slit an entrance in the back wall of the tent with his dagger, voices from inside stopped him.

"Leave us," commanded Karim Singh.

Conan opened a small slit only, parting it with his fingers. A last Vendhyan soldier was bowing himself from the silk-walled chamber within. Karim Singh stood in the middle of the chamber, a cavalryman's sword in his hand, and before him knelt a Vendhyan bound hand and foot. The kneeling man wore the robes of a merchant, though they hardly seemed consistent with his hard face and the long scar that crossed his nose and cheek.

"You are called Sabah?" the *wazam* asked in an easy tone.

"I am Amaur, Excellency, an honest merchant," the kneeling man said, "and even you have no right to simply seize my goods without cause." The harsh, rasping voice made Conan stiffen in memory. The rider in the dunes. He would listen for a while before killing Karim Singh.

The *wazam* set the point of his sword against the other's throat. "You are called Sabah?"

"My name is Amaur, Excellency. I know no one called—" The kneeling man gasped as the point pressed closer, bringing a trickle of blood.

"An honest merchant?" Karim Singh laughed softly. As he spoke, he increased the pressure of the blade. The kneeling man leaned back but the sword point followed. "Within the bales of silk you carry were found chests sealed with lead. You are a smuggler, at least. Who are the chests destined for?"

With a cry, the prisoner toppled. From his back he stared with bulging eyes. The sword still was at his throat and there was no farther he could go to escape it. The hardness of his face had become a mask of fear. "I . . . I cannot say, Excellency. Before Asura, I swear it!"

"You will say or you will face Asura shortly. Or, more likely, Katar." The *wazam*'s voice became conspiratorial. "I know the name, Amaur. I know. But I must hear it from your lips if you would live. Speak, Amaur, and live."

"Excellency, he . . . he will kill me. Or worse!"

"*I* will kill you, Amaur. This sword is at your throat, here, and *he* is far away. Speak!"

"N . . . Naipal!" the man sobbed. "Naipal, Excellency!"

"Good," Karim Singh said soothingly. But he did not move the sword. "You see how easy it was. Now. Why? Tell me why he wants these chests."

"I cannot, Excellency." Tears rolled down Amaur's cheeks now and he shook with weeping. "Before Asura, before Katar, I would tell you if I could, but I know nothing! We were to meet the ship, kill all on board and bring the chests to Ayodhya. Perhaps Sabah knew more, but he is dead. I swear, Excellency! I speak truly, I swear!"

"I believe you," Karim Singh sighed. "It is a pity." And he leaned on the sword.

Amaur's attempt to scream became a bubbling gurgle as steel slid through his throat. Karim Singh stared at him as though fascinated by the blood welling up in his mouth and the convulsions that wracked his bound form. Abruptly the *wazam* released the sword. It remained upright, its point thrust through man and carpets into the ground, shaking with Amaur's final twitching.

"Guards!" Karim Singh called, and Conan lowered the dagger with which he had been about to lengthen the slit. "Guards!"

Half a score of Vendhyans rushed into the chamber with drawn blades. Staring at the sight that greeted them, they hastily sheathed their weapons.

"The other spies," the *wazam* said. "The giant, in particular. He has been taken? He cannot be mistaken, for his size and his eyes set him apart."

"No, Excellency," one of the soldiers replied deferentially. "Four of that party are dead, but not the giant. We seek the others."

"So he is still out there." Karim Singh spoke as though to himself. "He seemed a stark man. A slayer born. He will seek me now." He shook himself and glared at the soldiers as if angered that they had overheard. "He must be found! A thousand pieces of gold to the man who finds him. All of you, and ten others, will remain with me until he is dead or in chains. And he who does not die stopping the barbarian from reaching me will die wishing that he had. Have someone dispose of this,'' he added with a nod toward Amaur's corpse.

The *wazam* strode from the chamber then, the guards clustering about him, and Conan sagged where he crouched outside. Against a score of guards he might not even reach Karim Singh before he was cut down. He had known men who embraced a brave but useless death; he was not one of them. Death was an old acquaintance to him and had been long before he found himself with Patil's poison in his blood. Death was neither to be feared nor sought, and when he met it, the meeting would not be without purpose. Besides, he now had a name, Naipal, the man who had begun all of this. That was another who must die as well as Karim Singh.

Silently Conan slipped back into the night.

CHAPTER XVI

A horse and a water bag were what he needed now, Conan knew. In this land a man afoot and without water was a man dying or dead. There were far more camels than horses in the caravan, however, and many of the horses were animals suitable for show but not for a man who needed to travel far and fast. Moreover, word of the reward must have been spreading quickly, for the soldiers were now more assiduous in their searching. Twice he located suitable mounts only to be forced to abandon them by turban-helmed patrols.

Finally he found himself in the nobles' portion of the encampment. Most of the tents were dark and the silence was as complete as in the merchants' part. He wondered if the soldiers had been as brusque here in quieting curiosity as they had been with the merchants.

Something moved in the darkness, a shadow heaving, and he froze. A grunt came from the shadow, and the rattle of a chain. Conan peered more closely and then stifled a laugh. It was Vyndra's dancing bear. On sudden impulse, he drew his dagger. The bear, sitting in a sprawl, eyed him as he cautiously approached. It did not move as he sawed at the leather collar about its neck.

"It is a harsh land," he whispered, "with many ways to die." He felt foolish in talking to an animal, but there was a need, too. "You may find hunters or stronger bears. If you do not run far enough, they will chain you again and make you dance for Vyndra. The choice is yours, to die free or to dance for your mistress."

The bear stared at him as the collar fell loose, and he held the dagger ready. Just because it had not attacked him so far did not mean it would not, and the shaggy creature was half again as large as he. Slowly the bear got to its feet and lumbered into the dark.

"Better to die free," Conan grinned after the beast.

"And I say I saw something move."

Conan stiffened at the words, cursing his impulses.

"Take ten men around the other way and we will see."

In an instant the Cimmerian's blade made a long slit in the tent wall behind him, and he went through as footsteps rounded the tent. Within was as deep a darkness as outside, though his keen eyes, already used to the night, could make out shadowy shapes and mounds on the carpet spread for flooring. The footsteps halted on the other side of the thin wall, and voices muttered indistinguishably. One of the mounds moved.

Not again, Conan thought. Hoping it was not another bear, he threw himself on the shifting shape. The grunt that came when he landed was nothing at all like that of a bear. Soft flesh writhed against him beneath a thin linen coverlet, and his hand frantically sought a mouth, finding it just in time to stifle a scream. Bringing his face close, he looked into big dark eyes filled with a mixture of fear and rage.

"Alyna is not here now, Vyndra," he whispered and moved his hand from her lips.

As her mouth opened once more for a scream, he stuffed it with the ball of her hair that he had gathered with his other hand. Quickly he felt around the bed mat until he found a long silk scarf, which he tied across her mouth to keep her from spitting the hair out. Bound and gagged, he thought, she could raise no alarm until he was far away. With luck, she would not be found until morning.

Stripping off the linen coverlet, he was forced to stop and stare. Even when covered in shadows, the lush curves of her were enough to take his breath away. He found it quickly, though, jerking his head back barely in time to save his eyes from clawing nails.

"This time the sport is not of your choosing," he said softly, catching her flailing arm and deftly flipping her onto her stomach. He found another scarf and used it to bind her wrists behind her. "You may not dance for me," he chuckled, "but this is almost as enjoyable." He felt her quiver and did not need the angry, muffled sounds coming from behind the gag to tell him it was with rage.

As he searched for something to tie her ankles with, he became aware of voices in the front of the tent. Hastily he dragged his struggling prisoner closer to where he could listen.

"Why do you wish to see my mistress?" came Alyna's voice. "She sleeps."

A man answered with weary patience. "The *wazam* has learned that your mistress entertained a spy earlier tonight. He would talk with her of it."

"Can it not wait until morning? She will be angry if she is wakened."

Conan did not wait to learn the outcome. If Vyndra was found now, the soldiers would know he was close by before her gag was fully out of her mouth. Half-carrying the wriggling woman, he darted to the rear of the tent and peered cautiously through the slit by which he had entered. The searchers were gone. It was possible they were even the same men now in the front of the tent.

"I am sorry," he told her.

He was glad for the gag as he pulled her through the slit. The violent protesting noises she made were bad enough as it was. Despite her struggles, he lifted her into his arms, running as fast as he could manage while making sure he did not speed into the midst of a patrol or trip over tent ropes.

Well away from her tent, he put her on her feet, careful to keep a grip on one slender arm. If they were discovered, he had to be able to fight without being burdened with her. And there would be no need to prevent her escape then.

Finding a horse was still his first concern, but when he tried to start out again, he found he was dragging a bent-over, crouching woman who seemed to be attempting to make herself as small as possible while simultaneously refusing to move her feet.

"Stand up and walk," he said hoarsely, but she shook her head furiously. "Crom, woman, I've no time to ogle your charms." She shook her head again.

A quick look around revealed no evidence of anyone both near and awake. All of the surrounding tents were dark. His full-armed swing landing on her buttock produced a louder smack than he would have liked, not to mention the sounds she produced, but it brought her onto her toes and half-erect. When she tried to crouch again, he held his open hand in front of her face.

"Walk," he whispered warningly.

Her glare was enough to slay lions, but slowly she straightened. Without so much as a glance at the beauties she had revealed, he hurried her on. He was not young enough to be a complete fool over a woman.

Ghosting among the tents, they more than once barely avoided the searching Vendhyan soldiers. At first Conan was surprised that Vyndra made no effort to escape when the turban-helmed warriors were close, nor even to attract them with noise or struggle. In fact, she had become as silent as he, eyes constantly searching for what might trip or betray. Then it came to him. Escaping him was one thing, being rescued while garbed in naught but two scarves quite another. He smiled gratefully, accepting anything that made his own escape easier.

Once more he was in the merchants' area, so deathly still that he knew all there were huddled breathlessly, not daring to make a sound that would attract the soldiers. A destination had come to his mind, a place where there might be horses and a place the soldiers would not be searching if he had but a particle of luck.

Movement in the shadows ahead again sent him to hiding, dragging a compliant Vyndra behind. This was no patrol, he saw quickly, but a lone man padding furtively. Slowly the shadow resolved into Kang Hou, half-crouched with his hands in his sleeves. As Conan opened his mouth, two more shapes appeared behind the first. Vendhyan cavalrymen, afoot and carrying their lances like spears.

"Searching for something, Khitan?" one called.

Smoothly Kang Hou pivoted, hands flickering out of concealment. Something flew through the air, and the two Vendhyans dropped soundlessly. Hastily the merchant ran to crouch above the bodies.

"You are a dangerous man for a merchant," Conan said softly as he stepped into the open.

Kang Hou spun, a throwing knife in each upraised hand, then slowly slid the knives from sight within his sleeves.

"A merchant must often travel in dangerous company," he said blandly. He ran his eyes over Vyndra and raised an eyebrow. "I have heard it said that some warriors favor women above all other loot, but under these circumstances, I find it strange."

"I do not want her," Conan said. Vyndra growled through her gag. "The problem is, where can I leave her and be sure she'll not be found before I have gotten a horse and left this place?"

"A quandary," the Khitan agreed. "You have considered where to find this horse? The soldiers check the picket lines constantly and a missing animal will not go long undiscovered."

"At the last place they will look for one of us," Conan replied. "The picket line behind your tent."

Kang Hou smiled. "Admirable reasoning. Having led my original pursuers a way from the encampment, I am now returning there. Will you accompany me?"

"In but a moment. Hold her."

Thrusting Vyndra at the startled Khitan, Conan hurried to the dead Vendhyans. Quickly he dragged them into the deeper darkness beside a tent—no sense in leaving them to be easily found—and when he returned to the others, he carried one of the soldiers' cloaks. Kang Hou wore a small smile, and Vyndra's eyes were squeezed tightly shut.

"What happened?" the Cimmerian asked. He draped the cloak around the woman as best he could with her hands bound. Her eyes flew open, giving him a look of mingled surprise and gratitude.

"I'm not entirely certain," the merchant said, "but it seems that her belief is that if she cannot see me, I cannot see her." Even in the dark her blush at his words was evident.

"We have no time for foolishness," Conan said. "Come."

A thousand gold pieces was a powerful spur when added to the command of a man such as Karim Singh, but even that spur lost its sharpness when the searchers began to believe their quarry had already escaped from the encamped caravan. Patrols of Vendhyans began to grow fewer, and those who still hunted did so in desultory fashion. Many no longer even went through the motions, gathering instead in easily avoided knots to talk in low voices.

Short of the Khitan's camp Conan halted, still hidden in the darkness among the other merchants' tents. Vyndra obeyed his grip on her arm with seeming docility, but he maintained his hold. The fire was only coals now, and bales of velvet lay ripped open among carpets unrolled and scattered about. If anyone had died there—the Cimmerian remembered the report to Karim Singh of four dead—their bodies had been taken away. The picket line was only a murky mass but some of those shadows moved in ways he did not like. Kang Hou started forward, but Conan caught his arm.

"Horses move even in the night," the Khitan whispered, "and the soldiers would not hide. We must hurry."

Conan shook his head. Pursing his lips, he gave the call of a bird found only on the plains of Zamora. For an instant there was silence, then the call came back, from the picket line.

"Now we hurry," Conan said and ran for the horses, hauling Vyndra behind him.

Hordo stepped out to meet him, motioning for greater quickness. "I hoped you had made it, Cimmerian," he said hoarsely. "Hell has come to sup, it seems." Two other shadows became men, Enam and Prytanis.

"I heard there are four dead," Conan said. "Who?"

"Baltis!" Prytanis spat. "The Vendhyan scum cut him to shreds. I *said* you brought us all to our deaths."

"He followed me," Conan agreed, to the slit-nosed man's evident surprise. "It is another debt I owe."

"Baltis died well," Hordo said, "and took an honor guard with him. A man can ask no more of dying than that. The other three," he added to the Khitan, "were your servants. I have not seen your nieces."

"My servants were not fighting men," Kang Hou sighed, "but I had hoped. . . . No matter. As for my nieces, Kuie Hsi will care for her sister as well as I could. Might I suggest that we take horses and continue this talk elsewhere?"

"A good suggestion," Conan said.

The stallion was still there; Conan had feared that such a fine mount would have been taken by the Vendhyans. He heaved the saddle onto the animal's back one-handed but fastening the girth would require two hands. Giving Vyndra a warning look, he released her but kept a sharp eye on her as he hastily strapped the saddle tight. To his surprise, she did not move. No doubt, he thought, she still dreaded being found clothed as she was, even if it did mean rescue.

"The wench," Hordo said curiously. "Do you have a purpose with her, or is she just a token to remember this place by?"

"There is a purpose," Conan said, explaining why he could not leave her yet. "It may be I must take her all the way to Vendhya with me, for I doubt she'd survive long if I left her to make her own way on the plain." He paused, then asked with more casualness than he felt, "What of Ghurran?"

"I've not seen the old man since the attack," Hordo replied regretfully. "I am sorry, Cimmerian."

"What is, is," Conan said grimly. "I must saddle a horse for the woman. I fear you must ride astride, Vyndra, for we have no sidesaddle." She merely stared at him, unblinking.

It was a silent procession that made its stealthy way through the tents of the encampment, leading their horses. The animals could walk more quietly without burdens, and they all would have been more noticeable mounted. The Vendhyan patrols, half-hearted and noisy, might as well not have been there. Conan, first in line, had the reins of his horse and Vyndra's in one hand and her arm firmly in the other. Discovery would end the need for keeping her, as he was sure she must know, and he was not about to trust the odd passivity she had shown so far.

The edge of the caravan encampment appeared before him, and ingrained caution made him signal a halt. Prytanis began to speak, but Conan angrily motioned him to silence. There was a faint noise, almost too low to hear. The soft tread of horses. Perhaps all of the Vendhyans had not given up on the hunt.

A glance told Conan the others had heard as well. Swords were in hand—Kang Hou held one of his throwing knives—and each man had moved alongside his horse to be ready to mount. The Cimmerian tensed, ready to heave Vyndra aside to relative safety and vault into his saddle, as the other horses appeared.

Five animals were in the other pary as well, and Conan almost laughed with relief when he saw those leading the beasts. Shamil and Hasan, each with a protective arm about one of Kang Hou's nieces, and old Ghurran hobbling in the rear.

"It is good to see you," Conan called softly.

The two younger men spun, clawing for their swords. Hasan was somewhat hampered by Chin Kou clutching at him, but Kuie Hsi came up with a knife poised to throw. A dangerous family, the Cimmerian thought. Ghurran merely watched expressionessly as though no fear remained in him.

The two groups joined, everyone attempting whispered conversation, but Conan silenced them with a hiss. "We talk when we are safe," he told them softly, "and that is far from here." Lifting Vyndra into her saddle, he adjusted the soldier's cloak to give her a modicum of decency. "I will find you something to wear," he promised. "Perhaps you will dance for me yet." She stared at him above the gag, the expression in her eyes unreadable.

As Conan swung into his own saddle, a wave of dizziness swept over him, and he had to clutch the high pommel to keep from falling.

Ghurran was at his side in an instant. "I will compound the potion as soon as I can," the old herbalist said. "Hang on."

"I've no intention of anything else," Conan managed through gritted teeth. Leading Vyndra's horse by the reins, he kneed his own mount to motion, into the night toward Vendhya. He would not let go.

There were debts to pay, and two men to kill first.

CHAPTER XVII

Naipal looked at the man facing him, a thin, hard-eyed Vendhyan who could have been a soldier, and wondered at what motivated him. Neither personal gain nor power seemed to impress the other man. He showed no signs of love or hate or pride, nor of any other emotion. It made the wizard uneasy, confronting a man who exposed so little by which he might be manipulated.

"You understand, then?" Naipal said. "When Bhandarkar is dead, the oppression will end. Shrines to Katar will be allowed in every city."

"Have I not said that I understand?" the nameless representative of the Katari asked quietly.

They were alone in the round chamber, its shallow-domed ceiling a bas-relief of ancient heroes. Golden lamps on the walls gave soft illumination. No food or drink had been brought, for the Katari would not eat in the dwelling of one who invoked the services of his cult. They stood because the Katari did, and the wizard did not want the other looming over him. A standing man had the advantages of height and position over a seated man.

"You have not said it will be done." Naipal was hard pressed to keep irritation out of his voice. There was so much to be done this day, but this part was as important as any and must be handled delicately.

Along with the other things that did not impress or affect one of the Katari was the power of a sorcerer. Spells could destroy a Katari as quickly as any other man, but that meant little to one who believed to his core that death, however it came, meant instantly being taken to the side of his goddess. It all gave the wizard an ache in his temples.

"It will be done," the Katari said. "In return for what you have promised, Bhandarkar, even on his throne, will be dedicated to the goddess. But if the promises are not kept . . ."

Naipal ignored the threat. That was an aspect he could deal with later. He certainly had no intention of giving additional power to a cult that could, and assuredly would, undermine him. The *khorassani* could certainly protect him against the assassin's knife. Or a bodyguard of resurrected warriors from King Orissa's tomb.

"You understand also," the wizard said, "that the deed must be done when I signal it? Not before. Not an hour before."

"Have I not said that I understand?" the other repeated.

Naipal sighed. The Katari had the reputation of killing in their own time and their own way, but even if Bhandarkar had not protected himself against spells, there could be nothing of sorcery connected with his death. The appearance of clean hands would be essential to Naipal, for he wanted a land united willingly under the supposed leadership of Karim Singh, not one ravaged by opposition and war. And who would believe a wizard would use the Katari when he could slay so easily by other means?

"Very well," Naipal said. "At my sign, Bhandarkar is to die by Katari knives, on his throne, in full view of his nobles and advisers."

"Bhandarkar will die."

With that Naipal had to be satisfied. He offered the Katari a purse of gold, and the man took it with neither change of expression nor word of gratitude. It would go to the coffers of the Katari, the wizard knew, and so was no cord to bind the fellow, but habit made him try.

When the assassin was gone, Naipal paused only to fetch the golden coffer containing the demon-wrought dagger, then made his way hurriedly to the gray-domed chamber far below the palace. The resurrected warrior stood his ceaseless vigil against a wall, unsleeping, untiring. Naipal did not look at him. The newness was gone, and what was a single warrior to the numbers he would raise from the dead?

Straight to the ivory chest he went, unhesitatingly throwing back the lid and brushing aside the silken coverings. In the mirror there was a single campfire, seen from a great height. For seven days the mirror had shown a fire by night and a small party of riders by day, first on the plains beyond the Himelias, now in the very mountains themselves. Almost out of them, in fact. They moved more slowly than was necessary. It had taken some time for him to realize that they actually followed the caravan bringing the chests to him. Salvation and potential disaster would arrive together.

Seven days of seeing the proof of Karim Singh's failure had taken much of the sting away though. It no longer affected him as it had, watching possible doom approach. In truth, except for the pain behind his eyes that had come while talking to the Katari, Naipal felt almost numb. So much to do, he thought as he closed the box, and so little time remaining. The strain was palpable. But he would win, as he always did.

Moving quickly, he arranged the *khorassani* on their golden tripods. The incantations of power were spoken. Fires brighter than the sun leaped and flared and formed a cage. The summoning was cried and with a thunderous clap, Masrok floated before him in the bound void, weapons glowing in five of its eight obsidian fists.

"It is long, O man," the demon cried angrily, "since you have summoned me. Have you not felt the stone pulse against your flesh?"

"I have been busy. Perhaps I did not notice." Days since, Naipal had removed the black opal from about his neck to escape that furious throbbing. Masrok had to be allowed to ripen. "Besides, you yourself said that time did not matter to one such as you."

Masrok's huge form quivered as though on the point of leaping at the fiery barriers constraining it. "Be not a fool, O man! Within the limits of my prison have I been confined, and only its empty vastness on levels beyond your knowing has saved me. My other selves know that one of the Sivani is no more! How long can I flee them?"

"Perhaps there is no need to flee them. Perhaps your day of freedom is close, leaving those others bound for eternity. Bound away from you as well as from the world."

"How, O man? When?"

Naipal smiled as he did when a man brought to hopeless despair by his maneuverings displayed the first cracks before shattering. "Give me the location of King Orissa's tomb," he said quietly. "Where lies the centuries-lost city of Maharastra?"

"No!" The word echoed ten thousand times as Masrok spun into an ebon blur, and the burning walls of its cage

howled with the demon's rage. "I will never betray!
Never!"

The wizard sat, silent and waiting, until the fury had
quieted. "Tell me, Masrok," he commanded.

"Never, O man! Many times have I told you there are
limits to your binding of me. Take the dagger that I gave
you and strike at me. Slay me, O man, if that is your wish.
But I will never betray that secret."

"Never?" Naipal tilted his head quizzically, and the
cruel smile returned to his lips. "Perhaps not." He touched
the golden coffer, but only for an instant. "I will not slay
you, however. I will only send you back and leave you
there for all of time."

"What foolishness is this, O man?"

"I will not send you back to those levels vaster than my
mind can know, but to that prison you share with your
remaining other selves. Can even a demon know fear if its
pursuers are also demons? I can only slay you, Masrok.
Will they slay you when at last they overtake you? Or can
demons devise tortures for demons? Will they kill you, or
will you continue to live, to live until the end of time under
tortures that will make you remember your prison as the
most sublime of paradises? Well, Masrok?"

The huge demon stared at him malevolently, unblinking,
unmoving. Yet Naipal knew. Were Masrok a man, that man
would be licking his lips and sweating. He *knew!*

"My freedom, O man?" the demon said at last. "Free
of serving you as well?"

"When the tomb is located," Naipal replied, "and the
army buried there is within my grasp, you will have your
freedom. With, of course, a binding spell to make certain
you can neither harm nor hinder me in the future."

"Of course," Masrok said slowly.

The part about the binding spell was perfect, Naipal

thought. A concern for his own future safety was certain to convince the demon he meant to go through with the bargain.

"Very well, O man. The ruins of Maharastra lie ten leagues to the west of Gwandiakan, swallowed ages past by the Forests of Ghendai."

Victory! Naipal wanted to jump to his feet and dance. Gwandiakan! It must be an omen, for the first city at which Karim Singh's caravan would rest once across the Himelias was Gwandiakan. He must contact the *wazam* with the scrying glass. He would race to meet the chests there and go immediately to the tomb. But no wonder the ruins had never been found. No road had ever been hewn through the Forests of Ghendai, and few had ever tried to cut its tall trees for their wood. Huge swarms of tiny, stinging flies drove men mad and those who escaped the flies succumbed to a hundred different fevers that wracked the body with pain before they killed. Some men would rather die than enter those forests.

"Maps," he said suddenly. "I will need maps so my men will not go astray. You will draw them for me."

"As you command, O man."

The demon's weary defeat was triumphal music to Naipal's ears.

CHAPTER XVIII

From the hills overlooking Gwandiakan, Conan stared at the city in amazement. Alabaster towers and golden domes and columned temples atop tiered, man-made hills of stone spread in vast profusion, surrounded by a towering stone wall leagues in circumference.

" 'Tis bigger than Sultanapur," Enam said in awe.

" 'Tis bigger than Sultanapur and Aghrapur together," Hordo said.

Kang Hou and his nieces seemed to take the city's size as a matter of course, while Hasan and Shamil had eyes only for the Khitan women.

"You judge by the smallness of your own lands," Vyndra mocked. She sat her horse unbound, for Conan had seen no reason to keep her tied once they were away from the caravan. She wore robes of green silk from bundles of clothing the Khitan women had gathered for themselves. They were smaller women than she, and the tightness of her current garb delineated her curves to perhaps greater perfection than she might have wished. "Many

186

cities in Vendhya are as large or larger," she went on.
"Why, Ayodhya is three times so great."

"Are we to sit here all day?" Ghurran demanded
grumpily. As the others had grown tired with journeying,
the herbalist had seemed to gain energy, but all of it went
to irritability.

Prytanis jumped in with still nastier tones. "What of
this palace she has been telling us of? After days of living
on what we can snare, with naught to drink but water, I
look forward to wine and delicacies served by a willing
wench. Especially as the Cimmerian wants to keep this
one for himself."

Vyndra's face colored, but she merely said, "I will take
you there."

Conan let her take the lead, though he kept his horse
close behind hers as they wended their way out of the
hills. He was far from sure of what to make of the Vendhyan
woman or her actions. She had made no attempt to escape
and ride to the caravan, even when she knew it was just
out of sight ahead of them, with a plain trail showing the
way. And he often caught her watching him, a strange,
unreadable look in her dark eyes. He had made no ad-
vances to her, for it seemed wrong after he had carried her
away bodily. She would see a threat behind any words he
might say, and she had done nothing to earn that. So he
watched her in turn, uneasily, wondering when this strange
calm she affected would end.

Their way led toward the city for only a short time, then
turned to the west. Before they came out of the hills,
Conan could see many palaces in that direction, great
blocks of pale, columned marble gleaming in the sun in
the midst of open spaces scattered over leagues of forest to
the north and south. Still farther to the west, the trees grew
taller, and there were no palaces there that he could see.

Suddenly the trees through which they rode were gone, and before them was a huge structure of ivory spires and alabaster domes, with rising terraces of fluted columns and marble stairs at the front a hundred paces wide. On each side was a long pool bordered by broad marble walks and reflecting the palace in its mirror-smooth waters.

As they rode toward the great expanse of deep-run stairs, Vyndra spoke suddenly. "Once Gwandiakan was a favored summer resort of the court, but many came to fear the fevers of the forests to the west. I have not been here since I was a child, but I know there are a few servants still, so perhaps it is habitable." She bounced from her saddle and bounded up the broad stairs, needing two paces to a single stairstep.

Conan climbed down from his horse more slowly, and Hordo with him. "Does she play some Vendhyan game with us?" the one-eyed man asked.

Conan shook his head silently; he was as uncertain as his friend. Abruptly a score of men i white turbans and pale cotton tunics appeared at the head of the stairs. The Cimmerian's hand went to his sword, but the men ignored those at the foot of the stair and bent themselves almost double bowing to Vyndra, murmuring words that did not quite reach Conan's ear.

Vyndra turned back to the others. "They remember me. It is as I feared. There are only a few servants, and the palace is much deteriorated, but we may find some bare comforts."

"I know the comforts I want," Prytanis announced loudly. "The three prettiest wenches I can find. Strip them all and I'll choose."

"My serving women are to be gently treated," Vyndra said angrily.

"You forget you are a prisoner, wench!" the slit-nosed man snarled. "Were the Cimmerian not here, I would—"

"But I am here," Conan said in hard tones. "And if she wants her serving girls treated gently, then you will treat them like your own sisters."

Prytanis met the Cimmerian's iron gaze for only a moment, then his dark eyes slid away. "There are tavern wenches in the city, I'll wager," he muttered. "Or do you wish them treated like sisters as well?"

"Have a care if you go into the city," Conan told him. "Remember, foreigners are all considered spies in this land."

"I can look after myself," the Nemedian growled. Sawing at the reins, he jerked his horse around and galloped off in the direction of Gwandiakan.

"Another must go as well," Conan said as he watched Prytanis disappear. "I'd not trust him to discover what we must know, but information is needed. The caravan entered the city, but how long will it remain? And what does Karim Singh do? Hordo, you see that none of Vyndra's servants run off to tell of strangers here. There has been nothing to indicate Karim Singh knows we follow, so let us see that that does not change. I will go into—"

"Your pardon," Kang Hou broke in. "It will take long for an obvious outlander such as yourself to learn anything of interest, for talk will die in your presence. On the other hand, my niece, Kuie Hsi, has often passed as a Vendhyan woman in aid of my business. If she can obtain the proper clothing here . . ."

"I cannot like sending a woman in my place," Conan said but the Khitan only smiled.

"I assure you I would not send her if I thought the danger were too great for her."

Conan looked at Kuie Hsi, standing straight and serene beside Shamil. In her embroidered robes she looked plainly Khitan, but with her dusky coloring and the near lack of an epicanthic fold on her eyes, it seemed barely possible. "Very well," he said reluctantly. "But she is only to look and listen. Asking questions could draw the wrong eyes to her and I'll not let her take that chance."

"I will tell her of your concern," the merchant said.

Servants came—silent turbaned men bowing as they took away the horses, even more deeply bowing men and women, smiling as they proffered silver goblets of cool wine and golden trays with damp towels for dusty hands and faces.

A round-faced, swarthy man appeared before Conan, bobbing quick bows as he spoke. "I am Punjar, master, steward of the palace. My mistress has commanded me to see personally to your wishes."

Conan looked for Vyndra and could not see her. The servants made a milling mass about the Cimmerian's party on the stairs, asking how they might serve, speaking of baths and beds. Momentary thoughts of devious traps flitted through his mind. But Kang Hou was following a serving girl in one direction while his nieces were led in another and Conan had few remaining doubts of the merchant's ability to avoid a snare. Ghurran, he saw, had retained his horse.

"Do you mistrust this place, herbalist?" Conan asked.

"Less than you, apparently. Of course she is both a woman and a Vendhyan, which means that she will either guard you with her life or kill you in your sleep." Days in the open had darkened and weathered the old man's skin, making it less parchmentlike, and his teeth gleamed whitely as he grinned at Conan's discomfort. "I intend to ride into Gwandiakan. It is possible I might find the ingredents for your antidote there."

"That old man," Hordo grumbled as the herbalist rode away, "seems to live on sunlight and water, like a tree. I do not think he even sleeps."

"You merely grow jealous as you catch up to him in age," Conan said and laughed as the one-eyed man scowled into his beard.

The corridors through which Punjar led him made the Cimmerian wonder at Vyndra's comment that the palace was barely habitable. The varicolored carpets scattered on polished marble floors, the great tapestries lining the walls, were finer than any he had seen in palaces in Nemedia or Zamora, lands noted in the West for their luxury. Golden lamps set with amethyst and opal hung on silver chains from ceilings painted with scenes of ancient heroes and leopard hunts and fanciful winged creatures. Cunningly wrought ornaments of delicate crystal and gold sat on tables of ebony and ivory inlaid with turquoise and silver.

The baths were pools mosaicked in geometric patterns, but among the multi-hued marble tiles were others of agate and lapis lazuli. The waters were warm in one pool, cool in another, and veiled serving girls in their servant's pristine white scurried to pour perfumed oils into the water, to bring him soaps and soft toweling. He kept his broadsword close at hand, moving it from the side of one pool to the side of the next as he changed temperatures, and this set the women twittering softly to one another behind their veils. He ignored their shocked looks; to disarm himself was to show more trust than he could muster.

Refusing the elaborate silken robes—including, he saw with some amusement, the long lengths of silk to wind into a turban—that they brought to replace his dusty, travel-stained garb, Conan chose out a plain tunic of dark blue and belted on his sword over that. Punjar appeared again, bowing deeply.

"If you will follow me, master?" The round-faced man seemed nervous and Conan kept a hand on his sword-hilt as he motioned the other to lead.

The chamber to which Conan was taken had a high vaulted ceiling and narrow columns worked in elaborate gilded frescoes. Surely such columns were too thin to be meant for support. At the top of the walls intricate lattice-work had been cut in the marble; the scrolled openings were tiny, Conan noted, but perhaps still large enough for a crossbow bolt.

The floor, of crimson and white diamond-shaped tile of marble, was largely bare, though a profusion of silken cushions was scattered to one side. Placed beside the cushions were low tables of hammered brass bearing golden trays of dates and figs, a ruby-studded golden goblet and a tall crystal flagon of wine. Conan wondered if it were poisoned and then almost laughed aloud at the thought of poisoning a man already dying of poison.

"Pray be seated, master," Punjar said, gesturing to the cushions.

Conan lowered himself but demanded, "Where is Vyndra?"

"My mistress rests from her travels, master, but she has commanded an entertainment for you. My mistress begs that you excuse her absence, and begs also that you remember her request that her serving women be treated gently." Bowing once more, he was gone.

Abruptly music floated from the latticework near the ceiling—the thrum of citherns, the piping of flutes, the rhythmic thump of tambours. Three women darted into the room with quick, tiny steps to stand in the center of the bare floor. Only their hands and feet were not covered by thick layers of many-colored silk, and opaque veils covered their faces from chin to eyes. To the sound of the music they began to dance, finger-cymbals clinking and tiny golden bells tinkling at their ankles.

Even for a Vendhyan, Conan thought, this was too

elaborate a way to kill a man. Filling the goblet with wine, he reclined to watch and enjoy.

At first the dancers' steps were slow but by tiny increments their speed increased. In flowing movements they spun and leaped, and with each spin, with each leap, a bit of colorful silk drifted away from them. Graceful jumps in unison they made, with legs outstretched, or they writhed with feet planted and arms twined above their heads. The length and breadth of the floor they covered, now moving away from him, now gliding almost to the cushions. Then all the silks were gone save their veils, and the three lush-bodied women danced in only their satiny skins, gleaming with a faint sheen of perspiration.

At the sharp clap of Conan's hands, the dancers froze, rounded breasts heaving from their exertions. The musicians, unseeing and unaware of what transpired, played on.

"You two go," the Cimmerian commanded, indicating his choices. "You stay and dance." Dark eyes exchanged uncertain glances above veils. "Your mistress commanded an entertainment for me," he went on. "Must I drag the three of you through the palace in search of her to tell her you will not obey?" The looks that passed between the women were frightened now. The two he had pointed out ran from the chamber. The third woman stared after them as though on the point of running also. "Dance for me," Conan said.

Hesitantly, reluctantly, she found her steps again. Before, the dancers had seemed more aware of the music than of Conan, but now this woman's head turned constantly, independent of her dance, to keep her dark eyes on his face. She flowed across the floor, whirling and leaping as gracefully as before, but there was a nervousness, too, as though she felt his gaze as a palpable caress on her nudity.

As she came close to him, Conan grabbed a slim, belled

ankle. With a squeal she toppled to the cushions and lay staring at him over her veil with wide eyes. For long moments there was no sound but the music and her agitated breathing.

"Please, master," she whispered finally. "My mistress asks that her serving women—"

"Am I your master then?" Conan asked. Idly he ran a finger from slender calf to rounded thigh, and she shivered. "What if I send for Punjar, saying you have not pleased me? What if I demand he switch you here and now?"

"Then I . . . I would be switched, master," she whispered and swallowed hard.

Conan shook his head. "Truly, Vendhyans are mad. Would you really go so far to hide the truth from me?" Before she could flinch away, he snatched the veil from her face.

For an instant Vyndra stared up at him, scarlet suffusing her cheeks. Then her eyes snapped shut, and frantically she tried to cover herself with her arms.

"It did not work with Kang Hou," Conan laughed, "and it does not work with me." Her blush deepened and her eyes squeezed tighter. "This time your playing at games has gone awry," he said, leaning over her. "One chance, and one chance only, will I give you to run and then I will show you what men and women do who do not play games."

The crimson did not leave her cheeks, but her eyes opened just enough for her to look at him through long lashes. "You fool," she murmured. "I could have run from you any day since my hands were unbound."

Throwing her arms about his neck, she pulled him down to her.

CHAPTER XIX

As shadows lengthened with the sinking sun, Conan left Vyndra sleeping on the cushions and went in search of more wine.

"Immediately, master," a servant said in response to his request, adding at his next question, "No, master, the two men have not yet returned from the city. I know nothing of the Khitan woman, master."

Finding a chamber with tall, arched windows looking to the west, Conan sat with his foot on the windowsill and his back against its frame. The sun, violent red in a purpling sky, hung its own diameter above the towering trees in the distance. It was a grim sight, fit for his mood. The day had been useless. Waiting in the palace, even making love to Vyndra, however enjoyable, now seemed time wasted. At least in following the caravan this far there had been the illusion of doing something about the poison in his veins, of hunting down the men whose deaths he must see to before his own. One of those men, at least, was in the city, not a league distant, and here he sat, waiting.

"Patil?"

At the soft female voice, he looked around. An unveiled Vendhyan woman stood in the doorway of the chamber, her plain robes of cotton neither those of a servant nor of a noble.

"You do not recognize me," she said with a smile, and abruptly he did.

"Kuie Hsi," he gasped. "I did not believe you could so completely—" Impatiently he put all that aside. "What did you learn?"

"Much, and little. The caravan remained in the city only hours, for the merchants' markets are in Ayodhya and the nobles are impatient to reach the court. Karim Singh, however," she added as he leaped to his feet, "is yet in Gwandiakan, though I could not learn where."

"He will not escape me," Conan growled. "Nor this Naipal, wizard though he be. But why does the *wazam* remain here rather than going on to the court?"

"Perhaps because, according to rumor, Naipal has been in Gwandiakan for two days. As his face is known to few, however, this cannot be confirmed."

Conan's fist smacked into his palm. "Crom, but this cannot be other than fate. Both of them within my grasp. I will finish it this night."

The Khitan woman caught his arm as he started from the chamber. "If you mean to enter Gwandiakan, take care, for the city is uneasy. Soldiers have been arresting the children of the streets, all of the homeless urchins and beggar children, supposedly on the orders of the *wazam*. Many are angered, and the poorer sections of the city need but a spark to burst into flame. The streets of Gwandiakan could run with blood over this."

"I have seen blood before," he said grimly, and then

he was striding down the tapestried corridors. "Punjar!
My horse!"

But half-awake, Vyndra stretched on the cushions, not-
ing lazily that the lamps had been lit and night was come.
Abruptly she frowned. Someone had laid a silken coverlet
over her. With a gasp she clutched the covering to her at
the sight of Chin Kou. The Khitan woman's arms were
filled with folds of many-colored silk.

"I brought garments," Chin Kou said.

Vyndra pulled the coverlet up about her neck. "And
what made you think I would need clothing?" she demanded haughtily.

"I am sorry," Chin Kou said, turning to leave. "No
doubt when you wish to cover yourself, you will summon
servants. I will leave you the coverlet since you seem to
desire that."

"Wait!" Blushing, Vyndra fingered the coverlet. "I did
not know. As you have brought the garments, you might
as well leave them."

Chin Kou arched an eyebrow. "There is no need to take
such a tone with me. I know very well what you were
doing with the *cheng-li* who calls himself Patil." Vyndra
groaned, the scarlet in her cheeks deepening. After a
moment the merchant's daughter took pity. "I was doing
the same thing with the *cheng-li* who calls himself Hasan.
Now I know your secret and you know mine. You fear
only shame before your servants. My uncle's switch pro-
duces a much greater smarting than mere shame."

Vyndra stared at the other woman as though seeing her
for the first time. It was not that she had been unaware of
Chin Kou, but the Khitan was a merchant's niece and
surely merchants' nieces did not think and feel in the same

way as a woman born of the Kshatriya blood. Or did they? "Do you love him?" she asked. "Hasan, I mean?"

"Yes," Chin Kou said emphatically, "though I do not know if he returns my feelings. Do you love the man called Patil?"

Vyndra shook her head. "As well love a tiger. But," she added with a mischievousness she could not control, "to be made love to by a tiger is a very fine thing."

"Hasan," Chin Kou said gravely, "is also very vigorous."

Suddenly the two women were giggling, and the giggles became deep-throated laughter.

"Thank you for the clothing," Vyndra said when she could talk again. Tossing aside the coverlet, she rose. Chin Kou aided her in dressing, though she did not ask it, and once she was garbed, she said, "Come. We will have wine and talk of men and tigers and other strange beasts."

As the Khitan woman opened her mouth to reply, a shrill scream echoed through the palace, followed by the shouts of men and the clang of steel on steel.

Chin Kou clutched at Vyndra's arm. "We must hide."

"Hide!" Vyndra exclaimed. "This is *my* palace and I will not cower in it like a rabbit."

"Foolish pride speaks," the smaller woman said. "Think what kind of bandits would attack a palace! Do you think your noble blood will protect you?"

"Yes. And you also. Even brigands will know that a ransom will be paid, for you and your sister as well, once they know who I am."

"Know who you are?" came a voice from the doorway, and Vyndra jumped in spite of herself.

"Kandar," she breathed. Pride said to stand her ground defiantly, but she could not stop herself from backing away as the cruel-eyed prince swaggered into the chamber, a bloody sword in his fist. In the corridor behind him were turban-helmed soldiers, also with crimson-stained weapons.

He stooped to take something from the floor—the veil she had worn while dancing—and fingered it thoughtfully as he advanced. "Perhaps you think you are a noble-woman," he said, "perhaps even the famous Lady Vyndra, known for the brilliance of her wit and the dazzling gatherings at her palaces? Alas, the tale has been well told already of how the Lady Vyndra fell prey beyond the Himelias to a savage barbarian who carried her off, to death perhaps, or slavery."

"What can you possibly hope to gain by this farce?" Vyndra demanded, but the words faded as six veiled women, swathed in concealing layers of silk, entered the room. And with them was Prytanis.

Smirking, the Nemedian leaned against the wall with his arms crossed. "The gods are good, wench," he said, "for who should I find in Gwandiakan but Prince Kandar, who was interested to learn of the presence of a certain woman nearby. A purse of gold he offered for the nameless jade, and I could only accept his generosity."

Annoyance flashed across Kandar's face, but he seemed otherwise unaware of the other man. "Prepare her," he commanded. "Prepare both of them. I will not refuse an extra trifle when it is put before me."

"No!" Vyndra screamed.

She whirled to run, but before she had crossed half the chamber, three of the veiled women were on her, pushing her to the floor. With a corner of her mind she was aware of the other three holding Chin Kou, but panting desperation flooded every part of her. Frantically, futilely, she fought, but the women rolled her this way and that, stripping away her so-recently donned robes with humiliating ease. When she was naked, they would not allow her to regain her feet but dragged her writhing across the floor with kicking legs trailing behind her. At Kandar's feet they forced her to her knees and his gaze chilled her to the bone, turning her muscles to water, stilling her struggles. Chin Kou was knelt beside her, as naked as she and sobbing with terror, but Vyndra could not take her eyes from Kandar's.

"You cannot hope to get away with this," she whispered. "I am not some nameless—"

"You *are* nameless," he snapped. "I told you, the Lady Vyndra is gone"—slowly he fastened the veil across her face by its tiny silver chain—"and in her place is a new addition to my *purdhana*. I think I will name you Maryna."

"Your sister," Vyndra panted. She had had no trouble with the veil while dancing; now it seemed to restrict her breathing. "I will free Alyna. I will—" His slap jerked her head sideways.

"I have no sister," he growled.

"What of my gold?" Prytanis demanded suddenly. "The wench is yours, and I want my payment."

"Of course." Kandar took a purse from his belt, tossing it to the slit-nosed man. "It is satisfactory?"

Prytanis eagerly untied the purse strings and spilled some of the golden coins into his palm. "It is satisfactory," he said. "If only Conan could see—" His words ended in a grunt as Kandar's sword thrust into his middle. Gold rang on the floor tiles as he grabbed the blade with both hands.

Kandar met the Nemedian's unbelieving gaze levelly. "You gazed on the unveiled faces of two women of my *purdhana*," he explained. The razor steel slid easily from the dying man's grasp, and Prytanis fell atop his gold.

Face smarting, Vyndra gathered the last shreds of her courage. "To kill your own hirelings and take back the gold is like you, Kandar. You were always a fool and a worm." His dark gaze made her realize it *had* been the last of her courage. She clenched her teeth with the effort of facing him.

"He saw your face unveiled," the prince said, "and that of the Khitan woman, so he had to die, for my honor. But he earned the gold and I am no thief. You will be beaten once for that and again for each of the other insults."

"I am of the Kshatriya blood." Vyndra spoke the words for her own benefit, as though to deny what had happened, and no one else seemed to notice them.

"This was the last of your strange companions," Kandar continued. "The others are already dead. All of them."

A whimper rose in Vyndra's throat. The vanishing of a small hope she had not know was there until it was gone, the hope that the huge barbarian would rescue her, left her now truly with nothing. "You will never break me," she whispered and knew the emptiness of the words even as they left her lips.

"Break you?" Kandar said mockingly. "Of course not. But there must be some small training in obedience. Some small humbling of your pride." Vyndra wanted to shake her head in denial, but his eyes held hers like a serpent mesmerizing a bird. "On the morrow you will be placed on a horse, garbed as now, and paraded through the streets of Gwandiakan so that all may see the beauty of my new possession. Bring them!" he snapped at the women.

With all of her heart Vyndra wanted to muster a shout of defiance, but she knew, as she was dragged to the horses, that it was a wail of despair that echoed in the halls of her palace.

CHAPTER XX

At a crude plank table by himself in the corner of a dirt-floored tavern, Conan was reminded of Sultanapur as he tugged the hood of his dark cloak, borrowed from a groom at Vyndra's palace, deeper over his face. Wondering when he would next be in a city without the need to hide his features, he emptied half the cheap wine in his wooden tank in one long swallow.

The others in the tavern were Vendhyans all, though far from the nobles or wealthy of Gwandiakan. Carters who smelled of their oxen rubbed elbows with masons' apprentices in tunics stained with gray splashes of dried mortar. Nondescript turbaned men hunkered over their wine or talked in hushed tones with black eyes darting to see who might overhear. The smell of sour wine warred with incense, and the muted babble of voices did not quite mask the tinkle of bells at the wrists and ankles of sloe-eyed doxies parading through the tavern. Unlike their sisters in the West, their robes covered them from ankle to neck, but those robes were of the sheerest gossamer, concealing nothing. The jades found few customers, though, and the usual frivolity of taverns was absent. The air was filled with a tension darker than the night outside the walls. The Cimmerian was not the only man to keep his face hidden.

Conan signaled for more wine. A serving wench, her garb but a trifle more opaque than that of the trulls, brought a rough clay pitcher, took his coin and hurried away without a word, obviously eager to return to her cubbyhole and hide.

That tightly wound nervousness had been evident in the entire city from his arrival, and it had grown tighter as the night went on. Soldiers were still arresting homeless waifs and beggar children, such few as had not gone to ground like pursued foxes, carrying them off to the fortress prison that stood in the center of Gwandiakan. But even the soldiers could sense the mood of the sullen throngs. Patrols now often numbered a hundred men, and they moved as though expecting attack at any moment.

The streets had been full of talk earlier, full of rumor, and the Cimmerian had no trouble in hearing of the men he sought. Quickly he learned the location of Prince Kandar's palace, one of the few east of the city, and of that where Karim Singh was said to be staying. Before he had gone a hundred paces, however, he heard of another palace said to house the *wazam*, and fifty paces beyond that a third, both widely separated from each other and from the first. Each corner brought a new rumor. Half the palaces of Gwandiakan were said to contain Karim Singh. Tongues could be found to name *every* palace as housing Naipal, and many spoke of an invisible palace constructed in a night by the mage, while still others claimed the wizard watched the city from above, from the clouds. In the end it was frustration that had sent Conan into the tavern.

A wave of dizziness that had nothing to do with the

wine swept over him, not for the first time that night, clouding his vision. Grimly he fought it off, and when his eyes cleared, Hordo was sliding onto a bench across the table from him.

"I have been looking for you for hours," the one-eyed man said. "Kandar attacked Vyndra's palace with a hundred lancers and took Vyndra and the Khitan's niece, Chin Kou. Prytanis was with him."

With a snarl Conan smashed his wooden tankard to the dirt floor. Momentary silence rolled through the room, and every eye swiveled to him. Then, hastily, talk began again. It was not a night to become involved in a stranger's anger.

"The men?" Conan asked.

"Nicks and cuts. No more. We managed to get to the horses and Kuie Hsi found us a place to hide, an abandoned temple on something called the Street of Dreams, though miserable dreams they must be. A day or two of rest and healing and we'll see what can be done about the wenches."

Conan shook his head, as much to clear it as in negation. "I do not have a day or two. Best you return to this temple. They will need you if they are to make it back to Turan."

"What are you about?" Hordo demanded, but the Cimmerian only clapped his friend on the shoulder and hurried from the tavern. As Conan trotted down the darkened street, he heard the one-eyed man calling behind him, but he did not look back.

The Bhalkhana stallion was stabled near the city gate by which he had entered Gwandiakan, and a coin retrieved the big black from a wizened liveryman. The city gates themselves were massive, ten times the height of a man, and made of black iron plates worked in fanciful designs.

They would not be easily moved, and from the dirt that had accumulated along their bases, it had been years since they were closed. The city's ill ease hung on the turban-helmed gate guards as well, and they only watched him nervously, fingering their spears, as he galloped through.

The one bit of definite information he had learned in his night of listening, the one story that did not change—and the one he had thought least useful even at that—was the location of Kandar's palace. Rage filled him, but it was an icy rage. To die with sword in hand would be much preferable to succumbing to the poison in his veins, but the women must be freed first. Only when they were safe could he allow himself to think of his own concerns.

Short of the palace he rode into a copse of trees and tied the stallion's reins to a branch. Stealth and cunning, bred in his days as a thief, would better serve him now than steel.

Prince Kandar's palace, larger even than Vyndra's, shone in the night with the light of a thousand lamps, a gleaming alabaster intricacy of terraces, domes and spires. Reflection pools stretched on all sides and between them gardens of flowering shrubs reached the very walls of the palace, their myriad blossoms filling the darkness with a hundred perfumes.

Perfumes and blossoms did not interest Conan, but the shrubs served well to cover his silent approach. He was but one shadow among many. Fingers trained by climbing the cliffs of his native Cimmerian mountains found crevices in the seemingly smooth joining of great marble blocks, and he scaled the palace wall as another man might climb a ladder.

Lying flat atop the broad wall, Conan surveyed what he could of the palace—small courtyards with splashing fountains, intricately friezed towers thrusting toward the sky, colonnaded walks lit by lamps of cunningly wrought gold. Breath caught in his throat, and his hand went unbidden to his sword. Past the fluted columns of one of those colonnades walked a man in robes of gold and crimson with another in what seemed black silk. Karim Singh. And, if the gods were with him, Naipal. With a regretful sigh he released the sword-hilt and watched the two men walk on beyond his sight. The women, he told himself. The women first. Scrambling to his feet, he ran along the wall.

Height was the key, as experience in the cities of Nemedia and Zamora had taught him. A man glimpsed in the upper reaches of a structure, even one who obviously did not belong there, was often ignored. After all, without a right to be there, how could he have traveled so far? Too, entering on the upper levels meant that every step took a man closer to the ground and his route to escape. Escape was especially important this night, for the two women if not for him.

Cornices, friezes and a hundred elaborate workings of alabaster stone made a swift path for the big Cimmerian. Slipping through a narrow window just below the roof, he found himself in a pitch-dark stuffy room. By touch he quickly ascertained that it was a storeroom for carpets and bedding. The narrow door opened onto a corridor dimly lit by brass lamps. No gold hangings or fine tapestries here, for these upper floors were servants' quarters. Snores drifted from some of the rooms. As silent and grim as a hunting cat, Conan padded into the hall. Stairs led him down.

Sounds floated from other parts of the palace—an indistinguishable murmur of voices, the thrum of a cithern. Once the single deep toll of a gong echoed mournfully. The Cimmerian let them pass all but unnoticed, his eyes and ears straining instead for the flicker of shadow or hint of a soft footfall that might betray any who could give an alarm.

It was a bedchamber he sought, he was sure of that. From what he knew of Kandar, such would have been his first stop with the women, and it would no doubt suit his fancy to have them awaiting his return were he not still with them. Conan hoped that he was. Karim Singh and Naipal would certainly escape him this night but it would be good to deal with Kandar at least.

The first three bedchambers he found were empty, though golden lamps cast soft light in wait for their eventual occupants. As he stepped into the fourth, only a sense below the levels of understanding threw him into a forward roll an instant before razor steel slashed through the place where his head had been.

Conan came to his feet with broadsword in hand, and a vigorous cut made his attacker leap back. The Cimmerian stared at his opponent, for he had not seen the man's like before, not even in this strange land. A nasaled helm with a thick spike topped his dark expressionless face, and his armor was of leather studded with brass. A long straight sword was in his gauntleted right hand, a shorter curved blade in his left, and he moved as though he knew well the use of each.

"I am here for the women," Conan said in a taunting voice. If he could make the man exchange words with him, the other might not think to give an alarm even while they strove to slay each other. "Tell me where they are, and I'll not kill you." The man's silent rush forced him to throw up his blade in defense.

And it was defense, the Cimmerian realized in shock. His broadsword flashed and darted as swiftly as ever it had, but it was all in a desperate effort to keep the other's steel from striking him. For the first time in his life he faced a man faster than himself. Slashes with the speed of a striking viper forced him back. Snarling, he gambled, continuing the motion of a block with a smash of his fisted hilt to his opponent's face.

The strangely armored man was thrown back, an inlaid table crushed to splinters by his fall, but before Conan could take more than a single step to follow up his attack, the other sprang to his feet. Conan met him in the center of the room, and sparks were struck as steel wove a deadly lace between them. The Cimmerian poured all of his rage—at Kandar, at Naipal, at Karim Singh—into his attack, refusing this time to yield a step. Abruptly a slicing blow of his broadsword sheared through flesh and bone, but even as it did, he was forced to jump back to avoid a decapitating stroke.

Landing on guard and ready to continue, Conan felt the hair on the back of his neck stir. His last blow had stopped his opponent—and indeed it should have, as the short curved sword now lay on the carpet along with the hand that gripped it—but it was obviously only a temporary halt. That expressionless face had not changed in the least, and the dark flat eyes did not so much as glance at the severed wrist, a wound that gave not a single drop of blood. Sorcery, the Cimmerian thought. Suddenly the silence in which the other had fought took on eerie quality. And then the murderous assault began anew.

If the sorcerous warrior was accustomed to fighting with two swords, he seemed little less able with only one. Conan met each lightning stroke but his own were met as well. He could match the other now, the Cimmerian knew, one blade against one blade, but could mortal flesh outlast the endurance of sorcery?

Abruptly the severed stump struck the side of Conan's head with a force greater than he would have believed possible, flinging him back as though he were a child. It was his turn to find himself on his back amidst the ruins of a table, but before he could rise, his attacker was on him. Desperately Conan blocked a downward blow that would have split his skull. Among the wreckage of the table his hand closed on a hilt, and he thrust. The other man twisted like a serpent, and the blade cut through his leather armor, slicing across his ribs. As though his bones had melted, the dark warrior collapsed atop Conan.

Quickly the Cimmerian heaved the body from him and sprang to his feet with sword ready, fearing some trick. The leather-armored figure did not move; the flat black eyes were glazed.

In wonder Conan looked at the weapon he had taken up and almost dropped it as he cursed. It seemed a short-sword but the hilt was long enough for two hands, and blade and hilt alike were wrought of some strange silvery metal that glowed with unearthly light.

A smell made his nose twitch and he cursed again. It was the stink of putrefaction. Within the leather armor the corpse of his opponent was already half-decayed, white bone showing through rotted flesh. An ensorcelled warrior slain by an obviously ensorcelled blade. Part of his mind urged Conan to leave the foul thing but another part whispered that such might be useful against a sorcerer like Naipal. Mages were not always so easily slain as other men.

Sheathing his broadsword, he hastily tore silk from the coverlets on the bed and wrapped the silvery weapon, thrusting it behind his sword-belt. As he did so, he heard pounding boots approaching, many of them. The splintered tables, with scattered chests and broken crystal and shattered mirrors, were mute evidence that the battle had not been silent after all. Muttering imprecations, he ran for the windows, climbing through just as a score of Vendhyan soldiers poured into the room.

Once more alabaster ornamentations were his roadway along the wall, but behind him he heard cries of alarm. Upward he climbed, grasping a balustrade to pull himself onto a balcony . . . and stopping with one foot over at the sight of another dozen men in turbaned helms. A thrown spear streaked by his head and he threw himself desperately back as other arms were cocked.

Even with knees bent, the force of landing shook him to the bone. More voices took up the cry of alarm, and the thud of running boots came from both left and right. A spear lanced from above to quiver in the ground not a pace from him. He leaped away from the wall, and another spear shivered where he had stood. Bent double, he ran into the garden between the reflecting pools, becoming one with the shadows.

"Guards!" the cries rose. "Guards!"

"Beat the gardens!"

"Find him!"

From the edge of the trees Conan watched, teeth bared in a snarl. Soldiers milled about the palace like ants about a kicked anthill. There would be no entering that palace again tonight.

Pain ripped through him, muscles spasming, doubling him over. Gasping for breath, he forced himself erect. His hand closed on the silk-shrouded hilt of the strange weapon. "I am not dead yet," he whispered, "and it will not be over until I am." With no more sound than the wind in the leaves, he faded into the darkness.

* * *

Naipal stared at the ruin of his bedchamber in shocked disbelief, willing himself not to breathe the smell of decay that hung in the air. The shouts of searching soldiers did not register on his ear. Only the contents of that chamber were real at that moment, and they in a way that turned his stomach with fear and sent blinding pains through his head.

The leather armor held his eye with sickly fascination. A skull grinned up at him from the ancient helm. Bones and dust were all that was left of his warrior. His warrior who could not die. The first of an army that could not die. In the name of all the gods, how had it happened?

With an effort he pulled his gaze from the leather-clad skeleton, but inexorably it fell on the long golden coffer, now lying on its side amid splinters of ebony that had been a table, lying there open and empty. Empty! Shards of elaborately carved ivory were all that was left of the mirror of warning, and naught but a hundred jagged pieces remained of the mirror itself.

Grunting, he bent to pick up half a dozen of the mirror fragments. Each, whatever its size, was filled by an image, an image that would be on all the other pieces as well, an image that would never change now. Wonderingly, he studied that grim face in the fragments, a square-cut black mane held back by a leather cord, strange eyes the color and hardness of sapphire, a feral snarl baring white teeth.

He knew who it had to be. The man who called himself Patil. Karim Singh's simple barbarian. But the mirror, even now at the last, would show only what threatened his plans. Could a simple barbarian do that? Could a simple barbarian seek him out so quickly? Know to break the mirror and steal the demon-wrought dagger? Slay what could not be slain? The pieces fell from Naipal's fingers as he whispered the word he did not want to believe. *"Pan-kur."*

"What was that?" Karim Singh asked as he entered the room. The *wazam* carefully kept his eyes from the thing in leather armor on the floor. "You look exhausted, Naipal. Kandar's servants will clean this mess, and his soldiers will deal with the intruder. You must rest. I will not have you collapse before you can serve me as king."

"We must go immediately," Naipal said. He rubbed his temples with the tips of his fingers. The strain of the past days wore at him, and he would not now take the effort to feign servility. "Tell Kandar to gather his soldiers."

"I have been thinking, Naipal. What will it matter if we wait a few days? Surely it will rain soon, and the stinging flies are said to be better after a rain."

"Fool!" the wizard howled, and Karim Singh's jaw dropped. "You will have me serve you as king? Wait and you will not be king, you will be meat for dogs!" Naipal's eyes went to the scattered fragments of mirror and slid away. "And tell Kandar we must have more soldiers. Tell him to strip the fortress if need be. A simple spell will divert your fearsome flies."

"The governor is uneasy," Karim Singh said shakily. "He obeys but I can tell that he does not believe my reasons for ordering the street children arrested. Given the mood of the city, he might refuse such a command and even if he obeys, he will doubtless send riders to Ayodhya, to Bhandarkar."

"Do not fear Bhandarkar. If you must fear someone . . ." Naipal's voice was soft, but his eyes burned so that Karim Singh took a step back and seemed to have trouble breathing. "Tell the governor that if he defies me, I will wither his flesh and put him in the streets as a tongueless beggar to watch his wives and daughters dragged away to brothels. Tell him!'' And the *wazam* of Vendhya fled like a servant. Naipal forced his gaze back to the fragments of mirror, back to the hundred-times repeated image.

"You will not conquer, *pan-kur*," he whispered. "I will yet be victorious over you."

CHAPTER XXI

Hordo had been right about the Street of Dreams, Conan thought when he first saw it in the gray light of dawn. The stallion picked its way along the dirt roadway between muddy pools of offal and piles of rubble overgrown with weeds. The buildings were skulls, with empty windows for eye sockets. Roofs sagged where they had not fallen in. Walls leaned and some had collapsed, spewing clay bricks across the dirt of the street, revealing barren, rat-infested interiors. Occasional ragged, furtive shapes appeared in a doorway or darted across the street behind him. The people of the Street of Dreams were like scurrying rodents, fearful to poke their noses into the light. The stench of decay and mold filled the air. Ill dreams indeed, Conan thought. Ill dreams indeed.

The abandoned temple was not hard to find, a domed structure with pigeons fluttering through gaping holes in the dome. Once eight fluted marble columns had stood across its front, but now three had fallen. Two lay in fragments across the street, weeds growing thickly along their edges. Of the third only a stump remained. Part of the front wall had fallen too, revealing that what must have once seemed to be marble blocks were in truth only a stone facing over clay bricks. The opening widened and heightened the temple door enough for a man to enter on horseback. There was no sign of the smugglers but the gloomy interior could have hidden them easily. Or ten times their number of the area's denizens. Conan drew his sword. He had to duck his head as he rode through the gap in the wall.

Within was a large dim room, its cracked floor tiles covered with dust and broken bricks. The thick pillars here were of wood, all splintered with rot. At the far end of the chamber there was a marble altar, its edges chipped and cracked, but of whatever god it had been raised to, there was no evidence.

Before the stallion had taken three paces into the room, Hordo appeared from behind a pillar. "It is about time you got here, Cimmerian. I was all but ready to give you up for dead this time."

Enam and Shamil stepped out, too, with arrows nocked but not drawn. Both had bandages showing. "We did not know it was you," the young Turanian said. "There are pigeons roasting on a spit in the back, if you are hungry."

"We try to hide the smell of them," Enam said, spitting. "The people here are like vermin. They look ready to swarm over anyone with food like a pack of rats."

Conan nodded as he stepped down from the saddle. Once on the ground, he had to hold onto the stirrup leather for a moment; the pains and dizziness had not returned, but weakness had come in their place. "I have seen nothing like them," he said. "In Turan or Zamora it is a far cry from palace to beggar, but here it seems two different lands."

"Vendhya is a country of great contrasts," Kang Hou said, approaching from the rear of the ruined structure.

"It is like a melon rotting from within," Conan replied. "A fruit overripe for plucking." The weakness was lessening. It came in cycles. "Someday perhaps I will return with an army and pluck it."

"Many have said as much," the Khitan replied, "yet the Kshatriyas still rule here. Forgive my unseemly haste, but Hordo has told us you sought Prince Kandar's palace last night. You could not find my niece? Or Lady Vyndra?"

"I could not reach them," Conan said grimly. "But I will before I am done."

Kang Hou's face did not change expression, and all he said was, "Hasan says the pigeons must be taken from the fire. He suggests they be eaten before they grow cold."

"The man must have a heart like stone," Hordo muttered as the other two smugglers followed the Khitan out.

"He is a tough man for a merchant," Conan agreed. He tugged the silk-wrapped weapon from his belt and handed it to his friend. "What do you make of this?"

Hordo gasped as the cloth fell away, revealing the faintly glowing silvery metal. "Sorcery! As soon as I heard there was a wizard in this, I should have turned my horse around." His eye squinted as he peered at the weapon. "This design makes no sense, Cimmerian. A two-handed hilt on a short-sword?"

"It slew a man, or a thing, that my sword did not slow," Conan said.

The one-eyed man winced and hastily rebundled the silk about the weapon. "I do not want to know about it. Here. Take it." He chewed at nothing as the Cimmerian returned the weapon to its place tucked behind his sword-belt, then said, "There has been no sign of Ghurran. How did you pass the night without his potion?"

"Without missing the foul thing," Conan grunted. "Come. I could eat a dozen of those pigeons. Let us get to them before they are gone."

There were two large windowless rooms at the back of the temple, one without a roof. In that room was the fire; the other was used as a stable. Enam and Shamil squatted by the fire, wolfing down pigeon. The Khitan ate more delicately, while Hasan sat against a wall, clasping his knees and scowling at the world.

"Where is Kuie Hsi?" Conan wanted to know.

"She left before first light," Hordo told him around mouthfuls of roast pigeon, "to see what she could discover."

"I have returned," the Khitan woman said from the door, "again learning much and little. I was slow in returning because the mood of the city is ugly. Angry crowds roam the streets and ruffians take advantage. A woman alone, I was twice almost assaulted."

"You have a light step," Conan complimented her. He would wager that the men who had "almost" assaulted her rued the incident if they still lived. "What is this much and little you have learned?"

Still in her Vendhyan garb, Kuie Hsi looked hesitantly at Kang Hou, who merely wiped his lips with a cloth and waited. "At dawn," she began slowly, "Karim Singh entered the city. The wizard, Naipal, was with him, and Prince Kandar. They took soldiers from the fortress, increasing the number of their escort to perhaps one thousand lances, and left the city, heading west. I heard a soldier say they rode to the Forests of Ghelai. The chests in which you are so interested went with them on mules."

For an instant Conan teetered on the horns of decision. Karim Singh and Naipal might escape him. There was no way to tell how much time he had left before the poison overtook him completely. Yet he knew there was only one way to decide. "If they took so many soldiers," he said, "few can remain at Kandar's palace to guard Vyndra and Chin Kou."

Kuie Hsi let her eyes drop to the floor, and her voice became a whisper. "There were two women with them, veiled but unclothed, and bound to their saddles. One was Chin Kou, the other the Vendhyan woman. Forgive me, uncle. I could see her but could do nothing."

"There is nothing to forgive," Kang Hou said, "for you have in no way failed. Any failure is mine alone."

"Perhaps it is," Conan said quietly, "but I cannot feel but that neither woman would be where she is except for me. And that means it is on me to see them safe. I will not ask any of you to accompany me. Beyond the matter of a thousand soldiers, you know there is a wizard involved, and he will be where I am going."

"Be not a fool," Hordo growled, and Enam added, "The Brotherhood of the Coast does not desert its own. Prytanis never understood that but I do."

"He has Chin Kou," Hasan burst out. "Do you expect me to sit here while he does Mitra alone knows what to her?" He seemed ready to fight Conan if need be.

"As for me," Kang Hou said with an amused smile for Hasan, "she is only my niece, of course." The young Turanian's face colored. "This is a matter of family honor."

Shamil gave a shaky laugh. "Well, I'll not be the only one to stay here. I wanted adventure, and none can say this is not it."

"Then let us ride," Conan said, "before they escape us."

"Patience," Kang Hou counseled. "The Forests of Ghelai are ten leagues distant, and a thousand men ride more slowly than six may. Let us not fail for a lack of preparation.

There are stinging flies in the forests, but I know of an ointment that may abate their attack.''

"Flies?" Hordo muttered. "Stinging flies? Wizards are not enough, Cimmerian? When we are out of this, you will owe me for the flies.''

"And returning to Gwandiakan may not be wise," Kuie Hsi offered. "Soon there may be riots. A league this side of the forests there is said to be a well, thought to be a stopping place for caravans in ancient times but long abandoned. There I will await you with food and clothing for Chin Kou and Vyndra. And word if the city is safe. I will draw maps."

Conan knew they were right. How many times in his days as a thief had he sneered at others for their lack of preparation and the lack of success that went with it? But now he could only grind his teeth with the frustration of waiting an instant. Time and the knowledge of the poison in his veins pressed heavily on him. But he would see Vyndra and Chin Kou free—and Karim Singh and Naipal dead—before he died.

By Crom, he vowed it.

CRAPTER XXII

Riding beneath the tall trees of the Forest of Ghelai, Conan was unsure whether Kang Hou's ointment was not worse than the flies it was meant to discourage. There was no smell to it, but the feel on the skin was much like that after wading in a cesspool. The horses had liked having it smeared on them no more than had the men. He slapped a tiny fly that would not be discouraged—the bite was like a red-hot needle stabbing his arm—and grimaced at the glittering-winged swarms that surrounded the meager column. Then again, perhaps the ointment was not so bad.

The forest canopy was far above their heads, many of the trees towering more than a hundred and fifty feet. The high branches were thickly woven, letting little light through, and that seeming tinged with green. Streams of long-tailed monkeys flowed from limb to limb, a hundred rivers of brown fur rolling in a hundred different directions. Flocks of multicolored birds, some with strange bills or elaborate tail feathers, screamed from high branches while others in a thousand varied hues made brilliant streaks against the green as they darted back and forth.

"There are no such flies on the plains of Zamora," Hordo grumbled, slapping. "I could be there instead of here had I a brain in my head. There are no such flies on the steppes of Turan. I could be there—"

"If you do not shut your teeth," Conan muttered, "the only place you will be is dead, and likely left to rot where you fall. Or do you think Kandar's soldiers are deaf?"

"They could not hear themselves pass wind for those Mitra-accursed birds," the one-eyed man replied, but he subsided into silence.

In truth Conan did not know how close or how far the Vendhyans might be. A thousand men left a plain trail, but the ground was soft and springy with a thousand years of continuous decay, and the chopping that passed for hoofprints could have been five hours old or the hundredth part of that. The Cimmerian did know the day was almost gone though, for all he could not see the sun. The amount of time they had been riding made that plain, and the dim greenish light was fading. He did not believe the soldiers would continue on in the dark.

Abruptly he reined in, forcing the others behind to do so as well, and peered in consternation at what lay ahead. Huge blocks of stone, overgrown with vines as thick as a man's arm, formed a wide wall fifty feet high that stretched north and south as far as the eye could make out in the dim verdant light. Directly before him was a towered gateway, though the gates that once had blocked it had been gone for centuries by the evidence of a great tree rising in its center. Beyond he could make out other shapes among the forest growth, massive ruins among the trees. And the trail they followed passed through that gateway.

"Would they pass the night in there?" Hordo asked.

"Even the gods do not know what might be in a place like that."

"I think," Kang Hou said slowly, "that this might be where they were going." Conan looked at him curiously, but the slight merchant said no more.

"Then we follow," the Cimmerian said, swinging down from his saddle. "But we leave the horses here." He went on as mouths opened in protest. "A man hides better afoot, and we must be like ferrets scurrying through a thicket. There are a thousand Vendhyan lancers in this place, remember." That brought them down.

Leaving someone with the animals, Conan decided, was worse than useless. It would reduce their number by one and the man left behind could do nothing if a Vendhyan patrol came on him. All would enter the city together. Conan, sword in hand, was first through the ancient gateway, with Hordo close behind. Enam and Shamil brought up the rear with arrows nocked to their bowstrings. Alone of the small column, Kang Hou seemed unarmed, but the Cimmerian was ready to wager the merchant's throwing knives resided in his sleeves.

Conan had seen ruined cities before, some abandoned for centuries, or even millennia. Some would stand on mountain peaks until the earth shook and buried them. Others endured the sand-laden desert winds, slowly wearing away stone so that in another thousand years or two, unknowing eyes would see only formations of rock and believe chance alone made them resemble an abode of men. This city was different, however, as though some malevolent god, unwilling to wait for the slow wearing away by rain and wind, had commanded the forest to attack and consume all marks of man.

If they crept over the remains of a street, it was impossible to tell, for dirt and a thousand small plants covered all, and everywhere the trees. Much of the city was no more, with no sign that it had ever been. Only the most massive of structures remained—the palaces and the temples. Yet even they fought a loosing battle against the forest. Temple columns were so wreathed in vines that only the regularity of their spacing betrayed their existence. Here the marble tiles of a palace portico bulged with the roots of a giant tree, and there a wall of alabaster, now green with mold, buckled before the onslaught of another huge trunk. Toppled spires lay shrouded by conquering roots and monkeys gamboled on no-longer gleaming domes that might once have sheltered potentates.

The others seemed to feel the oppressiveness of the ruins, but neither Conan nor Kang Hou allowed themselves to be affected, outwardly at least. The Cimmerian would allow no such distractions from whatever time he had left. He ghosted through the fading light with a deadly intensity, eyes striving to pierce the layers of green and shadow ahead. And then there was something to see. Lights. Hundreds of scattered lights, flickering like giant fireflies.

Conan could see little from the ground, but nearby vines like hawsers trailed down from a balcony of what might have once been a palace. Sheathing his sword and shifting the silk-wrapped sorcerous weapon to a place behind his back, the Cimmerian climbed one of the thick vines hand over hand. The others followed as agilely as the monkeys of the forest.

Crouching behind a green-swathed stone balustrade, Conan studied the lights. They were torches atop poles stuck in the ground, forming a great circle. A knot of Vendhyan cavalrymen clustered around each torch, dismounted and fingering their swords nervously as they peered at the wall of growth surrounding them. Oddly, no insects fluttered in the light of the torches.

"Their ointment is better than yours, Khitan," Enam muttered, crushing one of the stinging flies. No one else spoke for the moment.

It was clear enough what the soldiers guarded. The great circle of torches surrounded a building more massive than any Conan had yet seen in the ruined city. Columned terraces and great domes rose more than twice as high as the tallest tree on the forest floor, yet others of the giant trunks rose in turn from those terraces, turning the huge structure into a small mountain.

"If they are in that," Hordo said softly, "how in Zandru's Nine Hells do we find them? It must have a hundred leagues of corridor and more chambers than a man could count."

"They are in there," Kang Hou said. "And I fear we must find them for more than their lives."

Conan eyed the merchant sharply. "What is it you know that I do not?"

"I *know* nothing," Kang Hou replied, "but I fear much." With that he scurried to the vines and began to climb back down. There was nothing Conan could do but follow.

Once on the ground again, the Cimmerian took the lead. The two women would be with Kandar, and Kandar would certainly be with Karim Singh and Naipal. In the huge building, Kang Hou said, and for all the denials, Conan was sure the man knew something. So be it, he thought.

It was a file of wraiths that flitted through the Vendhyan lines, easily avoiding the few soldiers who rode patrol among the clusters at the torches. Bushes and creepers grew from chinks between the marble blocks of the great structure's broad stairs and lifted tiles on the wide portico at their head. Tall bronze doors stood open, a thick wreathing of vines speaking of the centuries since they had been shifted from their present position. With his sword in advance, Conan entered.

Behind him he heard the gasps of the others as they followed but he knew what caused the sounds of astonishment and so did not look back. His eyes were all for the way ahead. From the huge portal a wide aisle of grit-covered tiles led between thick columns, layered with gold leaf, to a vast central chamber beneath a dome that towered hundreds of feet above. In the middle of that chamber stood a marble statue of a man, more than half the height of the dome and untouched by time. Conan's skin prickled at the armor on the figure, stone-carved to represent studded leather. Instead of a nasaled helm, however, a gleaming crown topped the massive head.

"Can that be gold?" Shamil gasped, staring up at the statue.

"Keep your mind to the matter at hand," Hordo growled, "or you'll not live long enough for worrying about gold." His eyes had a glitter though, as if he had calculated the weight of that crown to within a feather.

"I had thought it was but legend," Kang Hou breathed. "I had hoped it was but legend."

"What are you talking about?" Conan demanded. "This is not the first time you have indicated you knew something about this place. I think it is time to tell the rest of us."

This time the Khitan nodded. "Two millennia ago, Orissa, the first King of Vendhya, was interred in a tomb beneath his capital city, Maharastra. For five centuries he was worshiped as a god in a temple built over his tomb and containing a great figure of Orissa wearing a gold crown said to have been made by melting the crowns and scepters of all the lands he had conquered. Then, in a war of succession, Maharastra was sacked and abandoned by its people. With time the very location of the city was lost. Until now.''

"That is very interesting," Conan said dryly, "but it has nothing to do with why we are here."

"On the contrary," Kang Hou told him. "If my niece dies, if we all die, we must slay the wizard Naipal before he looses what lies in the tomb beneath this temple. The legends that I know speak vaguely of horrors, but there is a prophecy associated with all of them. 'The army that cannot die will march again at the end of time.' ''

Conan looked again at the carved armor, then shook his head stubbornly. "I am here for the women first. Then I will see to Naipal and the other two."

A boot crunched at one side of the chamber and Conan whirled, his broadsword coming up. A Vendhyan soldier, eyes bulging beneath his turbaned helm, clutched at the throwing knife in his throat and fell to lie still on the floor. Kang Hou hurried to retrieve his blade.

"Khitan merchants seem a tough lot," Hordo said incredulously. "Perhaps we should include him when we divide that crown."

"Matters at hand." Conan grunted. "Remember?"

"I do not say leave the women," the one-eyed man grumbled, "but could we not take the crown as well?"

Conan paid no heed. His interest lay in where the soldier had come from. Only one doorway on that side of the chamber, and that the nearest to the corpse, opened onto stairs leading beneath the temple. At the base of those stairs he could see a glimmer of light, as of a torch farther on.

"Hide the Vendhyan," he commanded. "If anyone comes

looking for him, they'll not think that wound in his throat was made by a monkey.''

Impatiently hefting his sword, he waited for Hasan and Enam to carry the corpse into a dark corridor and return alone. Without a word, then, he started down.

CHAPTER XXIII

In a huge high-ceilinged chamber far beneath the temple once dedicated to Orissa, Naipal again paused in his work to look with longing expectation at the doorway to his power. Many doorways opened into the chamber, letting on the warren of passages that crossed and criss-crossed beneath the temple. This large marble arch, each stone bearing a cleanly incised symbol of sorcerous power, was blocked by a solid mass of what appeared to be smooth stone. Stone it might appear, but a sword rang on it as against steel and left less mark than it would have on that metal. And the whole of the passage from the chamber to the tomb, a hundred paces in length, was sealed with the adamantine substance, so said the strange maps Masrok had drawn.

The wizard swayed with exhaustion, but the smell of success close at hand drove him on, even numbing the ache behind his eyes. Five of the *khorassani* he placed on their golden tripods at the points of a carefully measured pentagon he had scribed on the marble floor tiles with chalk made from the burned bones of virgins. Setting the largest of the smooth ebon stones on its own tripod, he threw wide his black-robed arms and began the first incantation.

"Ka-my'een dai'el! Da-en'var hoy'aarth! Khora mar! Khora mar!"

Louder the chant rose, and louder still, echoing from the walls, ringing in the ears, piercing the skull. Karim Singh and Kandar pressed their hands to their ears, groaning. The two women, naked save for their veils, bound hand and foot, wailed for the pain. Only Naipal reveled in the sound, gloried in the reverberations deep in his bones. It was a sound of power. His power. Eye-searing bars of light lanced from the largest *khorassani* to each of the others, then from each of those smaller stones to each of its glowing brothers, forming a pentagram of burning brilliance. The air between the lines of fire shimmered and rippled as though flame sliced to gossamer had been stretched there, and the whole hummed and crackled with fury.

"There," Naipal said. "Now the guardian demons, the Sivani, are sealed away from this world unless summoned by name."

"That is all very well," Kandar muttered. Actually seeing the wizard's power had drained some of his arrogance. "But how are we to get to the tomb? My soldiers cannot dig through that. Will your stones' fire melt that which almost broke my blade?"

Naipal stared at the man who would lead the army that was entombed a hundred paces away—at least the man the world would think led it—and watched his arrogance wilt further. The wizard did not like those who could not keep their minds focused on what they were about. Kandar's insistence that the women should witness every moment of his triumph—*his* triumph!—irritated Naipal. For the mo-

ment Kandar was still needed, but, Naipal decided, something painfully fitting would make way for the prince's
successor. At least Karim Singh, his narrow face pasty and
beaded with sweat, had been cowed to a proper view of
matters.

Instead of answering the question, Naipal asked one in
tones like the caress of a razor's edge. "Are you sure you
made the arrangements I commanded? Carts filled with
street urchins should have arrived by now."

"They will come," Kandar answered sullenly. "Soon. I
sent my body servant to see if they have come, did I not?
But it takes time to gather so many carts. The governor
might—"

"Pray he does only what he has been told," Naipal
snarled.

The wizard rubbed at his temples fretfully. All of his
fine plans, now thrown into a hodgepodge of haste and
improvisation by that accursed *pan-kur*.

Quickly he took the last four *khorassani* from their
ebony chest and placed them on tripods of gold. So close
to the demon's prison, they would do for the summoning.
He was careful to put the tripods well away from the other
five to avoid any interaction. A resonance could be deadly.
But there would be no resonance, no failure of any kind.
The accursed blue-eyed barbarian, the devil spawn, would
be defeated.

*"E'las eloyhim! Maraath savinday! Khora mar! Khora
mar!"*

Conan was grateful for the pools of light from the
distantly spaced torches, each only just visible from the
last. Seemingly hundreds of dark tunnels formed a maze
under the temple but the torches made a path to follow.
And at the end of that path must lie what he sought.

Suddenly the Cimmerian stiffened. From behind came the sound of pounding feet. Many pounding feet.

"They must have found the body," Hordo said with a disgusted glare that took in Hasan and Enam.

Conan hesitated only an instant. To remain where they were meant a battle they could not in all probability win. To rush ahead meant running headlong into the gods alone knew what. "Scatter," he ordered the others. "Each must find his way as he can. And Hanuman's own luck go with us all."

The big Cimmerian waited only long enough to see each man disappear down a separate dark passage, then chose his own. The last glimmers of light faded behind him quickly. He slowed, feeling his way along a smooth wall, placing each foot carefully on a floor he could no longer see. With the blade of his sword he probed the blackness ahead.

Yet abruptly that blackness did not seem as complete as it had. For a moment he thought his eyes might be adapting, but then he realized there was a light ahead. A light that was approaching him. Pressing his back against the wall, he waited.

Slowly the light drew closer, obviously bobbing in someone's hand. The shape of a man became clear. It was no torch he carried, though he held it like one, but rather what seemed to be a metal rod topped by a glowing ball.

Conan's jaw tightened at this obvious sorcery. But the man coming nearer looked nothing at all like the one he had seen at Kandar's palace, the man he had thought was Naipal. Recognition came to him in the same instant that the man stopped, peering into the darkness toward Conan was though he sensed a presence. It was Ghurran, but a Ghurran whose apparent age had been halved to perhaps fifty.

"It is I, herbalist," the Cimmerian said, stepping away from the wall. "Conan. And I have questions for you."

The no-longer-so-old man gave a start, then stared at him in amazement. "You actually have one of the daggers! How—? No matter. With that I can slay the demon if need be. Give it to me!"

A part of the silk wrapping had scraped loose against the wall, Conan realized, revealing the faintly glowing hilt of silvery metal. With one hand he pushed the cloth back into place. "I have need of it, herbalist. I will pass over how you have made yourself younger, and how that torch was made, but what do you do in this place, at this time? And why did you abandon me to die from the poison after coming so far?"

"There is no poison," Ghurran muttered impatiently. "You must give me the dagger. You know not what it is capable of."

"No poison!" Conan spat. "I have suffered agonies of it. Not a night gone but the pain was enough to twist my stomach into knots and send fire through my muscles. You said you sought an antidote, but you left me to die!"

"You fool! I gave you the antidote in Sultanapur! All you have felt is your body purging itself of the potions I gave you to make you think you were still poisoned."

"Why?" was all Conan said.

"Because I had need of you. My body was too frail to make this journey alone, but as soon as I saw the contents of those chests, I knew I must. Naipal prepares to loose a great evil on the world, and only I can stop him. But I must have that dagger!"

A widening of Ghurran's eyes warned Conan as much as did the increase in light. The Cimmerian dropped to a crouch and threw himself to one side, twisting and stabbing as he did. A Vendhyan tulwar sliced above his head, but his own blade went through the soldier's middle. The dying man fell, and his two fellows, rushing at his heels, went down in a heap atop Conan. The big Cimmerian grappled with them in the light of their fallen torch. Ghurran and his glowing rod had vanished.

In a struggling pile the three men rolled atop the torch. One of the Vendhyans screamed as the flames were ground out against his back, then screamed again as a dagger found his flesh. Conan's hands closed on the head of the soldier who had slain his companion by mistake. The sound of a neck breaking was a loud snap in the dark.

But it need not be total dark Conan thought as he climbed to his feet. Without hesitation he unwrapped the strange weapon. A dagger, Ghurran had called it, but what monstrous hand could use it so, the Cimmerian wondered. And it could slay the demon. What demon? But for whatever hand or purpose the silvery blade had been wrought, its faint glow was light of a sort in the blackness of the tunnel, if light of an eerie grayish-blue. By it Conan recovered his broadsword and again began a slow progress through the tunnels. Soon he heard voices, hollow echoes in the distant passages. With difficulty he determined a direction. Grimly he moved toward the source.

Thunder smote the chamber, and the obsidian form of Masrok floated in the void of its fiery cage. The silvery weapons held in five of its eight arms looked no different, yet in some fashion they had an aura of having been used recently, a pulsation that reached into the back of a human mind and whispered of violence and death. Karim Singh and Prince Kandar edged back from the huge figure, no matter that it was confined. The bound women seemed frozen with shock and fear.

"You slice matters too finely, O man," Masrok boomed.

Crimson eyes flickered to the blazing pentagram in what could not possibly have been nervousness. "A delay of but another beat of a human heart and my other selves would have been on me. Who would serve you then, O man?"

"Masrok, I command you—" Naipal began when half a score of Vendhyan soldiers burst into the chamber.

"Prince Kandar!" one of them cried. "Someone has—"

"You dare intrude!" Naipal howled. He spoke a word that made even him shiver, and lightning flared from the largest of the *khorassani*. A single shriek rent the air, and a cinder, only vaguely resembling the soldier who had shouted, fell and shattered into charred chunks on the stone floor. Turban-helmed men ran, screaming with terror.

Karim Singh and Prince Kandar both tried to speak at once.

"My men are not to be slain out of hand," Kandar shouted.

"The message could have been important," the *wazam* cried.

Both men clamped their teeth on further words as Naipal's dark eyes came to rest on them. "He dies whom I wish to die, and what is important is what I say is important. *This* is important!" The wizard turned his attention back to the demon, which had watched what had happened impassively. "You will open the way to the tomb for me, Masrok. I care not how."

"From within this cage?" Masrok replied with a hint of its former sarcasm.

"Open it!"

For a moment scarlet eyes met those of ebon, then the demon's mouth opened, and the sound that emerged sent shudders through human flesh. Only for an instant, however. The sound rose with blinding speed to send a stabbing pain in the ears, and beyond. Yet still Masrok's straining jaws told of a cry continuing.

Suddenly that call was answered. Suddenly there were— *things* in the chamber. What exactly or how many it was impossible to tell, for it pained the eye to gaze on them directly, and under a sidelong glance, the numbers and forms seemed to shift constantly. Impressions were all that could be made out, and they enough to bring a lifetime of nightmares. Fangs dripping spittle that bubbled and hissed on the stone. Razor claws gleaming like steel and needle spines glittering like crystal. Sparkling scales in a thousand hues and leathery wings that seemed to stretch farther than the eye could see, farther surely than the walls of the chamber.

Kandar stood ashen-faced, trembling almost as much as the women, who writhed against their bonds and wailed with frantic despair. Karim Singh's lips moved rapidly and silently, and Naipal realized with considerable amusement that the *wazam* prayed. The wizard realized as well that those monstrous forms, so terrifying to human eyes, cowered beneath Masrok's gaze. Perhaps, he thought, he had summoned and bound a greater power than he knew. It increased his resolve to see the demon returned to the prison it shared with its other selves.

Human skulls, dangling for ornament, swayed as Masrok raised one silvery, glowing spear and pointed with it to the blocked passage. Horrific forms flowed to the adamantine substance, clawing, gouging, devouring, a seething mass that slowly sank into the stone, leaving an open way behind it.

"Impressive," said a voice from one of the many entrances to the great room.

Naipal spun, ready to utter the word that drew lightning from the *khorassani,* and it seemed his heart had turned to ice in his chest. "Zail Bal," he gasped. "You are dead!"

"You never would believe your eyes, Naipal," the newcomer said, "when you wished to believe other than what you saw. Of course you have reason to believe as you do. You saw me carried off by *rajaie* while far from my implements." Zail Bal's dark eyes narrowed. "And some of my amulets had been most cunningly tampered with. Still, I managed to slay the demons, though not without cost, it is true. I found myself deposited on the shores of the Vilayet in an age-riddled body, too frail to travel a league." His gaze went from the imprisoned Masrok, once again watching the humans in silence, to the passage into which the summoned beings had now disappeared. "You have done well for me in my absence, apprentice. I had not managed to locate this place before my . . . accident."

"I am no longer the apprentice," Naipal snarled. "I am the court wizard! I am the master!"

"Are you?" Zail Bal's chuckle was dry. "Karim Singh may have his throne, and Kandar may call himself general, but the army that lies below will march for me, Naipal, not for you. The demon will serve me."

Naipal's eyes flickered to the *khorassani*. Did he dare? He had never known that Zail Bal sought Orissa's tomb, and that fact raised unpleasant possibilities. Could he risk that the former court wizard did not also know the words of power? Would the other have risked confronting him without that knowledge? So. If either began to speak the words, the other would also. The nature of the stones was to accept only one master at a time. If neither man gained control quickly enough, both would perish, as well as every living thing for leagues. Naipal had no interest in taking the other man with him as he died. He wanted victory, not death.

"You said your body was age-riddled," Karim Singh said suddenly in a voice that quavered, "yet you appear younger than I. No more than forty. I remember you well, and you were older than that when . . ." His voice trailed off at Zail Bal's chuckle. It was dry this time as well, like the dust of the grave.

"Yes, I am younger than I was and I will be younger still. But what of you, Naipal? Do you suffer from exhaustion that sleep will not cure? Are there pains behind your eyes, splitting your skull?"

"What have you done?" Naipal whispered, then screamed it. *"What have you done?"*

The other wizard laughed and as he spoke, his voice never lost its sound of amusement. "Did you think I kept no cords to my apprentice, Naipal? They were useless over the distance from Turan but once I was across the Himelias . . . aaah. Now I drain the vitality from you through those cords, Naipal, though not exactly as the *rajaie* drained it from me. You will not grow old. Merely tired. So tired you cannot stand or even hold your head up. But do not fear that I will let you die, Naipal. I would not do such to my *faithful* apprentice. No, I will give you eternal life. I will put you in a safe, dry place, with only the endless thirst to distract you from the pains in your head and the nibbles of the rats. Of course the rats will stop their nibbling when you wither sufficiently. You will be a desiccated husk, holding life until it crumbles to dust. And I assure you I will see that it takes a very long time."

Naipal had neither moved nor spoken during Zail Bal's recitation. The fool should have lulled him, he thought. Now he would have to take the gamble. There would come a moment when the *former* court wizard let his attention lapse and then Naipal would begin the words, in a whisper. By the time Zail Bal realized what was happening, it would be too late. It *must* be too late.

A gasp from Karim Singh caught a corner of Naipal's mind. The shifting mass of beings that Masrok had summoned had returned, flowing from the mouth of the passage to the tomb.

"They are done, O man," the eight-armed demon announced. "The way is clear."

All eyes went to the passage. Zail Bal stepped by the seething horror without looking at it, not as though the sight pained his eyes but rather as if he simply could not be bothered by it at the moment. Even Kandar and Karim Singh overcame their fear enough to move closer. Naipal began to whisper furiously.

Crouching near the end of one of the passages that let into the great underground chamber, Conan weighed the silvery weapon in his hand. A dagger, Ghurran had called it. Or Zail Bal, as he now named himself. And the Cimmerian could see the weapon's twin clasped by the huge eight-armed shape. Much had been said in that chamber that he would ponder later, but it was another thing that Ghurran/Zail Bal had said that was of interest now. The weapon he held could slay the demon, by which Conan assumed he had meant the towering obsidian form. Masrok, he had heard it called. Perhaps it could slay the others as well.

Once more Conan tried to look at the demons and found his eyes sliding away unbidden. Their sudden appearance from the other passage, just when he was on the point of entering while the men argued, had been a shock. But now that all eyes peered into the passage from which the monstrosities had come, it might just be possible for him to reach the women before he was even seen. As for what came then. . . . With a fatalistic grimness he hefted his broadsword in one hand and the large silvery dagger in the other. Then he must bar pursuit long enough for the women to flee. Treading with light swiftness, he moved into the subterranean chamber.

His eyes shifted constantly from the women to the others. Vyndra and Chin Kou, naked and bound at wrists and ankles, lay trembling with eyes squeezed shut above their veils. Naipal appeared to be muttering under his breath, watching the other men, and they in turn had eyes only for the passage. It led to an army, had Ghurran, or Zail Bal, claimed? Kang Hou's army that would come at the end of time perhaps? Warriors like the one he had faced? He could not waste time in worry over that now. The demons that had come from the tunnel seemed fixed on the huge ebon form floating in nothingness in the center of the chamber, while it—

Conan's breath caught in his throat. Those crimson eyes now followed him. He quickened his pace toward the women. If the demon called a warning, he might still. . . . The massive arms holding glowing spears moved back. Conan snarled silently. He could not dodge two thrown spears at once. Flipping the silvery weapon in his hand, he hurled it at the demon and threw himself toward the women.

A titanic blast rocked the chamber, and Conan landed atop the women as the earth heaved beneath his feet. Stunned, he fumbled desperately for his own dagger as he took in the horrific scene. The humans were staggering to their feet where the blast had flung them. Splintered shards of black stone lay in ten small pools of molten gold. And Masrok stood on the stone floor, the glowing dagger it had already held now mirrored by another.

"Free!" Masrok cried, and with gibbering howls of

demonic terror, the beings it had summoned fled, flowing up into the ceiling, melting into the floor. Scarlet eyes that now glittered went to Naipal. "You threatened me with this blade, O man." The booming voice was heavy with mockery. "How I wished for you to strike. From the inside your barriers were impervious but from the out-side. . . . Any unliving thing could cross from the outside easily, and the crossing of this demon-wrought blade, this metal of powers you never dreamed of, shattered all of your bonds. All!"

The cords on the ankles first, Conan told himself as he found his knife. The women could run with hands tied if need be.

"I always intended your freedom," Naipal said hoarsely. "We made a pact."

"Fool!" the demon snarled. "You bound me, made one of the Sivani your servant. And *you*!" The furious rubiate gaze pinned Zail Bal, who had been attempting to edge toward one of the passages. "You intended the same. Know, then, the price for daring such!"

Both wizards shouted incantations, but the glowing spears sped from Masrok's hands, transfixing each man through the chest. Almost in the same instant the silvery weapons leaped back to the demons' grasp, bearing their still-living burdens. Shrieks split the air, and futile hands clutched at glowing hafts now staining with blood.

"Know for all time!" Masrok thundered. And the de-mon spun, blurring into an obsidian whirlwind streaked with silver.

Then it was still once more and the wizards were gone. But a new skull dangled below the head of each spear, a skull whose empty sockets retained a glow of life, and the shrieks of the wizards, echoing faintly as though from a great distance, could yet be heard.

Slicing the last cord binding a wrist, Conan heaved the women to their feet. Weeping, they tried to cling to him, but he pushed them toward the one passage that showed the light of a torch. The marked path lay there, one they could follow even without his aid.

"You also," Masrok growled, and Conan realized the demon's eyes were now on him. Keeping his face to the creature, he began to follow the women, but slowly. If the worst happened, there must be distance between him and them. "You thought to slay me, puny mortal," the demon said. "You, also, will know—"

A sound like all the winds of the world crying through the maze of passages filled the great room, but no breath of air stirred. The rushing howl died abruptly, and at its ending a mirror image of Masrok stood at either end of the chamber.

"Betrayer!" they shouted with one voice, and it was as though a thunderhead had spoken. "The way that was to open at the end of time is opened beforehand!"

Masrok shifted slightly, that monstrous ebon head swiveling from one form to the other.

"Slayer!" they cried as one. "One of the Sivani is dead, by the deeds of a Sivani!"

Masrok raised its weapons. No particle of the demon's attention remained on Conan. The Cimmerian spun to hasten after the women, and he found them halted before the passage entrance, Kandar confronting them with the curved blade of his tulwar.

The Prince's face was pale and sweaty, and his eyes rolled to the tensing obsidian giants with barely controlled terror. "You can keep the Khitan wench," he rasped, "but Vyndra is mine. Decide quickly, barbarian. If we are still here when their battle begins, none of us will survive."

"I have decided already," Conan said, and his broadsword struck. Twice steel rang on steel and then the Vendhyan Prince was falling with a crimson gash where his throat had been. "Run!" Conan commanded the women. He did not look back as they darted into the tunnel. The ground rumbled beneath his feet. The battle of demons was beginning.

Sound pursued them in their flight through the subterranean passages. The crash of lightnings confined and the roar of thunder imprisoned. The earth heaved, and dirt and rock showered from above.

Sheathing his sword, Conan scooped up the women, one over each shoulder, and redoubled his speed, fleeing from the pool of light into the debris-filled darkness. The flames on distantly spaced torches wavered as the walls on which they hung danced.

Then the stairs were before him. He took them three at a time. In the vast-domed temple chamber, massive columns shivered and the towering statue swayed. Without slowing, Conan ran past the tall bronze doors and into the night.

Outside, the circle of torches remained, swaying as the ground heaved in swells like the sea, but the soldiers were fled. Trees a hundred and fifty feet high cracked like whips.

Conan ran into the forest until a root caught his foot and sent him sprawling with his burdens. He could not rise again, only cling as the earth shook and rippled in waves, but at last he looked back.

Bolts of lightning burst toward the sky from the temple, hurling great blocks of stone into the air, casting a blue illumination over the frenzied forest. And dome by dome, columned terrace by columned terrace, the huge temple fell, collapsing inward, ever sinking as it leaped like a thing alive. Lightning flashes revealed the ruin no higher than the flailing trees surrounding it, then half their height, then only a mound of rubble.

Abruptly there was no more lightning. The ground gave one final tortured heave and was still.

Conan rose unsteadily to his feet. He could no longer see even the mound. In truth he did not believe it was any longer there. "Swallowed by the earth," he said softly, "and the entrance sealed once more."

His arms filled suddenly with naked, weeping women, but his mind was on other matters. Horses. Whether or not the demons had been buried with the tomb, he did not intend to remain long enough to find out.

EPILOGUE

Conan rode through the dawn with his jaw set grimly, wondering if perhaps he could not find just a few Vendhyan soldiers who would try to contest his passage or perhaps question the Vendhyan cavalry saddle on his horse. It would be better than the icy daggers of silence being hurled against his back by Vyndra and Chin Kou. Of necessity he gripped the reins of their horses in one hand; the fool women would not have left the forest otherwise.

"You must find us garments," Vyndra said suddenly. "I will not be seen like this."

"It is not seemly," Chin Kou added.

Conan sighed. It was not the first time they had made the demand, though they had no idea as to where he might obtain the clothes. The past hour of silence had come from his retort that they had *already* been seen by half the populace of Gwandiakan. He twisted in the saddle to look back at them. The two women still wore the veils, if nothing else. He had asked why, since they obviously hated the small squares of silk, but they had babbled incomprehensively at him about not being recognized, and both had gone into such a frenzy that someone might be watching, for all it had been pitch dark in the middle of the forest at the time, that he did not mention it again. They stared at him now with dark, furious eyes peeping over the top of their veils, yet each sat straight in her saddle, seemingly unaware of the nudity of which she complained.

"We are almost to the old well," he told them. "Kuie Hsi should be there with garb for you both."

"The well!" Vyndra exclaimed, suddenly trying to hide behind the high pommel of her saddle. "Oh, no!"

"There might be people!" Chin Kou moaned as she, too, contorted.

Before they could slip from the saddles and hide—they had done that once already—Conan kicked his horse to a gallop, pulling theirs along behind, heedless of their wails of protest.

The wall of the old well remained, surrounded by trees much smaller than those of the forest. The well itself had long collapsed. A portion of a stone wall still stood nearby, perhaps once part of a caravansary. There were people there as well. Conan grinned as he ran his eye over them. Hordo and Enam tossing dice. Hasan and Shamil seated with their backs against the wall. Kang Hou sipping from a tiny cup held delicately in his fingers, while Kuie Hsi crouched by a fire where a kettle steamed. The men looked the worse for wear, sprouting bandages and poultices, but they sprang to their feet with glad shouts at his appearance.

Kuie Hsi did not shout but rather came running with bundles in her arms. The other two women, Conan saw, had slid from the saddles and were hiding behind their horses. He dismounted, leaving them to their flurry of silks, and went to meet the men.

"I thought you were dead for certain this time," the one-eyed man muttered gruffly.

"Not I," Conan laughed, "nor any of the rest of us it seems. Our luck has not been so bad after all." The smiles faded from their faces, producing a frown on his. "What has happened?"

"A great deal," Kang Hou replied. "My niece brought much news with her. For one thing, King Bhandarkar is dead at the hands of the Katari. Fortunately Prince Jharim Kar managed to rally nobles to Bhandarkar's young son, Bhunda Chand, who has been crowned as the new king, thus restoring order. On the unfortunate side, you, my *cheng-li* friend, have been condemned to death by Royal Edict, signed by Bhunda Chand, for complicity in the assassination of his father."

Conan could only shake his head in amazement. "How did this madness come about?"

The Khitan merchant explained. "One of Jharim Kar's first moves after the coronation—and that was a hasty affair, it seems—was to ride for Gwandiakan with the young King and all the cavalry he could muster. Supposedly he found evidence that Karim Singh was a leader of the plot, and thus must be arrested and executed before he could become a rallying point for disaffection. It is rumored, however, that the Prince blames the *wazam* for an incident involving one of his wives. Whatever the truth, Bhunda Chand's column met the caravan on which we and the *wazam* traveled. And one Alyna, a servant of the Lady Vyndra, gave testimony that her mistress and a pale-skinned barbarian called Patil had plotted with Karim Singh and spoken in her presence of slaying Bhandarkar."

A shriek of fury announced that Vyndra had just had the

same information from Kuie Hsi. The Vendhyan noble-woman stormed from behind the horses, clutching half-donned silken robes that fluttered after her. "I will strip her hide! That sow will speak the truth, or I will wear out switches on her!"

"I fear it is too late for any such action on your part," Kang Hou said. "Alyna—perhaps I should say the Lady Alyna—has already been confirmed in your titles and estates. The Royal Edict concerning you not only strips you of those possessions but gifts her with your life and person."

Vyndra's mouth worked silently for a moment, then she rounded on Conan. "You are the cause of this! It is all your fault! What are you going to do about it?"

"I am to blame?" Conan growled. "*I* enslaved Alyna?" Vyndra's eyes almost started from her head in fury and he sighed. "Very well. I will take you to Turan with me."

"Turan!" she cried, throwing up her hands. "It is a pigsty unfit for a civilized woman! It—" Suddenly it dawned on her that her gesture had bared her to the waist. Shrieking, she snatched the still-sliding silk and dashed for the shelter of the horses.

"A woman whose temper equals her great beauty," Kang Hou said, "and whose deviousness and vindictive-ness exceed both."

Conan waved the words aside. "What of Gwandiakan? Will it be safe to hide there for a day or two while we recuperate?"

"That will not be possible," Kuie Hsi said, joining them. "The people of Gwandiakan took the earthquake as a sign from the gods, especially when they discovered that carts had been assembled to take the children from the city to an unknown destination. A wall of the fortress had collapsed. The people stormed the fortress, freeing the imprisoned children. Soldiers who tried to stop them were torn limb from limb. Jharim Kar has promised justice in the matter, but in the meanwhile his soldiers patrol the streets heavily. I cannot believe any Western foreigner would long escape their notice.''

''I am glad for the children,'' Conan said, ''for all it had nothing to do with me, but this means we must ride for the mountains from here. And the sooner the better, I think. What of you, Kang Hou? Are you, too, proscribed?''

''I am but a humble merchant,'' the Khitan replied, ''and so, no doubt, beneath Alyna's notice. To my good fortune. As for your journey over the mountains, I fear that not all who came with you will return to Turan. You will pardon me?'' Bowing, he left before Conan could ask what he meant, but Hasan took his place.

''I must speak with you,'' the young Turanian said. ''Alone.'' Still frowning after Kang Hou, Conan let himself be drawn off from the others. Hasan pressed a folded square of parchment into the Cimmerian's hand. ''When you return to Sultanapur, Conan, take that to the House of Perfumed Doves and say it is for Lord Khalid.''

''So you are the one who will not return to Turan,'' Conan said, turning over the square of parchment in his hands. ''And what message is it you send to Yildiz's spy master?''

''You know of him?''

''More is known on the streets of Sultanapur than the lords of Turan would believe. But you have not answered my question.''

The Turanian drew a deep breath. ''I was sent to discover if a connection exists between the Vendhyans and the death of the High Admiral. Not one question have I asked concerning that, yet I know already this land is so full of intrigues within intrigues that no clear answer can ever be found. I say as much in the letter. As well I say that I can find no evidence connecting the 'fishermen' of Sultanapur with the matter, and that the rumors of a northland giant in the pay of Vendhyans is just that. A rumor. Lord Khalid will recognize my hand, and so know it for a true report. It is unsealed. You may read it if you wish."

Conan stuffed the parchment into his belt pouch. There would be time for reading—and for deciding whether to visit the House of Perfumed Doves—later. "Why are you remaining?" he asked. "Chin Kou?"

"Yes. Kang Hou has no objections to a foreigner marrying into his family." Hasan snorted a laugh. "After years of avoiding it, it seems I will become a spice merchant after all."

"Be careful," Conan cautioned. "I wish you well, but I do not believe the Khitans are much less devious than the Vendhyans."

Leaving the young Turanian, Conan went in search of Kang Hou. The merchant was seated on the wall of the caved-in well. "Soon you will be fleeing Vendhya," the Khitan said as Conan approached. "What of your plans to sack the land with an army at your back?"

"Someday perhaps. But Vendhya is a strange land, mayhap too devious for a simple northlander like me. It makes my thoughts whirl in peculiar fashions."

Kang Hou arched a thin eyebrow. "How so, man who calls himself Patil?"

"Just fragments, spinning. Odd memories. Valash, sitting in the Golden Crescent on the morning the High Admiral died. A very hard man, Valash. He would never have let two such beauties as your nieces leave his ship except to a slaver's block. Unless someone frightened him into it perhaps. But then, you are a very hard man for a poor merchant, are you not, Kang Hou? And your niece, Kuie Hsi, is an extremely able woman. The way in which she passed for a Vendhyan woman to seek information in Gwandiakan. And knowing Naipal was among those who rode to the Forests of Ghelai, though I have heard his face was known but to a handful. Were you aware that a Vendhyan woman was delivered to the High Admiral as a gift on the morning he died? She vanished soon after his death, I understand. But I have never understood why the Vendhyans would sign a treaty with Turan and kill the High Admiral within a day of it. Kandar seemed truly shocked at the news, and Karim Singh as well. Strange, would you not say, Kang Hou?''

All through the rambling discourse the Khitan had listened with an expression of polite interest. Now he smiled, tucking his hands into his broad sleeves. ''You weave a very fanciful tale for one who calls himself a simple northlander.''

Returning the smile, Conan put his hand on his dagger. ''Will you wager you are faster than I?'' he asked softly.

For an instant Kang Hou wavered visibly. Then, slowly, he brought his hands into the open. Empty. ''I am but a peaceful merchant,'' he said as though nothing had happened. ''If you would care to listen, perhaps I can weave a tale as fanciful as yours. Having, of course, as little to do with reality.''

''I will listen,'' Conan said cautiously, but he did not move his hand from the dagger hilt.

''I am from Cho-Hien,'' the Khitan began, ''a small city-state on the borders of Vendhya. The lifeblood of Cho-Hien is trade, and its armies are small. It survives by balancing its larger, stronger neighbors one against another. Largest, strongest and most avaricious of Cho-Hien's neighbors is Vendhya. Perhaps the land rots from within, as you say, but the ruling caste, the Kshatriyas, are fierce men with eyes for conquest. If those eyes turn to the north, they will fall first on Cho-Hien. Therefore Cho-Hien must keep the Kshatriyas' gaze to the east, or to the west. A treaty with Turan, for instance, might mean that Kshatriyan ambitions would look not toward the Vilayet but toward Khitai. My tale, I fear, has no more point than yours but perhaps you found it entertaining."

"Entertaining," Conan agreed. "But a question occurs to me. Does Chin Kou share Kuie Hsi's talents? That is," he added with a smile, "if Kuie Hsi had any talents out of the ordinary."

"Chin Kou's sole talent is that she remembers and can repeat every word that she hears or reads. Beyond that she is merely a loving niece who comforts an aging man's bones. Though now it seems she will comfort another."

"That brings another question. Does Hasan know of this?"

"Of my fanciful tale? No." A broad grin split the Khitan's face. "But he knew what I was, as I knew what he was, before ever we reached the Himelias. He will make a fine addition to my family. For a foreigner. Now I will ask a question," he added, the grin fading. "What do you intend concerning my fanciful tale?"

"A tale spun by a northlander and another spun by a Khitan merchant," Conan said musingly. "Who in Turan would believe if I told them? And if they did, they would find ten other reasons for war, or near to war. For there to be true peace between Turan and Vendhya, the Vilayet will have to expand to swallow Secunderam, perhaps enough to separate the two lands for all time. Besides, true peace and true war alike are bad for smugglers."

"You are not so simple as you claim, northlander."

"Vendhya is still a strange land," Conan replied with a laugh. "And one I must be leaving. Fare you well, Kang Hou of Cho-Hien."

The Khitan rose and bowed, though he was careful to keep his hands away from his sleeves. "Fare you well . . . Conan of Cimmeria."

Conan laughed all the way to the horses. "Hordo," he roared, "do we ride, or have you grown so old you have put down roots? Enam, to horse! And you, Shamil. Do you ride with us, or remain here like Hasan?"

"I have had my fill of travel and adventure," Shamil replied earnestly. "I return to Sultanapur to become a fisherman. For fish!"

Vyndra pushed her way past the men scrambling into saddles and confronted Conan. "What of me?" she demanded.

"You do not wish to go to Turan," Conan told her, "and you cannot remain in Vendhya. Except as Alyna's . . . guest. Perhaps Kang Hou will take you to Cho-Hien."

"Cho-Hien! Better Turan than that!"

"Since you have asked so nicely, if you keep me warm on the cold nights in the mountains, I will find a place for you dancing in a tavern in Sultanapur."

Her cheeks colored, but she held out her arms for him to lift her to her saddle. As he did, though, she pressed herself against him briefly and whispered, "I would much rather dance for you alone."

Conan handed her her reins and turned away, hiding a smile as he vaulted to his own saddle. There would be problems with this woman yet, but amusing ones he thought.

"What of the antidote?" Hordo asked. "And Ghurran?"

"I saw him," Conan replied. "You might say he saved all of us with what he told me." Ignoring the one-eyed man's questioning look, he went on. "But are we to sit here until the Vendhyans put all our heads on pikes? Come! There's a wench called Tasha waiting for me in Sultanapur." And with a grin for Vyndra's angry squawl, he booted his horse to a gallop, toward the mountains towering to the north.

CONAN
THE
INDESTRUCTIBLE

The greatest hero of the magic-rife Hyborian Age was a northern barbarian, Conan the Cimmerian, about whose deeds a cycle of legend revolves. While these legends are largely based on the attested facts of Conan's life, some tales are inconsistent with others. So we must reconcile the contradictions in the saga as best we can.

In Conan's veins flowed the blood of the people of Atlantis, the brilliant city-state swallowed by the sea 8,000 years before his time. He was born into a clan that claimed a homeland in the northwest corner of Cimmeria, along the shadowy borders of Vanaheim and the Pictish wilderness. His grandfather had fled his own people because of a blood feud and sought refuge with the people of the North. Conan himself first saw daylight on a battlefield during a raid by the Vanir.

Before he had weathered fifteen snows, the young Cimmerian's fighting skills were acclaimed around the council fires. In that year the Cimmerians, usually at one another's throats, joined forces to repel the warlike Gundermen who, intent on colonizing southern Cimmeria, had pushed across the Aquilonian border and established the frontier post of Venarium. Conan joined the howling, blood-mad horde that swept out of the northern hills, stormed over the stockade walls, and drove the Aquilonians back across their frontier.

At the sack of Venarium, Conan, still short of his full growth, stood six feet tall and weighed 180 pounds. He had the vigilance and stealth of the born woodsman, the iron-hardness of the mountain man, and the Herculean physique of his blacksmith father. After the plunder of the Aquilonian outpost, Conan returned for a time to his tribe.

Restless under the conflicting passions of his adolescence, Conan spent several months with a band of Æsir as they raided the Vanir and the Hyperboreans. He soon learned that some Hyperborean citadels were ruled by a caste of widely-feared magicians, called Witchmen. Undaunted, he took part in a foray against Haloga Castle, when he found that Hyperborean slavers had captured Rann, the daughter of Njal, chief of the Æsir band.

Conan gained entrance to the castle and spirited out Rann Njalsdatter; but on the flight out of Hyperborea, Njal's band was overtaken by an army of living dead. Conan and the other Æsir survivors were led away to slavery ("Legions of the Dead").

Conan did not long remain a captive. Working at night, he ground away at one link of his chain until it was weak enough to break. Then one stormy night, whirling a four-foot length of heavy chain, he fought his way out of the slave pen and vanished into the downpour.

Another account of Conan's early years tells a different tale. This narrative, on a badly broken clay prism from Nippur, states that Conan was enslaved as a boy of ten or twelve by Vanir raiders and set to work turning a grist mill. When he reached his full growth, he was bought by a Hyrkanian pitmaster who traveled with a band of professional fighters staging contests for the amusement of the Vanir and Æsir. At this time Conan received his training with weapons. Later he escaped and made his way south to Zamora (*Conan the Barbarian*).

Of the two versions, the records of Conan's enslavement by the Hyrkanians at sixteen, found in a papyrus in the

British Museum, appear much more legible and self-consistent. But this question may never be settled.

Although free, the youth found himself half a hostile kingdom away from home. Instinctively he fled into the mountains at the southern extremity of Hyperborea. Pursued by a pack of wolves, he took refuge in a cave. Here he discovered the seated mummy of a gigantic chieftain of ancient times, with a heavy bronze sword across its knees. When Conan seized the sword, the corpse arose and attacked him ("The Thing in the Crypt").

Continuing southward into Zamora, Conan came to Arenjun, the notorious "City of Thieves." Green to civilization and, save for some rudimentary barbaric ideas of honor and chivalry, wholly lawless by nature, he carved a niche for himself as a professional thief.

Being young and more daring than adroit, Conan's progress in his new profession was slow until he joined forces with Taurus of Nemedia in a quest for the fabulous jewel called the "Heart of the Elephant." The gem lay in the almost impregnable tower of the infamous mage Yara, captor of the extraterrestrial being Yag-Kosha ("The Tower of the Elephant").

Seeking greater opportunities to ply his trade, Conan wandered westward to the capital of Zamora, Shadizar the Wicked. For a time his thievery prospered, although the whores of Shadizar soon relieved him of his gains. During one larceny, he was captured by the men of Queen Taramis of Shadizar, who sent him on a mission to recover a magical horn wherewith to resurrect an ancient, evil god. Taramis's plot led to her own destruction (*Conan the Destroyer*).

The barbarian's next exploit involved a fellow thief, a girl named Tamira. The Lady Jondra, an arrogant aristocrat of Shadizar, owned a pair of priceless rubies. Baskaran

Imalla, a religious fanatic raising a cult among the Kezankian hillmen, coveted the jewels to gain control over a fire-breathing dragon he had raised from an egg. Conan and Tamira both yearned for the rubies; Tamira took a post as lady's maid to Jondra for a chance to steal them.

An ardent huntress, Jondra set forth with her maid and her men-at-arms to slay Baskaran's dragon. Baskaran captured the two women and was about to offer them to his pet as a snack when Conan intervened (*Conan the Magnificent*).

Soon Conan was embroiled in another adventure. A stranger hired the youth to steal a casket of gems sent by the King of Zamora to the King of Turan. The stranger, a priest of the serpent-god Set, wanted the jewels for magic against his enemy, the renegade priest Amanar.

Amanar's emissaries, who were hominoid reptiles, had stolen the gems. Although wary of magic, Conan set out to recover the loot. He became involved with a bandette, Karela, called the Red Hawk, who proved the ultimate bitch; when Conan saved her from rape, she tried to kill him. Amanar's party had also carried off to the renegade's stronghold a dancing girl whom Conan had promised to help (*Conan the Invincible*).

Soon rumors of treasure sent Conan to the nearby ruins of ancient Larsha, just ahead of the soldiers dispatched to arrest him. After all but their leader, Captain Nestor, had perished in an accident arranged by Conan, Nestor and Conan joined forces to plunder the treasure; but ill luck deprived them of their gains ("The Hall of the Dead").

Conan's recent adventures had left him with an aversion to warlocks and Eastern sorceries. He fled northwestward through Corinthia into Nemedia, the second most powerful Hyborian kingdom. In Nemedia he resumed his profession successfully enough to bring his larcenies to the notice of Aztrias Petanius, ne'er-do-well nephew of the governor. Oppressed by gambling debts, this young gentleman hired the outlander to purloin a Zamorian goblet, carved from a single diamond, that stood in the temple-museum of a wealthy collector.

Conan's appearance in the temple-museum coincided with its master's sudden demise and brought the young thief to the unwelcome attention of Demetrio, of the city's Inquisitorial Council. This caper also gave Conan his second experience with the dark magic of the serpent-brood of Set, conjured up by the Stygian sorcerer Thoth-Amon ("The God in the Bowl").

Having made Nemedia too hot to hold him, Conan drifted south into Corinthia, where he continued to occupy himself with the acquisition of other persons' property. By diligent application, the Cimmerian earned the repute of one of the boldest thieves in Corinthia. Poor judgment of women, however, cast him into chains until a turn in local politics brought freedom and a new career. An ambitious nobleman, Murilo, turned him loose to slit the throat of the Red Priest, Nabonidus, the scheming power behind the local throne. This venture gathered a prize collection of rogues in Nabonidus's mansion and ended in a mire of blood and treachery ("Rogues in the House").

Conan wandered back to Arenjun and began to earn a semi-honest living by stealing back for their owners valuable objects that others had filched from them. He undertook to recover a magical gem, the Eye of Erlik, from the wizard Hissar Zul and return it to its owner, the Khan of Zamboula.

There is some question about the chronology of Conan's life at this point. A recently-translated tablet from Asshurbanipal's library states that Conan was about seventeen at the time. This would place the episode right after that of "The Tower of the Elephant," which indeed is mentioned in the cuneiform. But from internal evidence, this event seems to have taken place several years later. For one thing, Conan appears too clever, mature, and sophisticated; for another, the fragmentary medieval Arabic manuscript *Kitab al-Qunn* implies that Conan was well into his twenties by then.

The first translator of the Asshurbanipal tablet, Prof. Dr. Andreas von Fuss of the Münchner Staatsmuseum, read Conan's age as "17." In Babylonian cuneiform, "17" is expressed by two circles followed by three vertical wedges, with a horizontal wedge above the three for "minus"—hence "twenty minus three." But Academician Leonid Skram of the Moscow Archaeological Institute asserts that the depression over the vertical wedges is merely a dent made by the pick of a careless escavator, and the numeral properly reads "23."

Anyhow, Conan learned of the Eye of Erlik when he heard a discussion between an adventuress, Isparana, and her confederate. He invaded the wizard's mansion, but the wizard caught Conan and deprived him of his soul. Conan's soul was imprisoned in a mirror, there to remain until a crowned ruler broke the glass. Hissar Zul thus compelled Conan to follow Isparana and recover the talisman; but when the Cimmerian returned the Eye to Hissar Zul, the ungrateful mage tried to slay him (*Conan and the Sorcerer*).

Conan, his soul still englassed, accepted legitimate employment as bodyguard to a Khaurani noblewoman, Khashtris. This lady set out for Khauran with Conan, another guard, Shubal, and several retainers. When the other servants plotted to rob and murder their employer, Conan and Shubal saved her and escorted her to Khauran. There Conan found the widowed Queen Ialamis being courted by a young nobleman who was not at all what he seemed (*Conan the Mercenary*).

With his soul restored, Conan learned from an Iranistani, Khassek, that the Khan of Zamboula still wanted the Eye of Erlik. In Zamboula, the Turanian governor, Akter Khan, had hired the wizard Zafra, who ensorcelled swords so that they would slay on command. En route, Conan encountered Isparana, with whom he developed a lust-hate relationship. Unaware of the magical swords, Conan continued to Zamboula and delivered the amulet. But the nefarious Zafra convinced the Khan that Conan was dangerous and should be killed on general principles (*Conan: the Sword of Skelos*).

Conan had enjoyed his taste of Hyborian-Age intrigue. It became clear that there was no basic difference between the opportunities in the palace and those in the Rats' Den, whereas the pickings were far better in high places. Besides, he wearied of the furtive, squalid life of a thief.

He was not, however, yet committed to a strictly law-abiding life. When unemployed, he took time out for a venture in smuggling. An attempt to poison him sent him to Vendhya, a land of wealth and squalor, philosophy and fanatacism, idealism and treachery (*Conan the Victorious*).

Soon after, Conan turned up in the Turanian seaport of Aghrapur. A new cult had established headquarters there under the warlock Jhandar, who needed victims to be drained of blood and reanimated as servants. Conan refused the offer of a former fellow thief, Emilio, to take part in a raid on Jhandar's stronghold to steal a fabulous ruby necklace. A Turanian sergeant, Akeba, did however persuade Conan to go with him to rescue Akeba's daughter, who had vanished into the cult (*Conan the Unconquered*).

After Jhandar's fall, Akeba urged Conan to take service

in the Turanian army. The Cimmerian did not at first find military life congenial, being too self-willed and hot-tempered to easily submit to discipline. Moreover, as he was at this time an indifferent horseman and archer, Conan was relegated to a low-paid irregular unit.

Still, a chance soon arose to show his mettle. King Yildiz launched an expedition against a rebellious satrap. By sorcery, the satrap wiped out the force sent against him. Young Conan alone survived to enter the magic-maddened satrap's city of Yaralet ("The Hand of Nergal").

Returning in triumph to the glittering capital of Aghrapur, Conan gained a place in King Yildiz's guard of honor. At first he endured the gibes of fellow troopers at his clumsy horsemanship and inaccurate archery. But the gibes died away as the other guardsmen discovered Conan's sledge-hammer fists and as his skills improved.

Conan was chosen, along with a Kushite mercenary named Juma, to escort King Yildiz's daughter Zosara to her wedding with Khan Kujula, chief of the Kuigar nomads. In the foothills of the Talakma Mountains, the party was attacked by a strange force of squat, brown, lacquer-armored horsemen. Only Conan, Juma, and the princess survived. They were taken to the subtropical valley of Meru and to the capital, Shamballah, where Conan and Juma were chained to an oar of the Meruvian state galley, about to set forth on a cruise.

On the galley's return to Shamballah, Conan and Juma escaped and made their way into the city. They reached the temple of Yama as the deformed little god-king of Meru was celebrating his marriage to Zosara ("The City of Skulls").

Back at Aghrapur, Conan was promoted to captain. His growing repute as a good man in a tight spot, however, led

King Yildiz's generals to pick the barbarian for especially hazardous missions. Once they sent Conan to escort an emissary to the predatory tribesmen of the Khozgari Hills, hoping to dissuade them by bribes and threats from plundering the Turanians of the lowlands. The Khozgarians, respecting only immediate, overwhelming force, attacked the detachment, killing the emissary and all but two of the soldiers, Conan and Jamal.

To assure their safe passage back to civilization, Conan and Jamal captured Shanya, the daughter of the Khozgari chief. Their route led them to a misty highland. Jamal and the horses were slain, and Conan had to battle a horde of hairless apes and invade the stronghold of an ancient, dying race ("The People of the Summit").

Another time, Conan was dispatched thousands of miles eastward, to fabled Khitai, to convey to King Shu of Kusan a letter from King Yildiz proposing a treaty of friendship and trade. The wise old Khitan king sent his visitors back with a letter of acceptance. As a guide, however, the king appointed a foppish little nobleman, Duke Feng, who had entirely different objectives ("The Curse of the Monolith," first published as "Conan and the Cenotaph").

Conan continued in his service in Turan for about two years, traveling widely and learning the elements of organized, civilized warfare. As usual, trouble was his bedfellow. After one of his more unruly adventures, involving the mistress of his superior officer, Conan deserted and headed for Zamora. In Shadizar he heard that the Temple of Zath, the spider god, in the Zamorian city of Yezud, was recruiting soldiers. Hastening to Yezud, Conan found that a Brythunian free company had taken all the available mercenary posts. He became the town's blacksmith because as a boy he had been apprenticed in this trade.

Conan learned from an emissary of King Yildiz, Lord Parvez, that High Priest Feridun was holding Yildiz's favorite wife, Jamilah, in captivity. Parvez hired Conan to abduct Jamilah. Meanwhile Conan had set his heart on the eight huge gems that formed the eyes of an enormous statue of the spider god. As he was loosening the jewels, the approach of priests forced him to flee to a crypt below the naos. The temple dancing girl Rudabeh, with whom Conan was truly in love for the first time in his life, descended into the crypt to warn him of the doom awaiting him there (*Conan and the Spider God*).

Conan next rode off to Shadizar to track down a rumor of treasure. He obtained a map showing the location of a ruby-studded golden idol in the Kezankian Mountains; but thieves stole his map. Conan, pursuing them, had a brush with Kezankian hillmen and had to join forces with the very rogues he was tracking. He found the treasure, only to lose it under strange circumstances ("The Bloodstained God").

Fed up with magic, Conan headed for the Cimmerian hills. After a time in the simple, routine life of his native village, however, he grew restless enough to join his old friends, the Æsir, in a raid into Vanaheim. In a bitter struggle on the snow-covered plain, both forces were wiped out—all but Conan, who wandered off to a strange encounter with the legendary Atali, daughter of the frost giant Ymir ("The Frost Giant's Daughter").

Haunted by Atali's icy beauty, Conan headed back toward the South, where, despite his often-voiced scorn of civilization, the golden spires of teeming cities beckoned. In the Eiglophian Mountains, Conan rescued a young woman from cannibals, but through overconfidence lost her to the dreaded monster that haunted glaciers ("The Lair of the Ice Worm").

Conan then returned to the Hyborian lands, which include Aquilonia, Argos, Brythunia, Corinthia, Koth, Nemedia, Ophir, and Zingara. These countries were named for the Hyborian peoples who, as barbarians, had 3,000 years earlier conquered the empire of Acheron and built civilized realms on its ruins.

In Belverus, the capital of Nemedia, the ambitious Lord Albanus dabbled in sorcery to usurp the throne of King Garian. To Belverus came Conan, seeking a patron with money to enable him to hire his own free company. Albanus gave a magical sword to a confederate, Lord Melius, who went mad and attacked people in the street until killed. As he picked up the ensorcelled sword, Conan was accosted by Hordo, a one-eyed thief and smuggler whom he had known as Karela's lieutenant.

Conan sold the magical sword, hired his own free company, and taught his men mounted archery. Then he persuaded King Garian to hire him. But Albanus had made a man of clay and by his sorcery given it the exact appearance of the king. Then he imprisoned the king, substituted his golem, and framed Conan for murder (*Conan the Defender*).

Conan next brought his free company to Ianthe, capital of Ophir. There the Lady Synelle, a platinum-blond sorceress, wished to bring to life the demon-god Al'Kirr. Conan bought a statuette of this demon-god and soon found that various parties were trying to steal it from him. He and his company took service under Synelle, not knowing her plans.

Then the bandette Karela reappeared and, as usual, tried to murder Conan. Synelle hired her to steal the statuette, which the witch needed for her sorcery. She also planned to sacrifice Karela (*Conan the Triumphant*).

Conan went on to Argos; but since that kingdom was at

peace, there were no jobs for mercenaries. A misunderstanding with the law compelled Conan to leap to the deck of a ship as it left the pier. This was the merchant galley *Argus,* bound for the coasts of Kush.

A major epoch in Conan's life was about to begin. The *Argus* was taken by Bêlit, the Shemite captain of the pirate ship *Tigress,* whose ruthless black corsairs had made her mistress of the Kushite littoral. Conan won both Bêlit and a partnership in her bloody trade ("Queen of the Black Coast," Chapter 1).

Years before, Bêlit, daughter of a Shemite trader, had been abducted with her brother Jehanan by Stygian slavers. Now she asked her lover Conan to try to rescue the youth. The barbarian slipped into Khemi, the Stygian seaport, was captured, but escaped to the eastern end of Stygia, the province of Taia, where a revolt against Stygian oppression was brewing (*Conan the Rebel*).

Conan and Bêlit resumed their piratical careers, preying mainly on Stygian vessels. Then an ill fate took them up the black Zarkheba River to the lost city of an ancient winged race ("Queen of the Black Coast," Chapters 2–5).

As Bêlit's burning funeral ship wafted out to sea, a downhearted Conan turned his back on the sea, which he would not follow again for years. He plunged inland and joined the warlike Bamulas, a black tribe whose power swiftly grew under his leadership.

The chief of a neighboring tribe, the Bakalahs, planned a treacherous attack on another neighbor and invited Conan and his Bamulas to take part in the sack and massacre. Conan accepted but, learning that an Ophirean girl, Livia, was held captive in Bakalah, he out-betrayed the Bakalahs. Livia ran off during the slaughter and wandered into a mysterious valley, where only Conan's timely arrival saved her from being sacrificed to an extraterrestrial being ("The Vale of Lost Women").

Before Conan could build his own black empire, he was thwarted by a succession of natural catastrophes as well as by the intrigues of hostile Bamulas. Forced to flee, he headed north. After a narrow escape from pursuing lions on the veldt, Conan took shelter in a mysterious ruined castle of prehuman origin. He had a brush with Stygian slavers and a malign supernatural entity ("The Castle of Terror").

Continuing on, Conan reached the semicivilized kingdom of Kush. This was the land to which the name "Kush" properly applied; although Conan, like other Northerners, tended to use the term loosely to mean any of the black countries south of Stygia. In Meroê, the capital, Conan rescued from a hostile mob the young Queen of Kush, the arrogant, impulsive, fierce, cruel, and voluptuous Tananda.

Conan became embroiled in a labyrinthine intrigue between Tananda and an ambitious nobleman who commanded a piglike demon. The problem was aggravated by the presence of Diana, a Nemedian slave girl to whom Conan, despite the jealous fury of Tananda, took a fancy. Events culminated in a night of insurrection and slaughter ("The Snout in the Dark").

Dissatisfied with his achievements in the black countries, Conan wandered to the meadowlands of Shem and became a soldier of Akkharia, a Shemite city-state. He joined a band of volunteers to liberate a neighboring city-state; but through the teachery of Othbaal, cousin of the mad King Akhîrom of Pelishtia, the volunteers were destroyed—all but Conan, who survived to track the plotter to Asgalun, the Pelishti capital. There Conan became involved in a polygonal power war among the mad Akhîrom, the treacherous Othbaal, a Stygian witch, and a company of black mercenaries. In the final hurly-burly of sorcery, steel, and blood, Conan grabbed Othbaal's red-haired mistress, Rufia, and galloped north (''Hawks Over Shem'').

Conan's movements at this time are uncertain. One tale, sometimes assigned to this period, tells of Conan's service as a mercenary in Zingara. A Ptolemaic papyrus in the British Museum alleges that in Kordava, the capital, a captain in the regular army forced a quarrel on Conan. When Conan killed his assailant, he was condemned to hang. A fellow condemnee, Santiddio, belonged to an underground conspiracy, the White Rose, that hoped to topple King Rimanendo. As other conspirators created a disturbance in the crowd that gathered for the hanging, Conan and Santiddio escaped.

Mordermi, head of an outlaw band allied with the White Rose, enlisted Conan in his movement. The conspiracy was carried on in the Pit, a warren of tunnels beneath the city. When the King sent an army to clean out the Pit, the insurrectionists were saved by Callidos, a Stygian sorcerer. King Rimanendo was slain and Mordermi became king. When he proved as tyrannical as his predecessor, Conan raised another revolt; then, refusing the crown for himself, he departed (*Conan: The Road of Kings*).

This tale involves many questions. If authentic, it may belong in Conan's earlier mercenary period, around the time of *Conan the Defender*. But there is no corroboration in other narratives of the idea that Conan ever visited Zingara before his late thirties, the time of *Conan the Buccaneer*. Moreover, none of the rulers of Zingara mentioned in the papyrus appear on the list of kings of Zingara in the Byzantine manuscript *Hoi Anaktes tês Tzingêras*. Hence some students deem the papyrus either spurious or a case of confusion between Conan and some other hero. Everything else known about Conan indicates that, if he had indeed been offered the Zingaran crown, he would have grabbed it with both hands.

We next hear of Conan after he took service under Amalric of Nemedia, the general of Queen-Regent Yasmela of the little border kingdom of Khoraja. While Yasmela's brother, King Khossus, was a prisoner in Ophir, Yasmela's borders were assailed by the forces of the veiled sorcerer Natohk—actually the 3,000-years-dead Thugra Khotan of the ruined city of Kuthchemes.

Obeying an oracle of Mitra, the supreme Hyborian god, Yasmela made Conan captain-general of Khoraja's army. In this rôle he gave battle to Natohk's hosts and rescued the Queen-Regent from the malignant magic of the undead warlock. Conan won the day—and the Queen ("Black Colossus").

Conan, now in his late twenties, settled down as Khorajan commander-in-chief. But the queen, whose lover he had expected to be, was too preoccupied with affairs of state to have time for frolics. He even proposed marriage, but she explained that such a union would not be sanctioned by Khorajan law and custom. Yet, if Conan could somehow rescue her brother from imprisonment, she might persuade Khossus to change the law.

Conan set forth with Rhazes, an astrologer, and Fronto, a thief who knew a secret passage into the dungeon where Khossus languished. They rescued the king but found themselves trapped by Kothian troops, since Strabonus of Koth had his own reasons for wanting Khossus.

Having surmounted these perils, Conan found that Khossus, a pompous young ass, would not hear of a foreign barbarian's marrying his sister. Instead, he would marry Yasmela off to a nobleman and find a middle-class bride for Conan. Conan said nothing; but in Argos, as their ship cast off, Conan sprang ashore with most of the gold that Khossus had raised and waved the king an ironic farewell ("Shadows in the Dark").

Now nearly thirty, Conan slipped away to revisit his Cimmerian homeland and avenge himself on the Hyperboreans. His blood brothers among the Cimmerians and the Æsir had won wives and sired sons, some as old and almost as big as Conan had been at the sack of Venarium. But his years of blood and battle had stirred his predatory spirit too strongly for him to follow their example. When traders brought word of new wars, Conan galloped off to the Hyborian lands.

A rebel prince of Koth was fighting to overthrow Strabonus, the penurious ruler of that far-stretched nation; and Conan found himself among old companions in the princeling's array, until the rebel made peace with his king. Unemployed again, Conan formed an outlaw band, the Free Companions. This troop gravitated to the steppes west of the Sea of Vilayet, where they joined the ruffianly horde known as the *kozaki*.

Conan soon became the leader of this lawless crew and ravaged the western borders of the Turanian Empire until his old employer, King Yildiz, sent a force under Shah Amurath, who lured the *kozaki* deep into Turan and cut them down.

Slaying Amurath and acquiring the Turanian's captive, Princess Olivia of Ophir, Conan rowed out into the Vilayet Sea in a small boat. He and Olivia took refuge on an island, where they found a ruined greenstone city, in which stood strange iron statues. The shadows cast by the moonlight proved as dangerous as the giant carnivorous ape that ranged the isle, or the pirate crew that landed for rest and recreation ("Shadows in the Moonlight").

Conan seized command of the pirates that ravaged the Sea of Vilayet. As chieftain of this mongrel Red Brotherhood, Conan was more than ever a thorn in King Yildiz's flesh. That mild monarch, instead of strangling his brother Teyaspa in the normal Turanian manner, had cooped him up in a castle in the Colchian Mountains. Yildiz now sent his General Artaban to destroy the pirate stronghold at the mouth of the Zaporoska River; but the general became the harried instead of the harrier. Retreating inland, Artaban stumbled upon Teyaspa's whereabouts; and the final conflict involved Conan's outlaws, Artaban's Turanians, and a brood of vampires ("The Road of the Eagles").

Deserted by his sea rovers, Conan appropriated a stallion and headed back to the steppes. Yezdigerd, now on the throne of Turan, proved a far more astute and energetic ruler than his sire. He embarked on a program of imperial conquest.

Conan went to the small border kingdom of Khauran, where he won command of the royal guard of Queen Taramis. This queen had a twin sister, Salome, born a witch and reared by the yellow sorcerers of Khitai. She allied herself with the adventurer Constantius of Koth and planned by imprisoning the Queen to rule in her stead. Conan, who perceived the deception, was trapped and crucified. Cut down by the chieftain Olgerd Vladislav, the Cimmerian was carried off to a Zuagir camp in the desert. Conan waited for his wounds to heal, then applied his daring and ruthlessness to win his place as Olgerd's lieutenant.

When Salome and Constantius began a reign of terror in Khauran, Conan led his Zuagirs against the Khauranian capital. Soon Constantius hung from the cross to which he had nailed Conan, and Conan rode off smiling, to lead his Zuagirs on raids against the Turanians ("A Witch Shall Be Born").

Conan, about thirty and at the height of his physical powers, spent nearly two years with the desert Shemites, first as Olgerd's lieutenant and then, having ousted Olgerd, as sole chief. The circumstances of his leaving the Zuagirs were recently disclosed by a silken scroll in Old Tibetan, spirited out of Tibet by a refugee. This document is now with the Oriental Institute in Chicago.

The energetic King Yezdigerd sent soldiers to trap Conan and his troop. Because of a Zamorian traitor in Conan's ranks, the ambush nearly succeeded. To avenge the betrayal, Conan led his band in pursuit of the Zamorian. When his men deserted, Conan pressed on alone until, near death, he was rescued by Enosh, a chieftain of the isolated desert town of Akhlat.

Akhlat suffered under the rule of a demon in the form of a woman, who fed on the life force of living things. Conan, Enosh informed him, was their prophesied liberator. After it was over, Conan was invited to settle in Akhlat; but, knowing himself ill-suited to a life of humdrum respectability, he instead headed southwest to Zamboula with the horse and money of Vardanes the Zamorian ("Black Tears").

In one colossal debauch, Conan dissipated the fortune he had brought to Zamboula, a Turanian outpost. There lurked the sinister priest of Hanuman, Totrasmek, who sought a famous jewel, the Star of Khorala, for which the Queen of Ophir was said to have offered a roomful of gold. In the ensuing imbroglio, Conan acquired the Star of Khorala and rode westward ("Shadows of Zamboula").

The medieval monkish manuscript *De sidere choralae*, rescued from the bombed ruins of Monte Cassino, continues the tale. Conan reached the capital of Ophir to find that the effeminate Moranthes II, himself under the thumb of the sinister Count Rigello, kept his queen, Marala, under lock and key. Conan scaled the wall of Moranthes's castle and fetched Marala out. Rigello pursued the fugitives nearly to the Aquilonian border, where the Star of Khorala showed its power in an unexpected way ("The Star of Khorala").

Hearing that the *kozaki* had regained their vigor, Conan returned with horse and sword to the harrying of Turan. Although the now-famous northlander arrived all but empty-handed, contingents of the *kozaki* and the Vilayet pirates soon began operating under his command.

Yezdigerd sent Jehungir Agha to entrap the barbarian on the island of Xapur. Coming early to the ambush, Conan found the island's ancient fortress-palace of Dagon restored by magic, and in it the city's malevolent god, in the form of a giant of living iron ("The Devil in Iron").

After escaping from Xapur, Conan built his *kozaki* and pirate raiders into such a formidable threat that King Yezdigerd devoted all his forces to their destruction. After a devastating defeat, the *kozaki* scattered, and Conan retreated southward to take service in the light cavalry of Kobad Shah, King of Iranistan.

Conan got himself into Kobad Shah's bad graces and had to ride for the hills. He found a conspiracy brewing in Yanaidar, the fortress-city of the Hidden Ones. The Sons of Yezm were trying to revive an ancient cult and unite the surviving devotees of the old gods in order to rule the world. The adventure ended with the rout of the contending forces by the gray ghouls of Yanaidar, and Conan rode eastward ("The Flame Knife").

Conan reappeared in the Himelian Mountains, on the northwest frontier of Vendhya, as a war chief of the savage Afghuli tribesmen. Now in his early thirties, the warlike barbarian was known and feared throughout the world of the Hyborian Age.

No man to be bothered with niceties, Yezdigerd employed the magic of the wizard Khemsa, an adept of the dreaded Black Circle, to remove the Vendhyan king from his path. The dead king's sister, the Devi Yasmina, set out to avenge him but was captured by Conan. Conan and his captive pursued the sorcerous Khemsa, only to see him slain by the magic of the Seers of Yimsha, who also abducted Yasmina ("The People of the Black Circle").

When Conan's plans for welding the hill tribes into a single power failed, Conan, hearing of wars in the West, rode thither. Almuric, a prince of Koth, had rebelled against the hated Strabonus. While Conan joined Almuric's bristling host, Strabonus's fellow kings came to that monarch's aid. Almuric's motley horde was driven south, to be annihilated at last by combined Stygian and Kushite forces.

Escaping into the desert, Conan and the camp follower Natala came to age-old Xuthal, a phantom city of living dead men and their creeping shadow-god, Thog. The Stygian woman Thalis, the effective ruler of Xuthal, double-crossed Conan once too often ("The Slithering Shadow").

Conan beat his way back to the Hyborian lands. Seeking further employment, he joined the mercenary army that a Zingaran, Prince Zapayo da Kova, was raising for Argos. It was planned that Koth should invade Stygia from the north, while the Argosseans approached the realm from the south by sea. Koth, however, made a separate peace with Stygia, leaving Conan's army of mercenaries trapped in the Stygian deserts.

Conan fled with Amalric, a young Aquilonian soldier. Soon Conan was captured by nomads, while Amalric escaped. When Amalric caught up again with Conan, Amalric had with him the girl Lissa, whom he had saved from the cannibal god of her native city. Conan had meanwhile become commander of the cavalry of the city of

Tombalku. Two kings ruled Tombalku: the Negro Sakumbe and the mixed-blood Zehbeh. When Zehbeh and his faction were driven out, Sakumbe made Conan his co-king. But then the wizard Askia slew Sakumbe by magic. Conan, having avenged his black friend, escaped with Amalric and Lissa ("Drums of Tombalku").

Conan beat his way to the coast, where he joined the Barachan pirates. He was now about thirty-five. As second mate of the *Hawk*, he landed on the island of the Stygian sorcerer Siptah, said to have a magical jewel of fabulous properties.

Siptah dwelt in a cylindrical tower without doors or windows, attended by a winged demon. Conan smoked the unearthly being out but was carried off in its talons to the top of the tower. Inside the tower Conan found the wizard long dead; but the magical gem proved of unexpected help in coping with the demon ("The Gem in the Tower").

Conan remained about two years with the Barachans, according to a set of clay tablets in pre-Sumerian cuneiform. Used to the tightly organized armies of the Hyborian kingdoms, Conan found the organization of the Barachan bands too loose and anarchic to afford an opportunity to rise to leadership. Slipping out of a tight spot at the pirate rendezvous at Tortage, he found that the only alternative to a cut throat was braving the Western Ocean in a leaky skiff. When the *Wastrel*, the ship of the buccaneer Zaporavo, came in sight, Conan climbed aboard.

The Cimmerian soon won the respect of the crew and the enmity of its captain, whose Kordavan mistress, the sleek Sancha, cast too friendly an eye on the black-maned giant. Zaporavo drove his ship westward to an uncharted island, where Conan forced a duel on the captain and killed him, while Sancha was carried off by strange black beings to a living pool worshiped by these entities ("The Pool of the Black Ones").

Conan persuaded the officials at Kordava to transfer Zaporavo's privateering license to him, whereupon he spent about two years in this authorized piracy. As usual, plots were brewing against the Zingaran monarchy. King Ferdrugo was old and apparently failing, with no successor but his nubile daughter Chabela. Duke Villagro enlisted the Stygian super-sorcerer Thoth-Amon, the High Priest of Set, in a plot to obtain Chabela as his bride. Suspicious, the princess took the royal yacht down the coast to consult her uncle. A privateer in league with Villagro captured the yacht and abducted the girl. Chabela escaped and met Conan, who obtained the magical Cobra Crown, also sought by Thoth-Amon.

A storm drove Conan's ship to the coast of Kush, where Conan was confronted by black warriors headed by his old comrade-in-arms, Juma. While the chief welcomed the privateers, a tribesman stole the Cobra Crown. Conan set off in pursuit, with Princess Chabela following him. Both were captured by slavers and sold to the black Queen of the Amazons. The queen made Chabela her slave and Conan her fancy man. Then, jealous of Chabela, she flogged the girl, imprisoned Conan, and condemned both to be devoured by a man-eating tree (*Conan the Buccaneer*).

Having rescued the Zingaran princess, Conan shrugged off hints of marriage and returned to privateering. But other Zingarans, jealous, brought him down off the coast of Shem. Escaping inland, Conan joined the Free Companions, a mercenary company. Instead of rich plunder, however, he found himself in dull guard duty on the black frontier of Stygia, where the wine was sour and the pickings poor.

Conan's boredom ended with the appearance of the

pirette, Valeria of the Red Brotherhood. When she left the camp, he followed her south. The pair took refuge in a city occupied by the feuding clans of Xotalanc and Tecuhltli. Siding with the latter, the two northerners soon found themselves in trouble with that clan's leader, the ageless witch Tascela ("Red Nails").

Conan's amour with Valeria, however hot at the start, did not last long. Valeria returned to the sea; Conan tried his luck once more in the black kingdoms. Hearing of the "Teeth of Gwahlur," a cache of priceless jewels hidden in Keshan, he sold his services to its irascible king to train the Keshani army.

Thutmekri, the Stygian emissary of the twin kings of Zembabwei, also had designs on the jewels. The Cimmerian, outmatched in intrigue, made tracks for the valley where the ruins of Alkmeenon and its treasure lay hidden. In a wild adventure with the undead goddess Yelaya, the Corinthian girl Muriela, the black priests headed by Gorulga, and the grim gray servants of the long-dead Bît-Yakin, Conan kept his head but lost his loot ("Jewels of Gwahlur").

Heading for Punt with Muriela, Conan embarked on a scheme to relieve the worshipers of an ivory goddess of their abundant gold. Learning that Thutmekri had preceded him and had already poisoned King Lalibeha's mind against him, Conan and his companion took refuge in the temple of the goddess Nebethet.

When the king, Thutmekri, and High Priest Zaramba arrived at the temple, Conan staged a charade wherein Muriela spoke with the voice of the goddess. The results surprised all, including Conan ("The Ivory Goddess").

In Zembabwei, the city of the twin kings, Conan joined a trading caravan which he squired northward along the desert borders, bringing it safely into Shem. Now in his late thirties, the restless adventurer heard that the Aquilonians were spreading westward into the Pictish wilderness. So thither, seeking work for his sword, went Conan. He enrolled as a scout at Fort Tuscelan, where a fierce war raged with the Picts.

In the forests across the river, the wizard Zogar Sag was gathering his swamp demons to aid the Picts. While Conan failed to prevent the destruction of Fort Tuscelan, he managed to warn settlers around Velitrium and to cause the death of Zogar Sag ("Beyond the Black River").

Conan rose rapidly in the Aquilonian service. As captain, his company was once defeated by the machinations of a traitorous superior. Learning that this officer, Viscount Lucian, was about to betray the province to the Picts, Conan exposed the traitor and routed the Picts ("Moon of Blood").

Promoted to general, Conan defeated the Picts in a great battle at Velitrium and was called back to the capital, Tarantia, to receive the nation's accolades. Then, having roused the suspicions of the depraved and foolish King Numedides, he was drugged and chained in the Iron Tower under sentence of death.

The barbarian, however, had friends as well as foes. Soon he was spirited out of prison and turned loose with horse and sword. He struck out across the dank forests of Pictland toward the distant sea. In the forest, the Cimmerian came upon a cavern in which lay the corpse and the demon-guarded treasure of the pirate Tranicos. From the west, others—a Zingaran count and two bands of pirates—were hunting the same fortune, while the Stygian sorcerer Thoth-Amon took a hand in the game ("The Treasure of Tranicos").

Rescued by an Aquilonian galley, Conan was chosen to lead a revolt against Numedides. While the revolution stormed along, civil war raged on the Pictish frontier. Lord

Valerian, a partisan of Numedides, schemed to bring the Picts down on the town of Schohira. A scout, Gault Hagar's son, undertook to upset this scheme by killing the Pictish wizard ("Wolves Beyond the Border").

Storming the capital city and slaying Numedides on the steps of his throne—which he promptly took for his own—Conan, now in his early forties, found himself ruler of the greatest Hyborian nation (*Conan the Liberator*).

A king's life, however, proved no bed of houris. Within a year, an exiled count had gathered a group of plotters to oust the barbarian from the throne. Conan might have lost crown and head but for the timely intervention of the long-dead sage Epimitreus ("The Phoenix of the Sword").

No sooner had the mutterings of revolt died down than Conan was treacherously captured by the kings of Ophir and Koth. He was imprisoned in the tower of the wizard Tsotha-lanti in the Kothian capital. Conan escaped with the help of a fellow prisoner, who was Tsotha-lanti's wizardly rival Pelias. By Pelias's magic, Conan was whisked to Tarantia in time to slay a pretender and to lead an army against his treacherous fellow kings ("The Scarlet Citadel").

For nearly two years, Aquilonia thrived under Conan's firm but tolerant rule. The lawless, hard-bitten adventurer of former years had, through force of circumstance, matured into an able and responsible statesman. But a plot was brewing in neighboring Nemedia to destroy the King of Aquilonia by sorcery from an elder day.

Conan, about forty-five, showed few signs of age save a network of scars on his mighty frame and a more cautious approach to wine, women and bloodshed. Although he kept a harem of luscious concubines, he had never taken an official queen; hence he had no legitimate son to inherit the throne, a fact whereof his enemies sought to take advantage.

The plotters resurrected Xaltotun, the greatest sorcerer of the ancient empire of Acheron, which fell before the Hyborian savages 3,000 years earlier. By Xaltotun's magic, the King of Nemedia was slain and replaced by his brother Tarascus. Black sorcery defeated Conan's army; Conan was imprisoned, and the exile Valerius took his throne.

Escaping from a dungeon with the aid of the harem girl Zenobia, Conan returned to Aquilonia to rally his loyal forces against Valerius. From the priests of Asura, he learned that Xaltotun's power could be broken only by means of a strange jewel, the "Heart of Ahriman." The trail of the jewel led to a pyramid in the Stygian desert outside black-walled Khemi. Winning the Heart of Ahriman, Conan returned to face his foes (*Conan the Conqueror*, originally published as *The Hour of the Dragon*).

After regaining his kingdom, Conan made Zenobia his queen. But, at the ball celebrating her elevation, the queen was borne off by a demon sent by the Khitan sorcerer Yah Chieng. Conan's quest for his bride carried him across the known world, meeting old friends and foes. In purple-towered Paikang, with the help of a magical ring, he freed Zenobia and slew the wizard (*Conan the Avenger*, originally published as *The Return of Conan*).

Home again, the way grew smoother. Zenobia gave him heirs: a son named Conan but commonly called Conn, another son called Taurus, and a daughter. When Conn was twelve, his father took him on a hunting trip to Gunderland. Conan was now in his late fifties. His sword arm was a little slower than in his youth, and his black mane and the fierce mustache of his later years were traced with gray; but his strength still surpassed that of two ordinary men.

When Conn was lured away by the Witchmen of Hyperborea, who demanded that Conan come to their stronghold alone, Conan went. He found Louhi, the High Priestess of the Witchmen, in conference with three others of the world's leading sorcerers: Thoth-Amon of Stygia; the god-king of Kambuja; and the black lord of Zembabwei. In the ensuing holocaust, Louhi and the Kambujan perished, while Thoth-Amon and the other sorcerer vanished by magic ("The Witch of the Mists").

Old King Ferdrugo of Zingara had died, and his throne remained vacant as the nobles intrigued over the succession. Duke Pantho of Guarralid invaded Poitain, in southern Aquilonia. Conan, suspecting sorcery, crushed the invaders. Learning that Thoth-Amon was behind Pantho's madness, Conan set out with his army to settle matters with the Stygian. He pursued his foe to Thoth-Amon's stronghold in Stygia ("Black Sphinx of Nebthu"), to Zembabwei ("Red Moon of Zembabwei"), and to the last realm of the serpent folk in the far south ("Shadows in the Skull").

For several years, Conan's rule was peaceful. But time did that which no combination of foes had been able to do. The Cimmerian's skin became wrinkled and his hair gray; old wounds ached in damp weather. Conan's beloved consort Zenobia died giving birth to their second daughter.

Then catastrophe shattered King Conan's mood of half-resigned discontent. Supernatural entities, the Red Shadows, began seizing and carrying off his subjects. Conan was baffled until in a dream he again visited the sage Epimitreus. He was told to abdicate in favor of Prince Conn and set out across the Western Ocean.

Conan discovered that the Red Shadows had been sent by the priest-wizards of Antillia, a chain of islands in the western part of the ocean, whither the survivors of Atlantis had fled 8,000 years before. These priests offered human sacrifices to their devil-god Xotli on such a scale that their own population faced extermination.

In Antillia, Conan's ship was taken, but he escaped into the city of Ptahuacan. After conflicts with giant rats and dragons, he emerged atop the sacrificial pyramid just as his crewmen were about to be sacrificed. Supernatural conflict, revolution, and seismic catastrophe ensued. In the end, Conan sailed off to explore the continents to the west (*Conan of the Isles*).

Whether he died there, or whether there is truth in the tale that he strode out of the West to stand at his son's side in a final battle against Aquilonia's foes, will be revealed only to him who looks, as Kull of Valusia once did, into the mystic mirrors of Tuzun Thune.

L. Sprague de Camp
Villanova, Pennsylvania
May 1984